Praise for Crow in Stolen Colors . . .

"An entertaining debut with a vivid setting and a brisk
pace."   —*Firsts Magazine*

"Great descriptive passages . . . Suspenseful twists and
turns . . . There is never a dull moment, never a breather,
never a wrong turn . . . Definitely a must-read!"
                                    —*About.com* Mysteries

"Readers who love the Kate Shugak mysteries will fully
enjoy *Crow in Stolen Colors*. The exciting novel describes
the beauty and danger that is Alaska . . . The protagonist is
an individualist that will garner much empathy by new fans
who will want her to make future appearances. Anyone who
enjoys an atmospheric mystery will gain immense pleasure
from this straight-lined, but exciting work."
                                    —*Midwest Book Review*

MORE MYSTERIES FROM THE
BERKLEY PUBLISHING GROUP . . .

DOG LOVERS' MYSTERIES STARRING HOLLY WINTER: With her Alaskan malamute Rowdy, Holly dogs the trails of dangerous criminals. "A gifted and original writer."—Carolyn G. Hart

by Susan Conant

DOG LOVERS' MYSTERIES STARRING JACKIE WALSH: She's starting a new life with her son and an ex-police dog named Jake . . . teaching film classes and solving crimes!

by Melissa Cleary

CHARLOTTE GRAHAM MYSTERIES: She's an actress with a flair for dramatics—and an eye for detection. "You'll get hooked on Charlotte Graham!"—*Rave Reviews*

by Stefanie Matteson

PEACHES DANN MYSTERIES: Peaches has never had a very good memory. But she's learned to cope with it over the years . . . Fortunately, though, when it comes to murder, this absentminded amateur sleuth doesn't forgive and forget!

by Elizabeth Daniels Squire

HEMLOCK FALLS MYSTERIES: The Quilliam sisters combine their culinary and business skills to run an inn in upstate New York. But when it comes to murder, their talent for detection takes over . . .

by Claudia Bishop

Sound Tracks

Marcia Simpson

BERKLEY PRIME CRIME, NEW YORK

This is a work of fiction. Names, characters, places, and incidents either are the product of the author's imagination or are used fictitiously, and any resemblance to actual persons, living or dead, business establishments, events, or locales is entirely coincidental.

SOUND TRACKS

A Berkley Prime Crime Book / published by arrangement with the author

PRINTING HISTORY
Berkley Prime Crime edition / May 2001

All rights reserved.
Copyright © 2001 by Marcia Simpson

The Penguin Putnam Inc. World Wide Web site address is www.penguinputnam.com

ISBN: 0-425-17944-3

Berkley Prime Crime Books are published by The Berkley Publishing Group, a division of Penguin Putnam Inc., 375 Hudson Street, New York, New York 10014.
The name BERKLEY PRIME CRIME and the BERKLEY PRIME CRIME design are trademarks belonging to Penguin Putnam Inc.

PRINTED IN THE UNITED STATES OF AMERICA

10 9 8 7 6 5 4 3 2 1

For Sheila, Dave, Brigid,
Evan, Louise, Christopher, and Bruce,
with love

Acknowledgments

My profound gratitude to Ben Stein, who gave me a Press Pass to the Acoustical Society of America meeting in Seattle, and to David, who told me exactly how to revise this manuscript.

Nothin' don't seem impossible once you've clapped
eyes on a whale.

Elizabeth Goudge, *Green Dolphin Street*

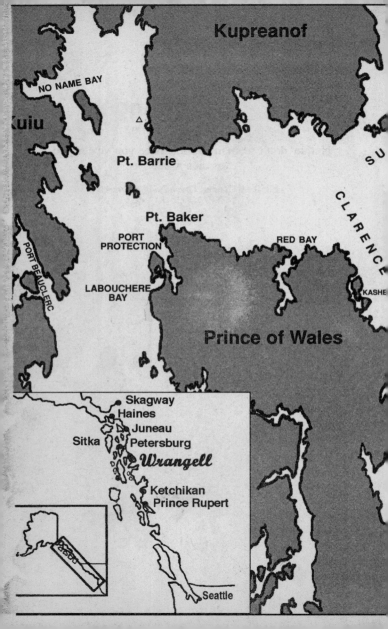

Mitkof
STRAIT
NER
Wrangell
ELEPHANT'S NOSE
STRAIT
SHOEMAKER BAY
Woronkofski
Zarembo
PASS
CHICHAGOF
ZIMOVIA
Wrangell Island
STIKINE
OF
SHEVAROF
STEAMER PT.
STRAIT
KINDERGARTEN BAY
STEAMER BAY
PASSAGE
STRAIT
Etolin

Prologue

ONCE UPON A TIME, THOUSANDS OF YEARS ago, humans beat their way across the ice to this land now called Alaska. Then the sea washed away their escape route, stranding them in a hostile place. Some made their way south to the new islands still breaking apart. There they carved pictures into the rocks of the birds and animals they found, and of the spirits whose protection they required, and of their own faces, lest the spirits in a moment of jest turn human life into sea snails.

Here at its ragged north edge, the earth pierces the sea to fourteen thousand feet. Trees grow as high as there is oxygen and warmth: Sitka spruce, western hemlock, Alaska cedar. Under their roof live a million smaller plants: kinnikinnick, salmonberry, thorny devil's club, tiny, red-helmeted British soldiers; even the plant names reflect the history of this rich, fierce land.

Every day, tugs named *Fred T. Archibald* and *Arctic Venture* pull barges into the small roadless towns of southeast Alaska, and cranes unload cars and refrigerators, steel beams and carpet and bags of cement. But rain upholsters boards in velvet and salt air rusts engines. Wind drives waves over breakwaters, tearing out docks and pilings. Avalanches thunder down and trees fall into the sea. Whales return to the long light of summer and salmon come back, but not as many as came before, and some years, not many at all.

The people who settle this northland acquire its characteristics like camouflage. Those who cannot hide never stay. Violence is here, and sorrow and unyielding purpose; also the softness of fog, the quiet of long darkness, the brilliance of sun stabbing from the surface of the sea. Those who stay know fury, depression, hopelessness, joy. Exhilaration pumps through their veins.

"Engine's overheating again," Joe said. "You gotta work on it some more."

Joe wrote in the log: November 4, Monday, 9:50 p.m. engine overheating.

"Turn on the sodium lights," Hank said.

"You think somebody's gonna see *Cash Buyer* out here?" Joe asked. "Somebody gonna sell us some fish out here?"

"No, stupid, we gotta have lights so we don't get overrun by some other boat."

Joe turned on the sodium lights while Hank went below to the engine room.

"Hot as hell in here," he shouted. "Water ain't pumping through. And there's water all over the floor. Hose is rotted out."

"We got a hose somewhere, a new one. You gotta put it on."

Hank went to work on it, finally clamped the new hose in place, and restarted the engine.

The packer was going from Sitka to Ketchikan along Sumner Strait, an L-shaped body of water running from the Pacific Ocean to the Stikine River delta. The packer was three miles from either shore—right out in the middle, it was, having just rounded Point Baker. It was long after the fishing season—they'd had jobs in Sitka, but the lumber mill had folded. The packer was on its way to Seattle to get the engine repaired, the hull repaired, the deck repaired. Everything repaired.

The water was choppy in the sodium lights and the tide was flooding, the current very strong. "Rock out there," Joe said. "Right in front of us."

"No rock showing on the chart," Hank said. "Looks like a deadhead to me."

The packer veered to port and passed whatever it was in the water. Joe went out and looked at it. "Orange mustang suit, looks like, floating all by itself."

Hank went out on deck and looked over. "There's a head there, and hands and feet sticking out. There's a *body* in that mustang suit. We're gonna have to pick it up." He rushed back to the wheelhouse and put the gears in neutral. Both the men hung over the side with boat hooks, trying to reach the body in the water. Eventually Hank hooked it and pulled it toward the packer.

"How we gonna get him out?" Joe asked.

"Gotta lower the hoist with one of those tubs for the salmon on it," Hank said. "Get the tote full of water, then pull it under him and lift."

Joe held the body against the boat while Hank lowered the hoist. Hank had to go over the rail with his boat hook, tipping the tote to get it full of water. It was difficult to get the tote under the body—the cables from the hoist kept getting in the way. Hank used his boat hook to try to drag the tote under the body, while Joe used his to position the body against the hull. At last they succeeded. Hank raised the hoist, the body came up, and Hank lowered him to the deck.

"What's the position on the GPS?" Hank asked. "Write the position in the log. And the time we found him. About 10:45."

Joe wrote: November 4, Monday, 10:45 p.m. found body floating: 56:25 north; 133:32 west.

"Hey, can we turn off those sodium lights now?" Joe asked. "Don't want to look like a *Cash Buyer* when we got a body aboard."

"So *do* it. Nobody'd think *Cash Buyer*—nobody'd be lookin' to sell *fish* this time 'a year. See any sign of a boat out there?"

Joe went out on deck, walked around it, came in and said, "Nothin'. No sign of a boat, nothin' floating, either."

Hank put the engine in gear. "Call the Wrangell police," Hank said. "Tell 'em we got a body aboard. Tell 'em he drowned."

1

"I DO NOT HAVE TO HAVE A SEA DOG,"
Liza Romero told Sam. "If you roll in one more dead fish,
you're history."

He grinned, tongue hanging to one side, and bounded
over the next rocky ledge, disappearing from view so she
couldn't continue to interfere with his significant pleasures.

At first light, the bay's green surface held a wind-carved
spruce and snow on a distant peak. A breeze fussed over the
reflection, making it shiver. The sun in early November was
so far south it barely rose above the horizon. Liza couldn't
see it from where she sat, but this was the first time in ten
days the sun had poked through the ironclad sky. She dab-
bled her fingers at the edge of the tide and stared out over
the bay. For the first time since early spring, she felt a surge
of something she could almost call hope. She whistled for
Sam, her big, copper-colored Lab/hound. Time to get
going—she had to go to Labouchere Bay and Sea Otter
Sound. The next day she'd go to No Name Bay, stay
overnight at the dock, then up Duncan Canal.

Lying awake one fall evening after she bought the *Salmon
Eye*, Liza had imagined a business that would allow her to
take both freight and books to the roadless villages and logging camps of southeast Alaska. And she had done it forth-

with. She'd resigned from the library and announced her business intentions to all the villages. She enjoyed the solitude, steering the boat through the passages and bays; she only had Sam for company, and he didn't speak very often.

The *Salmon Eye* was an old halibut schooner built in the early 1900s, originally named *Lituya Bay*. It had first been a sailing vessel, then had a gasoline engine put in around 1908. The man from whom Liza had bought her had renamed her *Salmon Eye*, and had packed salmon from the fishermen to the canneries. The *Salmon Eye* was narrow-beamed and rolled heavily in steep seas, but Liza was used to it, letting her knees take the roll; Sam lay flat on the floor when the waves were high.

They'd used dories for longlining, a very slow way to do it because the dories could only handle short lengths of line. The dories were nested on the aft deck. The *Salmon Eye* had had eight dories—Liza had read that in the earliest log, which was still aboard. She had all the logs up until 1990, when the man from whom she had bought it failed to keep one. She had gone back to keeping a log, every day telling where she was going, what she was passing, where she anchored at night.

Last evening, she had delivered freight to Point Baker and had also brought hydrophones for Henry Sizemore. They'd gotten to be friends in Shoemaker Bay, had had dinner together several times, and he'd asked her specifically to bring those hydrophones to Point Baker. Henry was from the Alaska State Wildlife Protection Agency. He was their whale expert. Something was damaging the whales, the humpbacks and orcas; they were driving headlong onto reefs and shores, and some had propeller wounds.

Henry told Liza it might be noise that was doing it, and he'd requested hydrophones so he could hear underwater.

Then, that very afternoon, he'd radioed her that he was on to something, would have to investigate before he could say for sure.

Point Baker was a tiny, roadless community on the northwest corner of Prince of Wales Island. There were a good many houses strung along the slopes above the inner bay, and in summer quite a few people resided there, but in winter the population dropped to less than a quarter of the summer people.

The Point Baker store, restaurant, sometimes functional bar, post office and telephone were strung out along the dock; boats were tied up on the outside of it. In the summer there were a lot of fancy yachts that fastened up for days or weeks at a time, but in the fall and winter, not many boats came into Point Baker. There was anchorage for only a few boats on the inner bay.

Henry's boat was tied at the dock and Liza moored the *Salmon Eye* ahead of it. There was a large black longliner coming in behind her; they went to the inner harbor, turned around, and came back to tie up facing the *Salmon Eye*. She unloaded her freight, whistled for Sam, then went to Henry's boat and pounded on the door, shouting, "Henry? Anybody aboard?"

She waited a minute and pounded again. No answer. Probably in the bar, she thought. Or the restaurant. It was pitch dark—in November the sun was down by four, and she'd gotten there around nine.

"Henry Sizemore?" she asked the bartender.

"He was here this afternoon," the bartender said. "But I haven't seen him since then."

"He was supposed to meet me here and pick up some hydrophones."

"Ahh, he'll be back," the bartender said. "Might have just gone out in the inflatable, looking for whales or something."

She ordered a beer, and sat there on the stool, sipping it. When her beer was gone, she said good-bye to the bartender and went out on the dock. Sam had been shut out of the bar and restaurant, and was overjoyed when Liza rejoined him, leaping and bounding around her, tail thudding against Henry's boat, his ears flying. She pounded on Henry's door again. "Henry? Anybody aboard?"

She went back to her boat, wrote him a note telling him the hydrophones were here and to contact her on the *Salmon Eye*. She got the Scotch tape, went back to Henry's boat, and taped the note to the door.

Then she noticed something. The inflatable was on the roof of the cabin. So he hadn't gone out in the inflatable and he wasn't in the restaurant or the bar. Where had he gone?

She went to bed at eleven. She had left Wrangell at five that morning and gone to Coffman Cove with freight, then to Kashevarof, then clear out to Point Baker. In the middle of the night Sam barked and Liza roused. She heard a roar as a big outboard started up. Sam barked again, but Liza listened no more.

In the morning, the longliner, as well as Henry's boat, was gone. He'd come back and gotten it—maybe that was the outboard she'd heard. Why hadn't he taken the hydrophones? She'd come all the way out there with them and now his boat was gone and he'd left the hydrophones on the *Salmon Eye*. She was extremely annoyed, furious at him, actually—why hadn't he picked them up? She'd left him a note, too.

She wrote in her log: November 5, Tuesday, 7:00 a.m. Henry's boat gone from Point Baker. Angry at him—I left a note on his door and he didn't pick up the hydrophones. What am I supposed to do with them?

*   *   *

The entrance to Point Baker was tortuous, with foul ground on either side, but Liza was accustomed to it and steered the *Salmon Eye* out through the narrow channel. She turned to port between Helm Rock and Mariposa Reef, and headed south from there.

She had just pushed the throttle up when something struck the hull. The wheel was yanked from her hands, the boat creaked and shuddered, and Sam was thrown against the binnacle holding the compass. He scrambled to his feet, barking, while Liza fought the wheel to center, adrenaline racing through her veins. Unmarked rocks? A deadhead? A sunken vessel?

She charged from the wheelhouse to the foredeck where the sun, firing darts off the water, blinded her. Shielding her eyes with her hand, she made out a geyser close to starboard; then tail flukes wider than the boat's beam. A humpback. From its dive, the whale erupted, fins extended like wings as it flew through the air.

Suspended above the boat, the huge animal was so close Liza could see barnacles on its corrugated jaw and smell its fetid odor. She held her breath—it was going to crash on the foredeck. But at the last instant it arched forward, hit the water on its side and sank from sight. Once more it breached. Then it rolled alongside and stared up at her with its great, inquiring eye.

"Hello," she called over the rail. The whale spouted again, a roaring volcano of glittering spray, then dove, silvery flukes poised like a waving fan.

Liza's whole body still reeled from the force of the impact. She put the engine in gear and turned out from the reef. They'd been carried far closer to the jagged rocks than she'd intended. As far as she could tell, though, the *Salmon Eye* had suffered no serious damage. No increased vibration from the propeller—the boat wasn't listing—no water poured through smashed planks.

Making her way south, she puzzled over the collision. In summer, humpbacks cruised the narrow straits of the Panhandle for krill, heading back to their breeding grounds in Hawaii in November and December. Sometimes they became entangled in the miles of drift nets that crisscrossed the North Pacific, but rarely if ever did they run into things they could hear. They disliked engine noise and were known to change course to avoid the huge oil tankers that hugged the coast. Why had that whale run into the *Salmon Eye*?

Sam had bayed his weird hound's wail when he saw a forty-ton bird soar over the rail. Now he stood pressed against the door of the wheelhouse, staring up. "It's okay, Sam," she told him, rubbing his silky ears. "Everyone lived." She turned to stare out the window, remembering those times when some had not.

2

PAUL HOWARD, LIEUTENANT IN THE Wrangell Police Department, was waiting at the Reliance dock in Wrangell when the packer came in around two in the morning. He swung his leg over the rail while they tied up. "Where's the body?" he asked.

"We took him below," Hank said. "Put him on a bunk."

Paul dropped down the ladder and went into the bunk room. He inhaled sharply when he saw the man. "It's the whale man," he said. "Henry Sizemore. I saw him just the other day. Got a wife and two kids up in Juneau. Don't know what I'll tell them." He shook his head. "Where'd you find him?"

"Middle of Sumner Strait," Hank said. "What was it, that position?"

Joe read from the log: "56:25 north; 133:32 west. And the time was 10:45."

"We'll get a copy of the log," Paul said. "Like to keep it for the record. We'll call the ambulance and take him to the hospital. He's for sure dead, but we gotta get an autopsy." He went to the phone outside the harbormaster's office and called.

"Sorry about this," Paul told the men. "Sorry you had to pick him up and bring him to Wrangell, and most of all, I'm sorry he's gone. I liked him. He was trying to see what was going wrong with the whales around here. Lot of 'em hitting props and beaching themselves. Well, don't mean to keep you up. Could you give me that log so I can make a copy of it?"

The men turned over the log to him, and he said he'd return it tomorrow sometime. "Catch you later," he said.

The next evening, Paul Howard went to the Coho bar. He had returned the log to the crew of the packer after he'd copied it, and told them he'd be at the Coho and buy them a drink.

Hank and Joe came in and Paul bought them drinks, which they both gulped down, waving their glasses at the bartender. Their second drinks followed the first in a matter of seconds. Paul wondered if he'd have to pay for all of them. They waved their glasses again as if there were no tomorrow. Now they were talking about finding the body.

"Found a body—catch of the day," Joe said.

The man on the stool next to him said, "Found a *body*?"

"Dumb old Joey thought it was a rock," Hank said. "I knew better."

"Ahh, you said it was a deadhead," Joe said.

"Well, it was."

"Where was it?" the man asked.

"Oh, way out there in Sumner Strait. Along off Point Baker," Joe said.

"Pulled it in with boat hooks, lowered the hoist, pulled him up with it," said Hank.

"Last night?"

"Yup. 'Bout ten forty-five last night."

The man shook his head. "Sorry to hear that," he said. "Got any idea who it was?"

Paul leaned across toward the man and said, "Henry Size-more. Know him?"

"Nope," the man said. "Never met him."

"He was the whale expert," Paul said. "Something going wrong with the whales around here." He asked the men where they were going.

"Seattle," they said simultaneously. Hank said, "Gotta get the whole packer repaired before we come back."

They split the bill in half and Paul made his farewells. He lifted his hand to the man at the bar before he left.

3

HOME, TO LIZA, WAS SHOEMAKER BAY. She slid the *Salmon Eye* into her slip, threw herself over the rail to tie the lines down, then climbed back and turned the engine off. She plugged the phone line in and the electric line for shore power. She thought about calling Paul Howard and telling him about the whale, but not right now—she was hungry and tired. She drove the four miles from Shoemaker Bay to town and parked the lime-green Chevy pickup on Front Street. The pickup was elderly and sported a crown of moss around the trim on the cab, It was dark and the false fronts of the buildings on Front Street lay in deep shadow. A mist had formed, swirling under the streetlights.

At Archie's, where Liza sometimes ate supper, the tables were crowded, so she sat at the counter next to a woman she'd never seen before. The woman had yellow hair, stiff from bleach, that stood out under her blue cap like an old broom. She wore a wool lumberman's red-and-black shirt, yellow bib rain pants, and brown fisherman's boots. Easily six feet tall, Liza thought. Her shoulders stretched the black and red squares of her shirt into curves.

The woman lit a cigarette and immediately stubbed it out in the ashtray. "Trying to quit," she said to Maggie, who was replacing the filter in the coffeemaker.

"Don't buy 'em," Maggie said. "Can't smoke 'em if you don't have 'em."

"Yeah," the woman said. "But I think about it more then. If I have them, I think, well, I'll wait because they're there if I have to—but if I don't have any, I start thinking, what'll I do, how am I going to do this—hey, no, I can't do it, I can't stand it. You know."

Liza waved the menu at Maggie and ordered the smoked salmon omelet, then took a paperback copy of *J Is for Judgment* from her purse and opened it on the counter. She hated to talk these days—she had nothing to say, wasn't interested in what the rest of the world wanted her to know.

The world was too much with her, "late and soon," she thought, dredging up her Wordsworth and thinking of Tango and his continuous flow of quotations. She'd try it out on him next time. He and Mink were about the only people on the planet she could tolerate at the moment. Well, and maybe Paul Howard. She squinted as she pictured Paul's longing eyes, his huge hands knotted up as he tried not to reach out for her.

"Something the way things get ahold, isn't it?" the woman said to no one in particular, or at least, Liza hoped, not to her. But the woman swiveled around in her chair and looked right at her. "You from around here?" she asked.

"Yup."

"Been here awhile?"

"Three years." She pointedly pulled her book closer as Maggie set coffee in front of her.

"Pretty much home, then."

"Another fifty and I'll stop being an Outsider."

"What d'you do around here?" the woman asked, as Maggie set an enormous Reuben sandwich in front of her and slid the ketchup bottle over for the french fries.

"I run a freight service and book-mo-boat."

The woman raised her eyebrows.

"Librarian in my former life," Liza said.

The woman's eyebrows were thick and dark and didn't match her stiff yellow hair at all. Under the brows, her eyes were brown. Liza wondered if the hair was a wig and eyed her to see if she could see a line at the edge.

"Is that like a bookmobile?" the woman asked.

"Yeah, except the water's the highway. I run out to the villages and logging camps. Only sometimes the weather fouls it up—in winter especially."

"You do it by yourself?" the woman said, sounding incredulous.

"Yup. Well, and my dog, Sam." She stared down at the book and turned a page she hadn't yet read.

The woman shook her head. "I wouldn't want to be out there alone, that's for sure. I'm scared to death the whole time, even though there's a bunch of us. We're scoping out the fishing."

Maggie grabbed Liza's smoked salmon omelet off the pass-through from the kitchen and set it in front of her. "Anything else?"

Liza shook her head and said, "No thanks—enough for two here."

Picking up the ketchup bottle, the woman covered the potatoes with a red stream. "Probably stay around here this winter, maybe longline. Halibut and black cod. I'm Jenny Andover." She held out her hand.

"Liza Romero." Liza shook her hand and nodded.

"What's the name of your boat?" Jenny asked.

"The *Salmon Eye*. Old halibut schooner."

Liza declined more coffee—she'd left Point Baker early and was ready for bed. Jenny, shoveling in the potatoes, was already eyeing the dessert menu.

The two jackets on the rack at the end of the counter

looked identical, yellow Helly-Hansens. Liza took one down to see if it was hers—she always wrote "Romero–Salmon Eye" in black marker inside her collar, in case she was washed ashore somewhere. This collar said "Andover, J." It had something very heavy in one pocket. She hung it back, surreptitiously feeling the pocket as she did so. Jenny Andover was carrying a gun.

4

"SO WHAT'S THIS ALL ABOUT?"

"Henry Sizemore drowned."

"No, no, no, he couldn't have drowned. I know him very well. He's Alaska's whale expert."

"Well, you're their whale expert now. Says right here, 'Scott Beringer assigned to Wrangell Wildlife Protection office.' Off to Alaska again."

"Oh, I hate this. Henry drowned? And I don't want to leave Sarah with Andrea—she works night and day."

"Take the kid with you."

"Andrea wouldn't think of letting Sarah go washing around the straits and passages in a dinky boat. I've never been to Wrangell. Juneau, Sitka, Ketchikan, lot of time spent drifting around Frederick Sound, Chatham Strait—all the high spots, never Wrangell."

"Lot of things going on there right now with the impending mill closure—troubled little burg at the moment. Pretty much a workingman's town, not prettified for tourists. Lot of Natives, totem poles, stuff like that. Fabulous setting. You're the whale expert now—you gotta go. Just grab the kid and take her."

*   *   *

Beringer thrashed all night, thinking about Henry, thinking about Sarah, thinking about his custody battle with Andrea. He didn't want to leave San Diego without Sarah because Andrea worked such long hours, but Sarah lived with Andrea now—she was demanding custody because Beringer went off for long periods of time on boats, large and small. He intended to keep her, though. He would share her with her mother—Andrea could have her a couple months a year, but Sarah had been his love, his responsibility, since birth, and he was going to win this one, dammit.

And how could Henry have drowned? He was a fantastic sailor, cool and competent, extremely hardy. He'd known him since they went to school together, known his wife and kids—oh, shit, he couldn't have drowned.

Well, he'd have to go up there, be the whale expert now that Henry was gone. On loan, though. Only on loan, till he found out what was going on with the whales. Henry had called him a couple months ago to tell him that the whales had gone into kamikaze mode, running into boats, beaching themselves, bashing into propellers. He'd have to go, but he'd be back soon.

At least they'd provided Beringer with a good boat. Fast and maneuverable. Small galley so he could cook. All the latest electronics: Global Positioning Satellite system with charts, radar, depth sounder, fish-finder, excellent radios. Enough room for him to sleep if he had to be on surveillance overnight.

Something wrong with the whales in this area. Maybe something toxic in the food chain—boats dumping ballast, spilling fuel—industrial pollution. The humpbacks seemed to be in trouble. Beringer knew that noise from drilling rigs off Nova Scotia had been tagged as a possible cause of humpbacks tangling in fish nets and damaging themselves against boats and shore, but there wasn't any drilling going on around here.

A dead orca whale had washed up on the beach on Warren Island with a round wound in its side, as though it had hit a propeller. He'd had a report on the radio. Then there'd been a report of a large number of dead fish floating on the surface—most of them bottom fish.

The reports were coming mainly from the west end of Sumner Strait and the Coronation Island area, where the humpback whales were getting ready to head back to Hawaii for the winter. He'd had a report from the BLM that somebody was running a covert gold-mining operation somewhere up the Stikine River. Maybe toxic waste was being carried by the river current, poisoning fish and krill and getting into the stomachs of the bigger animals.

Beringer had frantically listed the names of the larger boats most often in the area, and plotted their locations on his charts, but the area was large and the waterways twisted and complex. The tugs *Gerald Atkins* and *Defiance*; the four longliners *Wind Walker*, *Eva Sound*, *Sophie Marie* and *Tillikum*; the coastal freighter *Ocean Pride* and the small freighter, *Salmon Eye*. *If* it was a boat. He had never spotted dumping—no oily sheen on the water, no clouds of murk drifting back from a boat.

He peered through the heavy mist. What little light had broken through the thick sky today was going fast, and he needed to anchor for the night before dark drowned every landmark. He would anchor in Exchange Cove. He turned the boat in between the islands, watching the radar as he made his way over a sandbar that had silted up.

Inside, the bay opened out a bit and he headed close to the east shore before he stepped out on deck and dropped the anchor over. When the chain stopped running, he pulled out some additional lengths; the boat was light, though—it wouldn't drag on short scope. Then he shut the engine down, inhaling silence like a magic vapor.

Somewhere along the forested slope, a raven noted his arrival and passed along a warning with a hollow knocking sound, picked up by another and another, till the woods were filled with harsh percussion. Eight scoters edged the bay single file. Through the deepening gloom, he saw something large move through the high grass at the mouth of the creek that emptied into the head of the bay. He strained to see. Stepping inside, he took the binoculars and watched a black bear plunge into the stony streambed, bury his muzzle in the icy water and grab a fish, tossing it quickly to break its spine. When the bear walked up into the forest, he set the binoculars down.

In June, he'd flown with Sarah to Juneau on vacation and they'd chartered a boat similar to this one. He remembered when she'd seen her first bear. They'd been anchored in Pybus Bay on Admiralty Island only a few months ago. Old-growth hemlocks ranked up the steep slope till they pierced the low clouds; the cirque, left by a long-vanished glacier, was still filled with snow in late June. Huddled on the aft deck in her yellow rain gear, Sarah pointed at an orange lion's mane jellyfish bigger around than her head, pumping its way slowly through the black water.

Standing next to her, Beringer had scanned the shore, trees neatly trimmed by the tide, then a dip where the land flattened to release a stream. And there was the bear, a brown bear, nosing through the bright green eel grass where the salt flat ended. Sarah froze, only a sharp intake of breath giving away her delight. Without speaking, they watched the bear amble along the creek, turning over a rock here, digging in the mud there, till its bowlegged walk finally took it out of sight.

"Cool," Sarah whispered. "That's so cool, Dad. If you got

a job in Alaska, maybe I could come here at Christmas and not go back to San Diego ever again."

"You know your mother won't let you go till she has to."

"I know," she said, her jaw locked on her words.

Beringer noticed now that his fingers were locked on the wheel. He eased them open and flexed them. Dinner. Watching the bear reminded him. He'd caught a rockfish yesterday and there was enough left for tonight. He put a little butter in the skillet to sauté it, got a tomato out, sliced an onion and threw it in the pan, too. When the fish flaked in only a couple of minutes, he tilted everything onto a plate, got out a beer, and sat at the table.

When he finished eating he leaned back, stretching his legs out along the bench, imagining how he'd be crowding Sarah if she were here in her sleeping bag, how she'd giggle and sit up, her hair tousled, skinny as a heron inside the enormous sweatshirt she slept in. He and Sarah had been a team since her first colicky months twelve years ago, when he'd walked the floor and recited batting averages against her hot feathered skull.

Only five days since he was assigned to this ragged edge of the continent—three days since he'd stepped off the plane in Wrangell and been seized by the watery grandeur, islands so small the tide drowned them twice a day, rain blowing sideways through skyscraper trees, mist that draped the back of your neck and ran in cold rivulets down your arms. He'd stay here, trade his job for one with Alaska Wildlife. He could still do the job they'd set him. He was the only whale expert they had now. And he hoped Sarah would be living with him soon.

The radio sputtered at him—channel 16—ferry entering Wrangell Narrows from the south, *"Securité, Securité, all concerned traffic respond on thirteen or sixteen."*

He stood up and reached for the scanner. Always interested in the local radio traffic, fishermen chatting with each other, never giving an ounce of information about how they were doing, where they were setting net or hanging out waiting for the opening, but full of oblique comments that a buddy might be able to decode.

And suddenly there was the voice. The voice that yanked him away from Exchange Cove, Alaska, and dumped him, twenty-seven years and an ocean between, into elephant grass along the Mekong River.

"Alpha Four-two—we're taking some mortar fire—Victor Charlie—tree line."

He knew for a fact the voice couldn't exist. *"This is Alpha Four-two, Alpha Four-two. We're pinned down by mortar fire, request illumination."*

But he'd heard the voice three times now on these surveillance trips out of Wrangell. And twenty-seven years ago at Kien Van. He still didn't know if he could answer it.

5

Somehow Lieutenant Paul Howard's office at the Wrangell Police Department had gotten smaller, like plastic shrink-wrap or something. He flicked the stack of papers on his desk with his thumb and forefinger and watched with glum satisfaction as the pile cascaded off the opposite side and disappeared. Way to go. Get rid of dumb bureaucracy by snapping his fingers.

He flipped to the back of the Seattle paper he'd bought—yesterday's, of course—plane never got in before he came to work.

Help Wanted. He scanned the columns for something likely—caretaker for a South Pacific island, lifeguard at Waikiki. Nobody seemed to be looking for an elderly, over-weight, Native American police officer. Very nice personality, caring, jolly, no typing or windows.

Sheesh. Nothing seemed to catch his attention anymore. Not since that crazy shoot-out last spring, that crazy, exultant, heart-breaking moment when he'd tried to comfort Lizzie. Not that she'd even noticed, so distraught, so exhausted she couldn't even talk. Since then, he'd tried to keep her from going off alone in that old tub of a boat, pointed out the things that could happen, but no, of course she didn't listen. Why would she, anyway, him an old fart trying to tell her what to do.

He hauled himself to his feet, went around the desk and shuffled the papers together, picked the pile up from the floor, and set it down dead center again. Hey-hey—new way to occupy himself—better than darts at the uglies on his bulletin board.

Norma-with-the-syrup-voice called from the dispatch desk. "Trouble over at the trailer court, Paul."

"Pauu . . . llll." Ugh.

"Woman on the phone crying—says her neighbor has her kid locked up and won't let him go till she takes her dog to the pound—says the man claims the dog pees on his roses and bites his wife."

"Yeah, okay, I got it, Norma." He might as well do it himself—Luke was sitting back there in the outer office hanging out on the phone, but Paul needed air—maybe by the time he got back, the office would be too small to get into, shrinking at this rate. Maybe he'd have to find a different job. Retire, drop a line in the water and wait for a fish. Meanwhile, dog pee and roses. He grabbed his cap and headed out the door whistling "Granny, Does Your Dog Bite?"

He went out and climbed into the Blazer, heading for the trailer court. It was a delicate negotiation that required the dog to be tied up ("Forever," the man said— "he's gotta be tied there every day the rest of his life, which'll sure be short if he ain't") before the child could be released. Then he pointed the Blazer downhill, heading for the harbor.

He leaned on the rail next to the harbormaster's office. He watched a huge longliner taking on fuel over at the Union dock. Old wooden boat, big and beamy, tubs for the hooks and skates, and the baiting shed on the aft deck. She sported the foot-high black numbers of her fishing permit on the side of the wheelhouse. Big Zodiac swung on davits.

A couple of crew members were hosing off her decks. She'd finished fueling now, and a tall man in a tan windbreaker and blue cap was waiting for his change. The man climbed over the rail as the two crewmen let the lines off. He stepped into the wheelhouse and started the engine. A cloud of blue smoke poured from the stack, and the boat pulled away from the dock. She ran slowly toward the inner harbor, made a broken U-turn, and came back toward Paul, passing the dock below him before turning out between the red and green markers at the harbor entrance.

As she passed below, Paul looked down at her aftdeck. On each side of the canopy, blue oil drums lined the rails all the way to the bulkhead of the pilothouse. Coils of clear tubing were wedged between the oil drums. Odd-looking gear—he wondered if they were part of the spill recovery team. Some of the fishermen had signed on as volunteers for that program. He pushed off the rail and headed for the Blazer. He'd better get back to work.

Chief Woods waved at him as Paul came in and Paul lifted his hand. He went back to his cubicle, tossing his jacket on the hook inside the door.

"Line two, Pau . . . ulll."

He lifted the receiver. "Howard here."

"Paul?"

"Lizzie." His heart did peculiar things when he heard her voice. He tried to sound calm despite a tendency to hyperventilate.

"You got a minute?" she asked. "I wanted to tell you about a couple funny things."

"Oh, sure. More minutes'n I want, actually."

"Well, the first thing—a humpback ran into the *Salmon Eye* just as we came out of Point Baker."

"Ran into you? Bashed into the boat, you mean?"

"Yeah. It seemed really strange. Crashed into the hull so

hard I don't know why it didn't sink us. Then it breached a few times, rolled along beside us a few minutes looking us over, and disappeared."

"Weird. Seems like their hearing's too good for that. I know they've tipped over a kayak now and then—maybe don't hear 'em, but your engine oughta warn it."

"I know. I thought it was really odd. Oh well, like I told Sam, 'everyone lived.' But the other thing is, a woman was there at the counter at Archie's—kind of a strange-looking woman—enormous bleached blonde. Said she was off a longliner that's planning to fish down here this winter.

"But when I went to get my jacket off the rack, I accidentally picked hers up first. There was something super heavy in the pocket, and when I felt of it, I could tell it was a gun. What would she have a gun for? And why would she leave it hanging there in her coat where anyone could find it?"

"Anyone can get a permit for a concealed weapon in Alaska now."

"Paul . . . that isn't the point. Why would a woman like that be carrying a gun at all?"

"Some women expect to be assaulted at every street corner. And people think Alaska's full of bears that jump out of the woods and eat you up. Maybe she was aiming to hike the trails or something."

"I suppose. Yeah—a handgun in case she goes ashore and hikes around. But just leave it in the pocket of her coat and hang her coat out there on a public coat rack? Oh well, I'm sure you're right—I'm still jumpy, is all."

"Lizzie, I got some bad news for you. Henry Sizemore drowned."

"Oh, no! I was just out there at Point Baker and his boat was there, but in the morning his boat was gone. Oh, that's just *terrible*."

"His boat went down, likely. I don't know what happened. I really liked him."

"So did I. He came back to Shoemaker Bay frequently—he was a live-aboard there. I'm so sorry he's gone. I'll write to his wife. He was a very, very good sailor. What happened?"

"I don't know—all I know is that he drowned—the packer brought him in a few nights ago and wrote in the log the position where they found him and the time of night."

"Dreadful, dreadful."

"When you coming back?"

"Tomorrow. I'm going to leave Kashevarof around five A.M. I want to get an early start. Sounds like there's a front moving in."

"Yeah, well . . . maybe I'll come by and help you tie up."

"Pretty early for the elderly," she said.

"Take care, little child. Bogeyman'll get'cha if you don't watch out."

The cubicle had shrunk a bit more. The snapshots of Joey seemed to leap at him, the ragged holes that had once been Carolyn, smoothed into the background. Now he saw another woman in those holes, her dark eyes focused on something behind him. He glanced over his shoulder, but nothing was there.

6

ALL THE WAY TO KASHEVAROF, SHE KEPT thinking about that gun. A short, heavy revolver by the feel of it. Why would Jenny Andover be carrying a gun, and why would she leave it in a public place like the coat rack at Archie's?

North of Steamer Point, Liza put the boat on auto and went out on deck. There was the tiny rocky islet with the light, where, eight months ago, she'd come upon a dead man. Beyond the Point lay Kindergarten Bay. The tide was out and the rock visible where James had been that day. That day in her first life.

Paul Howard and Liza had met in the spring when events had swept away just about every connection Liza had ever had: lovers and friends, cops and robbers and Indian chiefs. The first month of their acquaintance, Paul could scarcely look at Liza without clenching his jaw. During *his* first life, he'd been married to a white woman from the south. They'd had one son before Carolyn decided that rain mildewed the mind. She left Paul and took his adored eight-year-old back to Texas. His custody battle failed—what could an Indian man, living at the edge of the earth, offer a "normal" child?

Paul's distrust of all white women was profound. He and "Lizzie," as he insisted on calling her, still had a very fractious acquaintance. Under his gruff manner was . . . a gruff manner. Or, as her friend Tasha once said, "Under that thick skin lies another thick skin." She tried to ignore the knot under her ribs caused by the sight of him.

Paul's immense, dark presence seemed to Liza like a genie she'd released from a bottle and couldn't put back. He was running to fat—Liza thought fifty pounds wouldn't be missed at all. His graying hair was clipped a quarter inch from the scalp; he had the black, almond-eyed gaze of his Tlingit ancestors, but his skin was beginning to crinkle like old newsprint around his eyes. How could she find this aging, crabby cop appealing?

The bay at Kashevarof was very shallow—she had to watch the tide to get across the sandbar. The shore was covered in a scraggly forest of twisted spruce that ran down to long, sulfuric-smelling tidelands. The village ran up a steep ledge and vanished at the top, the houses staggered along a rutted, muddy road.

At the dock in Kashevarof, Liza used the crane to unload two concrete septic tanks, a generator, three rolls of carpet and twelve pallets of canned goods. Moving things along the dock with the forklift, she stowed them in the metal shed at the top of the ramp. Before she had all the freight unloaded, a crowd was lined up for the library. But first she had to make a call to her friend; Paul. No, she wouldn't, yes, she would. She didn't want to be involved with another cop after Efren's death, but somehow . . . well, actually, yes, she did.

Paul had told her terrible news, Henry had drowned. His body had been picked up by a packer in the middle of Sumner Strait. She might have heard his boat start up—middle of the night, she thought, and it was gone the next morning, and he hadn't taken the hydrophones. He'd radioed her that he was on to something—maybe he was investigating that when his boat went down? But he was a very assured sea-man. What had happened?

When she got back to the boat, she opened the former captain's stateroom where she kept the books these days, and set the crates out for returns. They filled quickly. People browsed through the mysteries and peered over each other's shoulders at the new-book shelf. In all, thirty-seven people checked out books, a high percentage of the local popula-tion. At 5:00 P.M. she dropped the notebook and date stamp into the drawer with the cards, flipped the sign on the door to "Closed," and climbed the twisty mud road to the Velvet Moose.

"Mink," Minerva Michaels, owner of the Velvet Moose, was manning the griddle, while Jimmy Matsui tended bar. Minerva Michaels and Paul Howard were cut from the same cloth: overweight, armor-clad curmudgeons. How had she gotten stuck with two of them?

Directly over Liza's head was the bronze ship's bell from the S.S. *Robert Merton*, the sunken steamship, which rang to celebrate the fortunes of local fishermen, announce wed-dings and births, and toll over departures. A round of drinks for the house with every clang of the bronze.

Liza ordered a hamburger and a Coke, then shoved her way through the crowd to the back booth to rap with Tango. Tango's gray hair had receded slightly farther since spring, the long back strands fastened in a ponytail. His chessboard was half played out, his radio log spread beside it.

Tango was Mink's husband, one of those whose past was erased in the jungles of Vietnam. An air raid—"friendly fire," as it was called—wiped out most of his platoon, as well as Tango's former self. Mink took him on "as is."

"Tango," Liza said, "what's on?"

His eyes opened and he nodded at her. He picked up his radio again. Staring over Liza's shoulder, he said, "Alpha

Four-two here, put it down the center, man, they're blowing us out with 120 mike mike mortars. Raining downtown— Charlie by the river. Alpha Four-two out."

"Tango . . ." Liza said, "what's that rap now? Why don't you just give it up, eh?"

" 'Have not I made blind Homer sing to me?' "

Liza laughed and raised her hands in surrender. Suddenly the heavy door to the Velvet Moose was flung open. Jenny Andover stood framed in it. Silence consumed her audience as she struggled to jam a revolver into the pocket of her jacket.

7

THE TIDE WAS FLOODING WHEN BERINGER turned into Port Beauclerc, keeping Edwards Island to starboard. The wind in the strait was causing heavy surge along the shore. A huge log floated just off the gravel, pushed by each swell. He didn't want to tangle with drift logs—he'd had an exhausting day trying to track a pod of orcas as well as scan the few boats that crossed its path. He turned out and dropped the anchor closer to the center of the bay. Then he looked at the beach again. Something odd about that log— one end of it seemed to be moving up and down.

He went in and grabbed the binoculars. The giant log rolling in the surf was not a log at all. It was a humpback whale.

Throwing himself into the raft, he pulled toward shore, aiming at a point far beyond the whale, not wanting to add terror to its obvious distress. Pulling the raft up on the beach, he walked up to the tree line before turning back. He edged along behind some rocky outcroppings till he was opposite the whale. Then he climbed onto the rocks and looked down at it.

The whale's back was toward him, the blowhole visible, and now and then it blew as a wave broke over it, not the towering spout of a surfacing whale, but a weak sigh, water sprayed in a bubbly gasp. From time to time the whale made a violent effort to right itself, the tail flukes writhing and the heavy body arching toward deeper water, but the shallows had captured it.

Two things he could do—one essential. He got back in the raft and rowed hard for the boat. Grabbing the radio, he called for assistance: the Coast Guard, his office in Wrangell, the Wildlife Protection Agency in Sitka. There was no one close to him—all of them indicated several hours ETA.

He contemplated other solutions. The tide was about halfway in, according to his tide table. If the whale was too weak or disoriented, or injured, it couldn't resist the force of the water lifting it toward the beach, and when the tide began to ebb, the whale would be stranded.

What he had to do was build a fence behind it to keep it from being pushed farther. Then, when the tide was high— the tide table showed a 16.4-foot vertical rise—the whale would be floating and he might be able to use the boat to steer it out into the strait. But he'd have to hurry or he'd be in water over his head trying to lever rocks and logs into place behind the whale. Besides, it was beginning to get dark, the sun already behind the ridge on the west side of the cove.

Beringer dragged on his insulated exposure suit, which would help keep him warm if he wound up working underwater, leaving the zipper open because dragging drift logs would keep him warm too. He had a survival suit on board, as well, but the survival suit was a totally enclosed garment that kept you warm and dry, gloves and booties attached to it. He needed his hands free, so the Mustang suit was what he wanted, though it would get soaked if he had to work in the water. He took the axe and set out again for shore.

The whale had rolled slightly, its huge pleated jaw turned

toward the bottom in a normal swimming position, but the body forward of the dorsal fin was apparently on gravel, the water too shallow for escape. It dwarfed everything in sight and Beringer wondered if the weight of it, unsupported by water, would implode, crushing its bones in blubber.

He looked along the beach for material. Most of the logs that lay crisscrossed like pick-up sticks were enormous—much too big for him to handle alone. There was some alder at the edge of the forest—maybe he could cut some and stab it into the sand behind the whale.

He climbed behind the ledge to the alder. The trunks weren't very straight, but most of them were a couple inches in diameter. He could cut several, sharpen them and drive them firmly into the sandy bottom.

A fine mist was blowing onshore in the gusting wind, a distant early warning, he thought. A DEW line. Well, *Sarah* laughs at my puns, he said to the whale.

In twenty minutes Beringer had felled fifteen saplings. He hacked off the longer branches, and used his knife to make a point at the larger end, dragging them down the beach toward the whale.

What was the whale thinking? Beringer wondered. Did whales think? Of course they did—a humpback sang complex songs in a language that changed; learned another song each year—how could anyone believe a whale didn't think? Someday that song language, the notes and phrases and themes, would be decoded, and man and whale would speak to each other in the harmonics of an ocean world.

He began to hum as he got closer—would the whale prefer music to speech? Was either better than silence for his approach?

The whale thrashed as he got close to it and he could see bubbles forming at the blowhole. He waded in till he was up to his thighs in water, only two feet behind the whale, each swell forcing him to brace against it. One at a time he drove the long stakes as far into the gravel as he could get them, trying to drive them in hard, two of them striking rock only a few inches down so he had to pull them and try again.

Very slowly he built a vertical fence behind the whale. Waist-deep now, he could barely keep his balance in the surge. Next, rocks. There were boulders as large as he was—there was the rocky ledge that cropped out of the earth at the top of the beach, and there was gravel—pea-sized, walnut-sized, a few as big as grapefruit. He searched, finding only two that he could lift that were big enough to be useful. He lifted and rolled, trying to move them down to brace those stakes.

What wasted effort this was—that whale weighed thirty or forty tons and he was trying to hold it off the beach with a few alder saplings? But water displaced heavy objects. Archimedes had known all about displacement. Archimedes had moved a huge ship all by himself. Why couldn't Scott Beringer move a whale? He only needed to hold that whale where it was. Then, when the water rose enough to displace its weight, it would lift off the bottom.

He stepped forward and laid his hands against the whale, feeling the whale's skin ripple beneath his hands as a horse might shiver off a fly, knowing he could not move this giant creature with his bare hands but stroking, slipping his hands over its side with fingers barely touching, his eyes filling as he imagined some ancient connection.

He couldn't waste another minute—it might already be too late—but the dark wall that rose above his hands had a huge, slow-beating heart and arteries that carried blood like his own, and his hands were caressing it. He laid his face against the whale's side for an instant and hummed into the skin, inhaling the fishy smell, the sulphur smell of things exposed by the tide. Then he backed away. What a strange, silly reaction—his only purpose was to get that whale off the beach.

It was so dark now he could barely see his own hands. The mist had, as promised, turned to cold rain, and the wind flung it against his face. He took the flashlight from the inflatable and went back to searching for a long slender log. Hurry up, hurry up—the whale's weight would crush his little fence if he couldn't hold it off while the water rose.

Behind the huge logs at the west corner of the beach, he found a smaller sawlog, still yellow from the mill, and dragged it back along the beach. He ran to the raft, took the life jacket out of it and wrapped it around one end of the log, tying it as tightly as he could to cushion it against the whale's side. Propping the flashlight on a rock ledge so that it cast a dim circle of light across the whale, he began to walk into the water, humming as he waded forward.

He knew the whale was watching him. Its dark eye was submerged now in several feet of water, but he could feel it watching. Inquiring into the plan. The whale had ceased to struggle, having grown used to his presence, or perhaps having resigned itself to its fate. He pressed the end of the log with the life preserver into the whale's side behind the huge jaw. Then he let the log rest on the surface, his hands gripping the center. He pushed gently. The whale had moved against the alder stakes, which meant there was enough water under it to have floated it a foot or two toward the beach.

Beringer was waist-deep in the water. In half an hour he'd be up to his neck, unable to keep his feet down so he could exert force on the end of the log. He pressed a little harder and the whale moved.

Beringer took a deep breath and stepped forward, pushing as hard as he could, and the whale moved again. Holding the log firmly against the side of the whale, he inched his hands back till he was holding the opposite end. He threw his full weight forward against the end of the log. The whale's great head rose in the surf, then dropped down as its back arched. The long sleek pectoral fins drove downward, scooping backward against the bottom. Beringer imagined its finger bones pressing the gravel—whales had returned from land to water in the long saga of evolution.

He leaned on his end of the log again, feeling his feet sink in the soft bottom, water to his chin now as he drove forward against the whale's side. And then he was falling forward. The far end of the log was braced on nothing. His face submerged and his exposure suit turned him into an orange peel bobbing on the surface.

He fought his way back to the beach, the suit making him swim like a wounded walrus. Dragging himself to his feet, he saw a dark shape roll up close to his boat in the center of the bay.

For the first time, Beringer noticed how cold he was. He started to the raft, then stopped as a sound like a wheezing steam jet reached his ears. Breath released from a living engine. Humming, he walked to the raft and climbed in.

Aboard the larger boat, he turned the stove up to torch, peeled his soaked clothes from his chilled body, and scrubbed himself with a towel till his skin was red and tingling. He pulled on his long johns, put sweats over them and topped it all off with a wool sweater. He was still shivering. He poured himself a double shot of Scotch.

"To Archimedes," he said aloud, raising the glass to the darkened window. "It still works, man."

Celebration and recovery. He opened a can of chili. What had caused that whale to beach itself? At no time had he seen an injury, though the skin all along the lower edge of the jaw, where the baleen attached, had been scraped and raw from the whale's efforts to dig itself off the gravel.

He put the chili in a bowl, set a block of cheese and some crackers on the table, and splashed more Scotch in his glass. His legs were shaking. He stretched them out on the bench and leaned back, feeling the boat swing on her anchor as the tide began to ebb. He hadn't had much time before the tide turned—beautiful, it had been, that huge intelligent eye, the grooved jaw that could expand around tons of water, weave air into a fish net.

Smelled bad—fishy—it wouldn't smell bad underwater, though—what strange evolution, water to land to water— escaping traffic on the freeways—he understood—if he could escape into the sea, that would be where . . . he wasn't thinking very clearly, was he? Suffering from Scotch-diluted fatigue—there was the radio—the radio voice—*"Alpha Four-two here, put it down the center, man, they're blowing us out. . . ."*

Goddammit, that voice brought tears to his eyes. Who the hell was it? The man who owned that voice had died seventeen years ago. It was all a hallucination brought on by alcohol. From being alone too much. He rubbed his neck and shook his head as though he could empty it of that voice. *". . . mike mortars. Raining downtown—Charlie by the river. Alpha Four-two out."*

Well, why the hell not? He stood up and reached for the transmitter.

8

JENNY FINALLY MANAGED TO WEDGE THE revolver into her pocket, her face increasingly red. From embarrassment or effort, Liza wondered. With the gun concealed—Paul's voice reminded Liza that concealed weapons were legal in Alaska—she pushed her way over to the bar.

A man came in after her and stood behind her, almost as tall, but too thin to hide Jenny entirely. A small dark-haired woman came through the door followed by a short bald man. The woman squeezed up to the bar next to a local fisherman wearing a brown coverall, and the bald man stood behind her. No one Liza had ever seen before, except Jenny.

Lynnie and Jerry McGovern came in with a swarm of other fishermen and dragged Liza over to their table. Picking up Liza's hamburger, which had been cooling for some time, Mink slammed it down in front of her while she took the others' orders.

Liza could see Tango sitting sideways at the end of the bench in his booth. He was holding his right hand over his ear to shut out the bar noise, the radio clapped tightly to his left ear. His body was rigid with tension, and his eyes were staring in amazement as though he'd heard the approach of Armageddon.

Sometimes Tango's voices became too vivid or painful,

and Mink would order him to the storeroom to recover, providing him with a couple joints to ease what hurt. When Mink came back, Liza gestured under the table in Tango's direction. "Fire fight?" she whispered to Mink.

Mink glanced at him and looked away. "I don't know what he's got going now," she muttered. "Kinda funny—not like the usual. Keeps saying, 'Roger roger, I hear you. It's really you, isn't it?' And when I stopped by, he had tears in his eyes, and he held the radio toward me and said, 'It's him, it's him. I waited all this time.'"

Mink looked down at her tray, moved some glasses closer together so she'd have room to pick up more, glanced back at Tango again. "Think he was talking to God his very own self, whisperin' away, 'it's him, it's him.' Makes me all over funny feeling." She shuddered, sending shock waves along the red Alaska fisherman suspenders she always wore.

"Want me to go sit with him?" Liza asked.

"Yeah, that'd be good—I can't seem to break in on this one. Don't want to make a scene just to lock him in the storeroom." Mink looked down at her and Liza could see the worry in her eyes.

Liza carried her glass over to the booth and squeezed in opposite Tango. From the jukebox came the beginning throb of "Blue Bayou."

"Roger, repeat at ready," Tango was saying. He wrote a series of numbers, then scooted the notebook across the table and handed her the pen. He pointed at the book and repeated the numbers slowly and clearly.

Liza checked each number as he said it: "1-0-3-1-0-2 november 1-0-5-4-6-1-6 echo."

"Roger," he said into the radio. "That was it—that was it!" He shook himself and sat straighter. "Alpha Four-two, here. Roger." He waved a hand at Liza and she picked up the pen, writing "5-6-1-8-0-2 november 1-3-3-0-9-0-9 whiskey," as he said each number aloud. He checked to see if she had it and she nodded. "Roger," he said, "eight hundred. Repeat, eight hundred."

Liza wrote "800" in the book after the word "whiskey." Tango's eyes were fixed on some inner space, so concentrated Liza could see the moving finger write across his brain.

"Five six one eight," he said again. "One three three zero nine." Then he smiled and said, "'Yet meet we shall, and part, and meet again, where dead men meet on lips of living men.'"

Even though the radio was clamped tightly to his ear, Liza could hear a shout of laughter from it, and a staticky voice crackled, *"Oh, that's you for sure, you old grunt."*

Tango grinned broadly. "Heh-heyyyy, Baaarron. Alpha Four-two, out," he said, and laid the radio on the table as gently as if it were glass. He stared at Liza, not seeing her. "'Footfalls echo in the memory,'" he whispered, "'down the passage which we did not take.'"

His eyes filled with tears. Reaching across to take the notebook, he said, "'I have measured out my life in coffee spoons.'"

A shout came from the bar. Someone cursed and a stool fell over. Barbra Streisand's voice vaulted into the sudden silence.

People shifted back from the bar, trying to get distance on the fight that was brewing. The bald man, no taller than Liza's own five seven, stood in the cleared area—the ring, now—slightly crouched, his fists doubled and his feet making small, hunting movements that caused his upper body to twitch. Opposite him, the taller bearded man ran his fingers over the side of his jaw, his eyes narrowed to slits under dark, angry eyebrows. He spat words at the bald man that Liza couldn't hear over Barbra's piercing soprano.

"Outa here," Mink said, marching into the center with her wide shoulders squared. "Plenty 'a space out there in the road for mud wrestling." She grabbed the bearded fellow by one arm and moved toward the bald man, but as she turned, Liza saw the bald man flick open a knife and launch himself from his half crouch.

Liza shouted, "Mink, don't," and several in the crowd lunged forward, but he opened a brilliant stripe across the sleeve of Mink's white shirt before they had him. Blood spurted and dyed the whole sleeve while Mink stepped behind the bar, opened the drawer under the cash register, and leveled an old Colt .25 automatic pistol across the bar at the bald man, now struggling in the firm grasp of four locals.

"You get," Mink said. "Both 'a you. You get, and don't come back. That door's one way only for guys with a grudge."

"Want us to call Hap Farwell?" one of the men asked her. Hap was the Village Public Safety Officer of Kashevarof, Alaska.

"So what's he gonna do, throw 'em in the slammer?" Mink said, there being no such institution in town. "When Hap Farwell's got more muscle than this little jewel," she said, holding out the pistol to show off its ivory stock, "sure I'll call him. Now, get 'em outa here, fellas."

Liza saw Jenny push the door open and hold it for the short woman, others sliding out at the same time. The bald man, whose blood alcohol was clearly beyond toxic, was half singing a line of four-letter words as though he were making up new verses to an old song. The crowd dropped back to make way for him and his escorts.

Suddenly Tango was on his feet shouting, "You bastard— you're next, you're next," pointing his finger at him like a gun.

Baldy raised his head and looked over his shoulder at

Tango, his eyes searching but unfocused. His opponent, the tall, bearded man, whirled and stared across the crowd at Tango.

" 'Bald heads, forgetful of their sins,' " Tango raged across the renewed silence. " 'After such knowledge, what forgiveness?' "

Baldy's eyes found him, and he sagged forward, dragging the men on each arm toward the door. The tall man, watching Tango over his shoulder, slipped through the crowd and was gone. As the door swung shut after them, Liza looked at Tango. His eyes were narrowed, his body drawn like fine wire. An eagle poised to attack.

Mink. By the time Liza got to her, she was seated on a stool behind the bar and already had her shirt off. Janet Haynesworth, the nurse in Kashevarof, had applied a tourniquet.

"New shirt, too," Mink was grumbling. "Slit right through it, the dumb fuck."

"You gotta get that sewed up, lady," Janet said. "Tonight."

"Aw, the hell . . ."

"No shit from you, Mink. You're gonna get it sewed up, you hear? It's deep—way into the muscle. You need a medevac."

Mink looked up at Liza and tried to growl her customary objections, but her face was ashen, and her voice croaked when she spoke. "Listen at her. Nanny Jan, hunh."

"You want me to call or are you gonna do it?"

"Don't need no medevac—I can get over there to the hospital tomorrow."

"Well, maybe I can tie this up for tonight, but either you go out with the mail plane tomorrow, or you get somebody here to run you over to Wrangell."

"I can take you," Liza said. "I'll run you over first thing in the morning."

"She'll last unless the bleeding starts up again. If it does—" she glared at Mink—"it's medevac time. Damned right it is," she said, as Mink started to protest.

Tango shouldered past Liza then, and shuddered at the sight of so much blood on the floor. He gagged, swallowed hard, then shuddered again before he bent over Mink. "'The question is,' said Humpty Dumpty, 'which is to be master—that's all.'" He pressed his cheek against hers, then levered her to her feet. "What time you going?" he asked Liza.

"We'll leave at five and be in by ten."

"I get up at noon," Mink said. "Don't be a fool."

"She'll be there, Tango said. "'And a grey mist on the sea's face and a grey dawn breaking.'"

"Break my fucking back is what, getting down there by five."

"She'll be there, Liza. And listen . . ." He bent over and whispered in her ear, "Take care of her."

Liza waited for the quote, but it didn't come. When she looked at him, he was staring over her shoulder with angry eyes.

9

BERINGER LAY ON HIS BACK ON THE V-berth, staring up into darkness, feeling the deck there not two feet above his head like a coffin lid. The instant he'd said, "This is the Baron, the Baron calling Alpha Four-two, come in Alpha Four-two," he was screwed. He'd jammed the transmitter back on the hook, his hands shaking so hard he missed twice in a row, but the voice came right back at him calm as ever, calm as twenty-seven years ago.

Roger, Baron, this is Alpha Four-two.

That guy had never raised his voice. "Alpha Six-one, this is Alpha Four-two—we're pinned down here," he'd say quietly, saying, "Charlie in the tree line—need cover—need cover," saying, " 'Royal captain of this ruin'd band . . . delays have dangerous ends.' "

Only once had he screamed. "You're on *top* of us, you *fuckers*." Only once sobbed, "Fuckin' hell—there's nobody left."

Beringer knew his cheeks were wet but he couldn't lift his hand to wipe his tears. Ted Hilliard was dead. How, then, could Ted's voice be carried on the VHF?

Imprinted, that's all it was. When you're in terror of your life, detail becomes etched on your brain. Chicken feathers stuck in a child's bloody black hair. The steady creak of the pack on the man ahead. The calm voice of your RTO repeating, "This is Alpha Four-two, Alpha Four-two, we need fire over the center of concentration. Alpha Four-two, Alpha Four-two . . ." And they got it. But not over the center, to the left of center. To their center. To the very heart of them.

Beringer had been the lucky one—a helicopter grabbed him from hell with one leg half blown away. Hilliard hadn't fared so well. Better to walk with one short leg than have your mind blown, your past erased.

When Beringer got home, hobbled but moving, he'd gone to see Hilliard at the V.A. hospital. Ted had seemed to know him, called him the Baron, a nickname that had stuck since high school. Beringer had talked about setting out on the trail toward the river and the VC mortars, but Hilliard lived in a vacuum. Beringer could do nothing to pierce it, nothing that brought back one single recollection, only the quotations Hilliard had committed to memory before he left the English department for the jungles of Vietnam.

"'Oh dark, dark, dark, amid the blaze of noon,'" Ted had said. "'The end is where we start from.'"

After five days of talking, Beringer gave up. He had gone then to visit Hilliard's wife, Andrea. Tried to explain what had happened to erase Ted's memory. And she had understood, been gentle with him when he'd broken down trying to describe the indescribable.

They'd talked of the future, how if Ted's memory didn't return, she'd have to take over and provide for them, which was all right—she'd finished a law degree and was already a junior partner in a small firm in St. Louis.

A few weeks later, Ted had gone home, had clasped his radio rather than his wife, had taken to long, rambling walkabouts. Andrea and Beringer had begun a correspondence, writing first about Ted and his condition, branching out later to talk of their careers, then more personal matters, hopes and private thoughts. Two years later Andrea wrote to Beringer: Ted was dead—he had walked into the path of a truck out on the freeway. His parents were dead—there had been no service—she had scattered his ashes in the Mississippi River as he had wanted.

They'd exchanged more letters and finally Beringer had flown to St. Louis. After a year of visits, he married her, taking her back to San Diego where she joined a new law firm. And now she was Sarah's mother, battling him for custody.

Had Andrea invented Ted's death, or was he going to meet a stranger? The deck above his head had moved down so he could scarcely breathe. He raised trembling hands and pressed them on the cold fiberglass as though he could push up the lid of his coffin.

Faces, images of rotted boots and razor wire, the stink of it all—why had he answered that voice? Why had something like those coordinates for Kien Van come bursting from his lips?

Shit—he didn't want to meet this man, whoever he was. And who was it, anyway? Good god, who could it be?

10

IN THE MORNING, LIZA HAD THE ENGINE warmed up when Tango and Mink appeared, Mink looking like the Moose herself in black rain gear, a black baseball cap with the Kashevarof Volunteer Fire Department logo pulled low over her steel-wool hair. The jacket was tied at the neck and unzipped to allow her to keep her arm inside it. She moved cautiously, lumbering up the steps and onto the deck with Tango behind her, steadying herself with her good arm before she stepped into the cabin, careful not to brush the narrow doorway with her shoulder.

"Hurting some, aren't you?" Liza said.

"Ahh, shit, it's nothin'." She waved off sympathy, but allowed Tango to slip the jacket off. The right suspender of her rain pants dangled loose.

"Want those off?" he asked her.

"Nahh, way too much trouble to get 'em on again," she said, "and rain movin' in. I'll need 'em in Wrangell. You still got that swell vehicle you were drivin' last time?" she said to Liza, referring to the '64 Chevy pickup with moss growing from its crown. "Gotta wear full armor plate to ride in that thing."

"You bet. Best transportation on the island for the money."

Liza looked at Tango. "You might as well go with us," she said, as he hovered and twitched around Mink. The two of them seemed to fill the whole cabin with separation anxiety.

"You want him along stewing around like a beached whale?" Mink said. "Go on now—get lost, buddy."

Tango stood there clapping his hands together nervously, doing a little shrugging dance with his feet, nodding and shaking his head till Liza thought he was going to have a seizure.

"Boat's leaving in three minutes." Liza cupped her hands around her mouth and announced: "All those ashore who're going ashore." Then she turned her back on them and went to the wheelhouse, switched on the GPS and radar, looking at the depth finder, which read eleven feet. Not much depth—only the smaller fishing boats came in to the dock—the channel between the long tide flats was deeper, ranging from fifteen to forty feet, mean low tide, and most of the boats just anchored there. The *Salmon Eye* drew almost nine feet, and she watched the tide tables because she had to avoid Kashevarof on a minus tide.

A couple of minutes later, Tango walked up the dock, pausing at the end to wave back at them. Then he turned and jogged up the hill past the café and hardware store, disappearing around the curve where muddy Main Street made a sharp turn to the north past the grocery and the Velvet Moose.

Liza went out, threw the steps aboard, and released the mooring lines. In the cabin, Mink was slumped at the table. She was crying. "Shut the hell up," she said.

A fine mist was leaking from a colorless sky; forested islands came and went around the boat as they crossed from Kashevarof to Snow Passage. They swung past the Bushy Island light and jogged into the tide rips in the Pass. The cloud enveloped them, obscuring all but a single line of trees at the shoreline of Zarembo Island. Liza watched the radar obsessively since she couldn't see the kelp on the ledge along Zarembo. Oddly enough, she really liked to be able to see where she was going, but unfortunately, in southeast Alaska, often "visibility is reduced to near zero in rain and fog."

They were just opposite the Nesbitt Reef light when, steaming and rolling out of the mist, came a pod of killer whales. Liza put the engine in neutral and shouted, "Mink. Look out to starboard. Orcas."

Grabbing the binoculars, Liza dashed back to the main cabin to hand them to Mink, then back to the wheel to maneuver the boat away from the pod. Suddenly they were all around her, lazing along on the surface, blowing from time to time with great sighs like gusts of wind through dense forest. She went out on deck to look.

She counted nine tall gleaming dorsal fins and two small ones. As the *Salmon Eye* swung sideways and nosed into the current, they moved to the port side but didn't dive. She was surprised to see how quiet they were, close to the surface, almost motionless. They formed a large oval, nearly head to tail. The closest whale was no more than fifty feet from the boat.

Then she saw it. A small spout rose from the center of the pod; a head lifted and vanished and a dorsal fin arced up and over.

She stared through the binoculars and in a minute, the entire motion was repeated. The orca, when it appeared again, had a long, gaping gash in its side, blood trickling over the black-and-white geometry of the skin's surface before it sank again. The others were taking care of the injured one. Protecting it from predators. From the *Salmon Eye*. She returned to the wheelhouse, put the gears in reverse and backed slowly away.

"Hey! Liza, there's more whales over there on the reef," Mink shouted. "Lookit there—by the rocks on Point Nesbitt."

Liza looked across at the Point, but through the mist, and without the glasses, she could barely see the tip of the island. She put the engine in gear, throttled down, and punched in bearings on the autopilot that would keep a course some distance from the nearest whales. When the auto took over, she went back to stand next to Mink.

"Lookit," Mink said, holding out the glasses. "Right on the Point there. Orcas, aren't they? Look at those tall dorsal fins. Seems like one's thrashing around on the rocks."

Liza steadied her elbow against the window frame and scanned the Point. The steep triangular dorsal fins of two orca whales were visible, rising simultaneously. They arched over and sank. Beyond them the water churned up in a huge spray like a wave breaking on a rock, and suddenly she could see a third whale.

She pressed the glasses against the window to try to hold them absolutely steady, but the window glass was oily from salt spray, and made the image shimmer. She went out onto the aft deck and leaned against the bulkhead, trying to focus on the rocks where she thought she'd seen that whale.

Water churned up again, and as the spray dissipated, Liza could see an orca struggling on a ledge of rock running out between Point Nesbitt and the reef light. Beached? How would an orca become stranded on a reef? They were much too strong to be driven on by the current, and their direction finders were as good as those in a satellite system. Something had gone wrong with that whale. Two whales in trouble?

Liza went back in the cabin and handed the binoculars to Mink.

"Something wrong with those whales," she said, echoing

Liza's thought. "Shit, they never run into things. Lookit that whale they got in the circle. Gotta slit in his side makes the cut in my arm look like a hangnail."

"It's strange for sure. Lucky thing the tide's flooding. That orca on the rocks'll be floated off in another hour or less—that part of the reefs under water at mid-tide."

"Think that one guy hit somebody's prop?"

"You know, we got hit by a humpback several days ago. Ran straight into the side of the *Salmon Eye*, breached practically on top of us. I've never seen a humpback drive straight into a boat before."

"Yeah, well, all I know, there's something wrong with 'em. Shit, two beat up at once? And that guy running into you? No way. Somethin' wrong."

"I'll give Wildlife a call in Wrangell. They like to have sightings reported, and if there's something wrong with these pods, they'll want to know about it—at least they can check to see if that stranded one gets off."

She glanced once more at the whales, then turned the *Salmon Eye* east toward Wrangell. Mist enclosed the islands and she ran the strait on instruments, as though tracking the edge of the universe.

11

AT TEN THIRTY-FIVE A.M., THE *SALMON Eye* made her slip at Shoemaker Bay. In the next slip, the older couple on the *Nereia* were putting their sailboat to bed for the winter. From under the green canvas covers, a hand waved, and there was a muffled sound of greeting from the stern. Liza missed them when they went south for the winter—they were her best book customers, finding it more convenient to load up from the *Salmon Eye* before they set out on their summer wanderings than go to the library in town.

The boat harbor at Shoemaker had been added to Reliance Harbor, the main port of Wrangell, to make more room for boats. More people chose permanent moorage at Reliance Harbor because of the convenience to fuel, food and entertainment, but Liza liked the quieter setting at Shoemaker, four miles south.

Liza went out and plugged in the shore power and phone lines while Mink worked at getting her jacket on. The mist had turned to steady rain and the wind was picking up, driving the rain against the windows in gusty assaults. Liza went back into the cabin and found Mink leaning back against the seat, her good arm braced against the roll of the boat. Her face was drained of color and she was breathing rapidly.

"Not feeling too great, are you?" Liza said. "I think I should call the medics. How you going to climb up the ramp?"

"Shit, no. Let's go. Tide's in by now—ramp won't be steep."

She was right that the ramp wouldn't be much of a climb compared to low tide. With a sixteen- to eighteen-foot vertical rise and fall twice a day, the water changed the landscape like a painter with a broad brush. At the lower low tide, it was a hand-over-hand pull up the ramp, and you didn't want to be hauling gear off your boat at that time of day.

Liza dug her purse out of the drawer and leaned over Mink to help her to her feet. Her hand was clammy, and Liza dropped it and felt her forehead. "Little warm, aren't you?"

"Hell, I'm shivering like a jellyfish," she said. "How come there ain't no heat on this sinker?"

"You've got a fever, Mink. Come on, let's go. I want somebody else to be in charge of this, Ms. Michaels."

Between Liza hauling and Mink dragging on the rail, they managed to get her up the ramp, but the high step into the truck was not fun. Mink sank down and leaned her head back on the seat when she finally got in. The truck started with its usual deep growl, backfiring repeatedly in protest as they circled the pothole-ridden parking lot and headed into town along Zimovia Highway, the old blacktop, two-lane road that went past Shoemaker Bay.

Wrangell was fortunate to have a modern hospital with a long-term care wing and two doctors who served a huge area of bush communities, logging camps, and the floating population that reaps the sea. The same people, in fact, whom the *Salmon Eye* served.

The nurse in the emergency room found Mink's temperature to be 102.8°, and shook her head at the red streaks running up her arm. While they waited for the doctor, she gave Mink a tetanus shot, and Mink wound up with her head between her knees. The doctor took one look at the arm and said, "You'll stay with us a little while, I believe." He motioned to Liza and they went out into the hall.

"That arm's kind of angry-looking," he said. "And she's feverish. I'm going to admit her. You a relative?"

"A friend. She'll snort around and give you a hard time, but you better keep her because I live on a boat, which isn't the best accommodation under the circumstances. She's from Kashevarof, and the nurse there wanted her seen over here."

"She was right. A couple days, anyway. She won't push me around on this one, don't worry."

He went back to Mink and said, "I'm admitting you."

She looked up at him, sitting straighter and working up to her familiar rumble.

"And don't give me no shit, woman. I'm boss here."

"I gotta get home." She was talking to Liza, not the doctor, and it wasn't a roar of protest. She looked extremely anxious. "Tango's all by himself."

"He's a grown-up, Mink. He can take care of himself a couple days. And Jimmy's there to run the bar. I'll call Jimmy to tell him you're staying a few days, and he has to run the show."

"But Tango," she said. "You don't know him. I think Tango might go . . ."

All at once her eyes closed and the color drained from her face.

"Whoops," the doctor said. "Little shocky, here."

The nurse pumped the blood-pressure cuff and he bent over Mink with his own stethoscope. In a minute, Mink sighed and opened her eyes again. Liza looked at the doctor, asking for reassurance.

"She's septic," he said. "She's lost some blood, and she's got some infection there, but she'll be out there bulldozing around again before you know it. I'll have to clean that wound before I stitch it up. And we need to give her antibiotics I.V."

Liza leaned close to Mink and said, "I'll be waiting right outside. When they're done operating, I'll come to your room and you can tell me everything you need to tell me." Mink nodded and closed her eyes again.

While she waited, Liza called the Wildlife Protection office. She described the humpback hitting the boat, and said she thought she'd seen an orca stranded at Point Nesbitt on the way back to Wrangell.

"I wish somebody'd check on that one on the rocks. It must have gone on before the tide turned—it should have floated before half flood, I think, but the way it was thrashing around, it could have gotten pretty battered."

"We've had a lot of sightings reported out in Sumner," the woman said. "Some questions being asked. We've got a whale expert on loan from the Feds."

"Well, tell him I called."

Liza called Jimmy Matsui at the Velvet Moose. He would be okay cooking. "Certainly. No problem."

"Can I speak to Tango?"

"He's not here" Jimmy said. "He's not been in all day."

"He's not? He's always there. He's part of the decor."

"I haven't seen him. And his radio's right there on the table. I called his house—no answer. He's taking the day off. Mink's not here to push him around." Jimmy laughed and said, "I have to go now—the lunch people are coming," and he hung up.

Funny. Tango was always there—where else would he

be? He didn't work, didn't socialize, other than the people at the Moose who sometimes shoved a few pieces around on the chessboard.

Liza called the house and listened to the ring, let it ring seven or eight times before she gave up. Funny. Mink wouldn't like that—not at all. She'd get all worked up, get her blood pressure and her fever cranked again.

Maybe he was stoned or something, consoling himself over her absence. He'd show up eventually. Strange, though. Tango was a fixture, not a moveable feast.

She went to Mink's room and found her sound asleep. Making up for the early departure, Liza figured. No point waking her up to get her in a snit over Tango. Liza simply wouldn't tell her.

12

BERINGER HAD TROUBLE FINDING THE channel entrance to Kashevarof, obscured as it was in heavy mist. He passed a speeding Zodiac with two people in it just as he reached the sandbar. He had to slow down in their wake, so he was a few minutes late. He put the engine in neutral and drifted quietly toward the dock, spun the wheel and gave her a little nudge with the engine, then cut it off and stepped through the door onto the aftdeck, dropping the fenders over the side and grabbing the wood rail on the sagging dock. Flinging his line over the rail, he pulled it through, knotting it before he stepped onto the dock.

At the shore end of the dock was a metal shed, and he could see a dirt road running up the hill, the outlines of several buildings looming through the mist, a yellow security light stabbing out. The silence was profound—it must be too early for the residents of Kashevarof to be abroad.

He glanced at his watch. 8:20. Where was the man? He'd plotted the coordinates more than once and they crossed right here at the dock in Kashevarof. He climbed back on the boat, looking again at the chart, then turned the diesel stove higher to warm his hands.

8:47. Damn. He wasn't coming. The man must live around here somewhere. He could track him down, but maybe he wasn't ready to face the past either—maybe he'd funked it, decided it would rile up too many things, meeting up after all these years. Beringer, though, had to know the answer. So much depended on it.

Where was the truth of it? This was spinning his mind— it would turn out not to be Ted, of course, just a strangely familiar voice. Quotes, though. Hilliard had memorized the whole body of English literature. It had to be Ted—nobody else would pull quotations out of a hat like that.

Was he losing it? Inventing a voice for someone who didn't even exist? At least ask around, see what he could find out. He had to know.

The only place along the dirt street where he saw a sign of life was a bar and grill called the Velvet Moose. The Japanese barman was washing dishes behind the bar and shook his head. "Not open now," he said.

"I'm looking for someone. Man who talks on the VHF radio a lot, uses radio signals from Vietnam?"

The barman nodded. "The man who talks on the radio is married to Mink, the owner of the bar. Mink got cut bad last night—maybe Tango went to Wrangell with her. I haven't seen him today."

"They live around here?"

"They live on top of the hill. Brown house with a lot of steps."

Armed with directions and new information—Ted, if he was Ted, was called Tango now, and married to someone named Mink—he climbed the muddy road that wound back and forth up the hill. The brown house was obvious, an aging bungalow, shingled, no houses close to it, the forest leading on behind it over the ridge. Lights were on in the living room, and from the road, the door appeared to be ajar. He climbed the steps and knocked on the doorjamb, then turned to look out over the village from the porch.

Because of the steep, winding road up the center, none of the buildings seemed plumb—they listed and lurched like children running and tripping down the hill. Beyond the small shelf at the bottom of the hill, the narrow inlet lay like a dark finger pointing. Along the sides, rocky, forested slopes staggered back. Beyond the forests lay the chain of islands separating Kashevarof Passage from Clarence Strait.

He stared out at the water and thought he saw a spout against the shore of Shrubby Island. Then another and another. There was a whale pod out there. He should be on watch. Instead he was standing here in a cold wind waiting for someone he didn't want to meet to come to the door.

He pounded harder this time, and called, "Hello-o." No answer, no sound of footsteps coming to the door. Tango, whoever he was, must have taken Mink over to Wrangell—what had the man said? She "got cut bad." Beringer wouldn't wait, then. But he had to know. Had to be sure once and for all. He pushed the door open and stepped inside.

He knew instantly that he had the right man. There were books all over the floor around a dilapidated recliner—Homer, Tacitus, *The Sonnets* of Shakespeare. *Vietnam Voices*, *The Making of the Atomic Bomb*, a world atlas, *A Rumor of War* by Philip Caputo. A coffee mug lay on its side, coffee spilled from it

He bent and put his finger in the pool of coffee. Warm, warmer than room temperature. It hadn't spilled long ago. Maybe Hilliard was in the bathroom—hadn't heard the knock. He walked into the hall and shouted, "Hey, Ted—where are you?"

Silence. He walked through the hall and paused again to look down at the books and coffee mug. The books looked like they'd been tipped from a pile, cascading across the faded rug with their pages bent. Whoever was sitting there had been startled by something. He crouched and picked up *A Rumor of War*. In the margin of the open page, someone had written "*. . . we owe God a death.*" *Henry IV.*

13

DRIVING FROM THE HOSPITAL TO TOWN, Liza turned into the parking lot at the police station. Norma, the dispatcher, said she thought the lieutenant was over at the harbor master's office. Liza, wondering why she had such a compulsion to tell Paul Howard about the stabbing, drove down the hill and parked at the beginning of the plank road on pilings that extended Front Street to the harbor offices. To the left was the long foot bridge out to Chief Shakes Island with the Tribal House and circle of totem poles, the main tourist attraction in the summer when the cruise ships came in. Paul's Blazer was parked beyond it, out on the dock.

Liza walked past the office to the crane where the boats hoisted their gear, and looked down at the entrance channel. She turned around when Paul Howard came out of the harbor master's office. Jogging after him, she caught up to him as he reached the car.

"Lizzie," he said, jamming his hands in his pockets. "Told you the weather was gearing up. I checked in around ten—you weren't there, though. You back?"

"It would appear that I am back. Mink's in the hospital—I brought her over this morning. Got a later start than I intended."

"Yeah? What's wrong with her?"

"Got knifed. The wound isn't too bad, but it seems to be infected—the doctor says 'septic'; he's giving her antibiotics."

The police car radio began a staticky series of calls and Paul's beeper went off simultaneously. Paul pushed buttons to quiet it, and said, "I'm off at five today. Could we, like . . . maybe we could get together for dinner?"

"Yeah, sure."

"Meet you at the Coho?"

"Good—I'll be there—five-thirty?"

He nodded and flung himself at the car, a huge smile on his face transforming it like the rising tide.

Driving back to Shoemaker Bay, Liza passed the George house. Liza noticed Tasha's car perched in the drive below the house. It took a sharp eye to distinguish Tasha's yellow Rabbit from the litter of vehicles, crab traps, oil buckets, fish net and woodpiles that occupied the space around the old frame house.

Tasha was Liza's oldest friend in Wrangell. Tasha, faced with harsh realities, and after an early and checkered career involving drugs with initials for names, had gotten her act together, and now counseled others through the Community Services program.

Liza plowed through the boots, kindling, and cats on the back porch, and hammered on the door. Tasha waved her in.

"Say what, Skipper," she bellowed, her voice by far the largest thing about her. "You back for a while?"

"How come you're home?" Liza asked Tasha.

"I work this weekend," she said. "So I've got today and tomorrow off. What's new with Sea Adventures, Ink?"

Liza sank down in one of the chairs at the kitchen table, held together with duct tape. The planks on the table had been lengthened for the growing children, and the chairs had been snatched from curbside rubbish piles.

"Give you the dregs of the breakfast coffee," Tasha said, and poured two mugs. She set a gallon of milk on the table, three-quarters empty, and slammed the sugar bowl in the middle, spooning some into her coffee, pouring a large quantity of milk in, too.

"I had to bring Mink in—she got stabbed in the arm in a bar fight while I was over there, and it got infected so they're making her stay in the hospital till her temp's normal."

"Must have to tie her down," Tasha said. "Can't imagine she'd stay just on invitation."

"She doesn't like it, but she's too weak to do more than complain. And we haven't been able to get hold of Tango since I brought Mink over. He hasn't been in the bar all day, and he doesn't answer his phone at home. Mink will go nuts worrying about him when she hears this. Of course, she's feeling lousy, which will make her worry more. It isn't like him to disappear."

"Get him on the radio," Tasha said. "He can't hear anything that doesn't come over the radio."

"I'm going to try that as soon as I get to the boat. Only Jimmy says Tango's radio's still on the table at the Moose."

"That is peculiar," Tasha said, frowning. "I always thought his radio grew to the side of his head. Let me know—I can't believe Tango would just go off and not let Mink know."

"Of course, that's how he showed up ten years ago, you know. Just wandering along the beach, no history, no belongings, except some old Army gear and his radio."

"You think he might have gone the same way he came? I don't believe it. He's so attached to Mink he'd never leave deliberately."

"Deliberate is not a word I associate with Tango," Liza said. "Carpe diem. Ad lib. Tango has no agenda. Well, I gotta go."

"Poor Mink. I'll go see her, since you're leaving," Tasha said. "Lemme get my purse."

"Well, just don't tell her Tango's missing. She might not have found out yet. She'll go crazy when she does."

When Liza got back to the harbor, the wind was blowing a southeast gale, and the boats at Shoemaker were tossing in the choppy swells. She headed down the ramp. Across from the *Salmon Eye*, Jake Fremantle was pulling his net off the drum on the *Aquila*. Jake gillnetted the summer season, then crabbed and longlined in the winter, a true toiler of the sea. Jake had a perpetual war with officialdom. A man of few words and many growls, Jake tolerated her because of his fondness for Sam.

A huge mound of net suddenly rose and lurched at Liza. Startled, she stepped backward, teetering at the edge of the dock as Sam's smiling muzzle poked through the mesh.

"He was complainin'," Jake said as the pile of net hurled itself at her legs. "I let him out."

Liza braced herself against the onslaught and tried to move out of range of the tangle. "I can see he's been a big help," she said.

"Oh, he's okay. Likes to keep close, keep an eye on things. Old Sam boy."

Jake lifted the pile of net while Liza tried to disentangle Sam's feet. When he was finally clear, Jake dumped the net in a cart to drag it up the ramp. "See ya, Sam," he said, and trundled off.

On the way to meet Paul Howard, Liza stopped by the hospital to check on Mink.

"Look what came to dinner," Mink growled, lifting the metal warmer from the plate on her tray to reveal a piece of pale fish sprinkled with parsley flakes; a few small, shiny, cooked carrots; and half a baked potato. A toothpick stuck in the center of the fish bore a sign with a red heart and the words "Heart-Healthy" beneath it.

"It's good for you," Liza said. "That salad looks yummy." She pointed at the orange Jell-O with chips of cabbage floating in it like fine wood bark.

Wordless grunts of disgust erupted from Mink's mouth.

"I'll sneak you a steak tomorrow," Liza said.

"Don't bother—I'm outa here tomorrow, ma'am."

"The doctor said you could leave?" Liza asked her suspiciously.

"He God Almighty or somethin'? Didn't see no glittery little circle around his head. You call Tango and tell him I gotta stay overnight?"

"I talked to Jimmy. He says everything's fine. No problem. He can hold the fort till you get back."

"I'll give Tango a call this evening. Tell him I'll be back tomorrow. He can vacuum—it's his week."

"Your temp down? Seems pretty fast to get that infection controlled."

"Shit—it ain't nothin'. Set that phone over closer so I don't have to reach so far. Wanna see it?" she said, pulling up her sleeve to reveal a thick bandage. "Forty-three stitches," she said proudly. "Embroidered like Mabel Anderson's tea towels."

The bandage was broad and neat, but above it there were still red streaks tracking toward her shoulder, and after Liza admired the bandage, Mink dropped her head back on the pillow and poked at the tray table in front of her. "Get that slop out of here," she said. "Can you crank this bed down a little?"

"You've got the controls right here by the pillow," Liza said, holding up the cord.

"Yeah, well, put it around the other side. I can't punch all those button thingies when my arm's tied up to the dumb I.V. and my other arm's bandaged up."

Liza lowered the head of her bed and repinned the controls on the other side. She didn't move the phone—she didn't want Mink to call and discover that Tango was missing.

The *Wrangell Sentinel* came out on Thursdays. This was Tuesday, though. Liza stopped at the market and picked one up, five days late, before she went to the Coho. There was a front-page story about Henry Sizemore. The Coast Guard had searched forty-eight hours for his boat before they had given up. Liza couldn't read it. She had written to his wife in Juneau, but she couldn't read this story about him. She stuck it in the pocket of her rain jacket.

The Coho was almost empty, though a few of the regulars were sitting in the bar. Liza pulled up a stool and asked Hal for coffee, black. The door at the far end of the bar opened and there was Jenny with the broomstalk hair. She climbed onto the stool next to Liza and asked Hal for a Heineken.

Liza said, "Saw you over at the Moose last night. You had your revolver out."

"Yeah, I did. Something going on between those guys— they were fighting even before they got to the bar, so I just waved my gun at them and they quieted down. A lot."

"And they fought again, right out in the open. Kind of strange. Those guys usually tanked like that?"

"Way too much," Jenny said. "That guy that pulled the knife is about one minute from detox, if you ask me. Too bad. He's one of the smartest guys I've ever met, but he's got a chip on his shoulder the size of an old-growth hemlock. Hates everybody."

"I brought Mink over this morning—she's in the hospital with blood poisoning. She won't bring charges, probably—says risk goes with the territory—but it seems to me he should pay her medical bills at least."

Jenny smiled. "He'd spend his life in court before he'd pay a cent, even if he had to spend every penny he has to beat the claim. You just don't know Barney Ellis."

"That's his name? Barney Ellis? Why was he so pissed off at the other man?"

"Like I said, Barney hates everyone. Barney can't stand anyone telling him what to do, and he thinks Frank wimps out about where the boat can and can't go. Frank refused to go somewhere, so Barney locked himself in his room and drank till we came into town."

"Skipper's decision, isn't it?"

"Well, there's some bad feeling," Jenny paused and turned to look sideways at Liza.

Liza noticed that Jenny's hands were trembling. "Affect you?" she asked.

Jenny must have noticed too. She clutched the beer bottle tightly. She started to say, "Oh, well, yeah . . . ," then hesitated, sliding the Heineken bottle back and forth in front of her. Finally she shrugged. "Not exactly, but it's kind of a bummer. The investment's split up among several people—not just the usual crew split-up, so everybody's got to have their say."

Hal had filled Liza's cup at least three times and she headed for the rest room. Paul must have run into some emergency. Surreptitiously she felt the pocket of Jenny's rain jacket hanging on the rack by the door. The gun was still there. When she came back, Jenny Andover was gone, but Barney Ellis and the small, dark-haired woman were sitting at the end of the bar on the other side.

14

"Sorry," Paul said to Lizzie. "Call from Juneau—they're missing somebody they thought they had under surveillance—wanted to know if we'd seen him down here. I had to check with the others. Let's eat."

In the dining room of the Coho, they sat in a booth looking out over the strait, and Paul ordered a glass of white wine for Lizzie and a Red Hook for himself. He leaned back and tried to see her face without really looking at her. She looked tired and drawn—don't ask, he warned himself, knowing that eventually he would despite himself.

"So what happened?" he said. "I dropped in on Mink. Said somebody jumped her. Clearly didn't want to talk about it, though. Didn't like to press her on it when she's feeling rotten."

"One of the guys pulled a knife on the other and got Mink instead. This giant blonde woman named Jenny Andover, who was just in here, was in the Velvet Moose that night. Incidentally, she's still got a gun in the pocket of her rain jacket. She had it out when she appeared at the Velvet Moose—she said the guys were already fighting. She jammed it into the pocket of her rain jacket and it's still there. I felt the pocket when I went to the rest room. That's the gun I was telling you about."

The waitress came over and they ordered.

"Jenny told me that the name of the man who slashed Mink's arm is Barney Ellis. And he's sitting right there at the bar," she said, leaning across the table to whisper. "Sideways on the stool next to the dark-haired woman who was with him at the Moose. Look now."

Paul leaned back in his chair and glanced over his shoulder. The man was sitting at one end of the bar. Around the corner from him sat a man with curly gray hair, steel-rimmed glasses and a neatly trimmed beard. He seemed to be observing Ellis closely, and Paul wondered if he was one of his associates, crew member, whatever. The man in the glasses glanced over at Paul and Paul swung around. Looking at Lizzie, he nodded.

"A nasty drunk," she said, "but he seems to be drinking coffee at the moment. Probably still hungover from last night."

The waitress brought their salads and they ate a while without talking.

"Mink is a world-class fool. Tried to strong-arm both of 'em at once, didn't she?" Paul said.

"Well, she was on the wrong side of the bar to grab her gun, so she just walked right in between them."

"So did Farwell take 'em in? Drive 'em over to Craig?"

"Mink didn't even call him. Grabbed her gun and waved it around—the tall man slid out the door before anyone could grab him, and about ten of the locals escorted the other one, Ellis, the guy who stabbed her, down to the dock. I have no idea what happened after that."

"Nothing, likely. They'll both be running scared if they had knives out. Wouldn't stick around to find out if Mink was gonna bring charges. They'll be on good behavior for a while, you can bet on that."

Then Lizzie described the crowd at the Velvet Moose, and

the people at the bar. "Funny . . . Tango acted like he recognized Ellis. He jumped up and shouted something, and Ellis looked totally terrified when he finally spotted Tango in back of the crowd, Couldn't get through the door fast enough."

Paul's rib steak and french fries arrived with Lizzie's grilled salmon.

"You must exercise enough to keep the blood moving through your arteries anyway," she said, pointing her fork at his steak.

"Hey, all the little pleasures of being fat and jolly," he said, picking up the ketchup bottle.

"Jolly?" she said. "You'd make Edgar Allan Poe look jolly."

They looked at each other solemnly and said, simultaneously, "Who's Edgar Allan Poe?"

Paul looked over his shoulder again, watching Ellis glance at his watch, fling some bills down on the bar and walk out, followed by the woman. The man in the glasses turned sideways and watched them till the door slammed behind them.

"That guy in the glasses," Paul said. "Was he with Ellis over there at the Moose?"

"I don't remember seeing him but it was super crowded. It does seem like he was watching them closely just now. But after seeing Ellis in action, I wouldn't blame anyone for keeping an eye on him. Now he's leaving, too."

Paul turned just in time to see the man with the curly hair and glasses open the door and go out. He had a decided limp.

Paul noticed how Lizzie pushed the salmon around on her plate, flaking it apart, putting nothing in her mouth. "Lizzie?" he said, already hating himself. "You doing better?"

She shrugged, avoiding his eyes. "Maybe. Actually, I am doing better."

Paul set his fork down and leaned toward her, clenching his hands under the table. He wanted to touch her—he couldn't do it. Not here.

"People hide themselves in Alaska, don't they?" she said. "Maybe I should go someplace else, but the boat's my cocoon. Where I hide."

They had both put down their forks now. They stared out the window, avoiding eye contact.

"Weren't hungry?" the waitress asked, slapping the bill on the table.

"Hungry?" Paul repeated. He stared up at the woman, the word finally taking on meaning. Yes, in a way he was very, very hungry.

Outside, Paul took Lizzie's arm and pulled her toward his car, opening the door on the passenger side. "We need to talk," he said, but his pager shrieked and the car radio snorted out his name. He reached across her and grabbed the transmitter.

"Howard," he said. "Yeah, yeah, I'm here."

"Man's body found on Petroglyph Beach. Shot right through the heart. Very recent. Woman out walking her dog found him, called 911."

"Roger. Got it. You got an I.D.? Okay, I'll be down in a couple secs."

He reached across to hang up the transmitter. "Who the hell would walk a dog in the dark on a rocky beach?" He groaned. He reached toward her, dropped his hands again, and pushed himself off the car door. "They're waiting for me before they move him, because the chief's gone to Juneau. Sounds like the guy hasn't been there long. Maybe somebody will've heard the shot."

He put his arms around her then, kissing the top of her head, wanting her, wanting her to love him, to be only a little happier, no, to be truly happy, to want him, but she pulled away, looked up at him, forced him to meet her eyes. Then she pulled his face down to hers and he was holding her, his mouth on hers, time disappearing.

"Lizzie," he whispered to her. "It's . . . I . . ." Words had hidden themselves in his brain. "Lizzie? You know?"

"Yes," she said. "I know."

He parked the Blazer on the little stub of road above the beach, took the big flashlight out of the glove compartment and looked at his watch. Ten thirty-four and black as the bottom of a mine, what with the sun gone five hours and dense cloud cover. He made his way across the sandy part toward the rocks, listening to the creek that poured out of the forest and made its way beneath the rocks to the sea. A thin mist fell silently. He shone the light just ahead of his feet, then stopped to look along the beach. Three men stood over something lying on the sand.

He moved toward them slowly, his feet twisting on the slippery rocks, his light picking up some of the ancient carvings, blue jay and wolf and cormorant and that most ancient spiral design repeated in every culture on earth. So many of the petroglyphs gone now, once thousands on every beach and stream. He climbed over a rock ledge and dropped down onto the gravel, walking slowly over to the group of men.

Luke was there—he'd been on the radio. Jerry Adkins, the new sergeant, stood next to him, holding a flashlight. Badger, the photographer, was hauling over his portable lights. Badger adjusted the tripod, pushing the legs into the sand, and switched the lights on. The dark split open, blinding everyone.

Paul tried to shield his eyes so he could see the body. The

man was dressed in jeans and a tan windbreaker, a blue cap caught under his head, flipped sideways by the force of his fall. The bald man from the Coho bar. Close to his hand was a small pistol with an ivory handle.

15

THE SHAPELESS HOURS FROM ONE TO FOUR in the morning had roused all her dread. A violent death—Paul called in just at the moment when some elusive peace between them seemed about to settle. She couldn't have another policeman in her life. It wouldn't work. She could accept no more violence—her mind and body recoiled, turned in on themselves like snails. Efren Romero, her policeman husband, was shot and killed in a drug bust. She'd known everything before Sergeant Reynolds said the words to her. She thought she'd known even before it happened, that Efren, her husband, would die.

Liza changed into her jogging clothes, needing to clear her head of all the mutterings and confusion. It was pouring and blowing—maybe that would counter some of her internal misery. Her feet trod the pavement slowly, never forcing Sam into a trot. He meandered his zigzag course up and down the gully beside the road, his shoulders rising like pistons as he applied his nose to important messages in the grass.

She extended her arms and shook her hands loose as she ran past the institute's beach. Three herons stalked the edge of the tide. A raven, perched on the light pole at the picnic ground, broke into raucous amusement at the sight of her. Rain had beaten down the summer's brilliant fireweed and the silky white fluff of the seeds were plastered to the stems like limp sails.

At the south edge of the bay the red cranes of the lumber mill loomed over sawdust mountains and stacked planks. A tug was pulling out with a log-laden barge. Not many more would leave there, now that the mill was closing.

At the parking lot north of the lumber mill, she turned back, driving herself faster. Sam raised his head, observing the change, and finally broke into a trot. She wasn't succeeding at all in falling into the trancelike state she often did when jogging.

She started thinking about Henry Sizemore. His boat was at the dock in Point Baker and then it was gone, and Paul had told her he'd drowned. But he was a truly competent sailor. Very, very good. What had happened to him? It made her extremely uneasy.

At ten, Liza decided Mink had slept long enough, and headed back to town. If Mink was awake it would only be under protest—she laughed, thinking of Mink's sleep interrupted at dawn by a cheerful nurse asking, "And how are we feeling this morning?"

She walked in braced for battle, but it didn't come. Mink was lying back against the pillows, the tray table in front of her, the phone set in the middle of it. A box of tissues sat beside the phone, and crumpled ones covered the sheet by her elbow. One look at her face told the tale.

"He's not there," Mink said, her voice shaking with the effort to stave off tears. "I called Jimmy last night, and he said he hadn't been there all day, so I called home and he never answered."

"I know. I tried, too. He's upset, though, Mink. You're his lifeline. He's got a stash of pot and he's taking a break. 'Pause in the bombing,' like you always tell him when he gets in those firefights."

"Hunh-unh. Something's happened. You know what he was like Monday night? Talking to somebody on that radio like he actually knew him? 'It's him, it's him,' he kept saying. And he had you writing all that stuff in the book."

"Listen, Mink," Liza said, massaging her good shoulder while she stood next to her, "we don't know what he carries in his head. There's no reason to think he was actually onto somebody real this time."

But she remembered that shout of laughter and the voice crackling, "That's you for sure, you old grunt." Somebody was on that radio. What did it have to do with Tango's present whereabouts?

"He was different about this one. See him crying? Tango ain't cried since I took him off the beach and scrubbed him down. Somethin's happened." She grabbed Liza by the wrist. "I gotta get outa here, but the doctor says it's gonna be some more days. I gotta get home and find him."

"Your fever still up?"

"I guess—anyway, he won't let me—says I'll kill myself, the junk still running around my blood. That fucking little bald guy musta been dirty as well as mean. I tried to call you last night—you musta been sound asleep not to hear the phone ringing."

"Uhhh, well, uhhh . . ."

"Unh-hunh, so you weren't home. Don't explain, just because your friend's at death's door and needed help and you couldn't be bothered—don't apologize for running out—lotta people aren't always considerate—kind, thoughtful. . . ."

"Mink. You were asleep before I left."

"Yeah, well, I don't sleep around the clock, babe. I been sitting here since eight last night willing that phone to ring."

"Watched pot, Mink. Listen, if it's going to be a few more

days before you're out, I'll just go back over and see what I can find out. I've got some more freight, anyway. By the time I get there, Tango'll be sitting right there with his chessboard and newspaper, anxious to hear how you're doing."

"So where's Tango right now?" a voice rumbled from the doorway. Paul stood there, eyes narrowed, face grim.

Before Liza could stop her, Mink said, "He's gone. He's missing, and he's never, never gone away before."

Paul walked over to the bed. "You bring that gun of yours along on this trip?" he asked Mink.

"What gun? That old pistol I keep in the drawer over there? What'd I be doing with that?" She snorted loudly. "Shoot that doctor if I had it—wish I'd thought 'a bringin' it."

"You recognize it if you saw it?"

"What're you after, Paul Howard? How would I tell one from any other? It's pretty old—Colt. 25, has an ivory stock."

"Have any identifying marks you can remember?"

Mink glowered at him. "Do I gotta call my lawyer? What're you on about, for chrissake?"

Paul held up a plastic bag with a small pistol in it. "We found a Colt .25 bullet in somebody who isn't going anyplace soon. Shot right through the heart—contact wound. I heard there was a ruckus over at the Moose the other night. This your gun?"

She stared at the bag. "Yeah, could be. Has an ivory handle, anyway. But I dunno . . . could be somebody else's. Was it that bald guy got killed?" she said.

"The guy's bald, yeah. Could be more than one, I guess. But Lizzie pointed him out at the Coho last night—said he was the one came after you with a knife."

Liza felt betrayal burning through her like vinegar. How could she forget for a minute that Paul was first and forever a policeman? Like Efren. The way Efren had always been cop first, then lover and husband with what was left.

"He wasn't after me," Mink said. "I just got in his way, Lieutenant. And I been right here tied up to that pole you're leanin' on. Since yesterday noon. So no way did I take my little gun and shoot anyone."

"But you do own a Colt .25 automatic?"

"You please tell me how my old pistol came over here to Wrangell all by itself and shot the guy? It was sitting right there in the drawer when I left."

"Yesterday morning?"

"Well, shit, I didn't look again in the morning—you know what time we left? Middle of the night, it was."

"Mink," Liza said. "It was five-fifteen in the morning."

"Same as," Mink said with a snort.

"So you saw it last when?"

"When I dumped it back in the drawer after Janet tied up my arm."

"You sure? You sure you dumped it back in the drawer?"

Mink looked at the window and then stared fixedly at the phone. "Yeah," she said. "Sure I did. I remember I threw it on the bar while she was messing around with my arm, and then I tossed it in the drawer while Jimmy was mopping up the mess. Liza was there. You remember me throwing the gun back in the drawer, don'cha?"

"I'm sure you did," Liza said. "I was figuring out with Tango about bringing you over here, but I don't remember seeing it on the bar when we left. Seems like I even remember seeing you slam the drawer. And listen, Lieutenant Howard, I told you that blonde woman had a gun in her pocket."

"A small pistol?"

"Well, I just felt of it through her jacket."

"Lizzie, everyone knows the difference between a pistol and a revolver. Did it have a round chamber?"

"I don't know. How was I supposed to tell—it just felt heavy and gunlike."

He glared at her in exasperation. She could hear him thinking stupid woman—doesn't know the difference between a
pistol and a revolver. She did, of course; she knew it was a revolver. She'd felt it through Jenny's rain jacket, and seen it in
Jenny's hand before she wedged it into her pocket. But Paul
didn't need to know that right now. Once they'd found Tango,
and he'd explained where he'd been and had a sound alibi,
then Liza could talk guns with Paul.

Paul finally shrugged and asked Mink, "How come Tango
didn't come over with you?"

"You want him to have a nervous breakdown? That guy, he
can't stand the sight of blood. He woulda fainted away dead
on the floor. If you'd ever seen your whole platoon scattered
in little bitty pieces before your eyes you'd maybe get sick at
blood, too. He would give no joy around a place like this—no
way."

"You talked to him since you got over here?"

"He's helping Jimmy at the bar. They got enough to do, figuring out how to get that griddle cranked up without me bug-
ging hell out of 'em."

"Is that a yes or a no, Mink?"

"It's a goddamned hell no!"

"I'd like to get your okay to send somebody over to check
and see if your gun's there. 'Course, we could get a warrant,
but it'd take time, and it's to your advantage if your gun's in
the drawer."

"So just fucking do it."

Paul's face relaxed slightly and his mouth twitched in a sort
of smile. "I'm sure the gun didn't fly over here, but we gotta
check it out. I'll send somebody over since you're willing."

He turned to Liza. Paul's face was always a precise chart of
his brain. She could see that he wanted to tell her that this
homicide did, in fact, have nothing to do with her, but he
couldn't. Because it wasn't true. She'd seen the fight, wit-

nessed Mink's wounding, knew that Tango had threatened the man. She watched the haunted expression cross Paul's face, watched him shake his head, draw himself up all official and leave.

Liza stared at the open door. She wanted to run after him, wanted to hear his voice grumbling in her ear—wanted to touch him again. She shook her head and turned back to Mink.

"Tango wouldn't . . . just because you got hurt?" she said. "He wouldn't get it in his head he had to, like, avenge you, or something?"

"Listen. Tango's got no fight left in him. Every lick 'a mad got beaten outa him over there in 'Nam. He won't look at a gun, won't look at TV because of all the killings and stuff, has to put his head down if he scratches open a mosquito bite. Wouldn't even hit the mosquito that bit him. He's so gentle, Liza"—tears were flowing fast now—"he's all just tender and kind . . . nobody ever like him in my life before, that kind of loving . . . you wouldn't know to look at us, would you . . . the kind of loving goes on between us . . . you'd never think . . ." Her voice succumbed to tears, and she buried her face in the sheet.

"Mink. I can guess how it is between you. He couldn't bear to watch us leave yesterday. I'm going over there and find him and tell him you're okay. He's probably so scared he can't bring himself to hear."

"Yeah," Mink mumbled. "Prob'ly that's it. You go." She sobbed into the pillow, waving her hand a little to send Liza on her way.

16

SHEESH, THIS WAS GOING TO DESTROY every shred of his relationship with Lizzie. She always drew up inside that dark, lost part of her he couldn't reach. Why were they always at cross-purposes?

When he got back to the office, he found the chief standing in his door. "Hear you stirred up hornets soon as I turned my back," Woods said. "Shit, Howard, can't you keep the plate clean a minute?"

Paul glared at him. "Welcome," he said. "I'm retiring. Here's my badge, my gun—" he dug in a drawer searching among the manila folders—"my papers, wherever the hell they are—I'm getting outa here, man, gonna drop a line in the water and watch the fish rush in."

"Yeah. Sure you are. But just so I know what happened, why don't you fill me in a little before you hightail it."

Woods threw himself down in the chair on the other side of the desk and Paul leaned back, propping a foot on the open file drawer. "The guy was shot in the heart on Petroglyph Beach around ten P.M. last night. Name of Barney Ellis."

"You sure of that time?"

"Eleanor Sioske found him—well, actually, her dog found him, but Eleanor went back up to the house, which is only a couple places up the beach from where he was lying, and called nine-one-one. When Luke got there, the guy was still warm—small caliber, contact wound—so yeah, we're pretty sure it happened not long before ten o'clock."

"You got an I.D. pretty fast."

"He was pointed out to me at dinner—Coho bar. Seems he was involved in some kinda ruckus over at the Moose a couple nights ago, resulted in Mink Michaels getting cut. She's over here in the hospital, some kind of blood poisoning or something."

"Find the weapon?"

"Sure did. Colt .25 automatic, ivory handle. Sent the bullet up to Juneau with Taquan Air, and ballistics called around ten-thirty this morning."

"Odd weapon—not your standard handgun around here.

Paul said nothing and Woods looked at him sharply. "You got some idea, eh?"

"Yeah," Paul said. "I do."

"And the gun belongs to . . . here comes the drumroll . . . it belongs to . . ."

"Probably belongs to Mink herself."

"So you think she killed him because he injured her?"

"She was in the hospital tied up to an I.V. like a dog's leash. No, it wasn't Mink. But her husband, Tango, has disappeared like smoke through the roof. Not a trace."

"I remember him. Glued to that radio—kinda one oar short?"

"'Nam got him—left him amnesic."

"So he might have gone for the guy because the guy hurt Mink?"

"Sounds like Tango recognized Ellis from somewhere. Strange, that, because Tango doesn't seem to have any memory for things except Willie Shakespeare and whatever the voices tell him on that VHF. But we got one more thing to go on. There was a woman in the Moose that night and again at the Coho the evening before Ellis was killed. Seems she was a fellow crew member of his on some boat around here. Name's Jenny Andover."

"She was pointed out to you, too?"

"No, she'd just left, but the person I had dinner with said Andover told her Ellis was a mean turkey with a hot temper."

"And this person you had dinner with was . . ."

Paul stared at the snapshots of Joey and at the ragged holes that were Carolyn and at his boot propped on the file drawer. "It was Lizzie," he said finally. "But believe me, she doesn't have anything to do with it."

"Except proximity? She was there, right? At the Moose? And at the Coho before Ellis was killed? How come that woman's always around when something happens?"

Paul shrugged. "So how was your meeting?"

"We have to track down that boat the guy was on," the chief said, ignoring the question. "You know the name of it? What it looks like—what it's doing around here? Fishing boat? Tug? Cruiser?"

"I don't know anything about the boat. We've got calls out through the Coast Guard and the marine telephone operators regarding Ellis—we didn't want to say he's dead, so we've said 'urgent contact.' If we don't get a response, we'll try calling Andover and see if she answers."

"You won't hear from her. That boat's already short a crew member, and nobody's reported him missing, right? I'd say we better get some uniforms from the state. This ain't ours, Paul, even though the man was offed on our beach."

"Seems like our little jurisdiction keeps expanding, though."

"Hunh. All right. If you want to do it, then go for it. Maybe that'll keep you from retiring this week."

17

IT WASN'T RAINING YET WHEN LIZA steered the *Salmon Eye* out between the red and green markers at the Shoemaker Bay entrance. Dark clouds moved overhead in a shifting jet stream, and the sea, whitened by the Stikine River silt, was filled with those same dark clouds. She turned the bow across Zimovia Strait toward the entrance to Chichagof Pass, a shortcut between the islands.

Looking back at the arc of the bay, at the derelict Indian school and the soon-to-be-closed lumber mill, Liza thought how the tough little town had weathered the times. Pictures on rocks near Wrangell were carved eight thousand years ago— someone had been here ever since, building a shelter, raising a child, surviving at this green edge of the sea.

Sam was prancing around the deck and whining now—she needed to get him ashore, and it was well after four, way too late to get to Kashevarof before dark. Liza would have to spend the night in Kindergarten Bay.

The forest shadows lying across the water were black bars, and the east end of Kindergarten Bay, behind the islands, seemed cavernous by the time she'd anchored. No one came in here—other boats chose Steamer Bay around the corner, and there weren't many of them anyway this time of year. Sam hung over precariously as a seal popped through the surface of the water and turned its huge brown eyes on him, luxurious whiskers signaling its curiosity. Liza dragged the little inflatable raft off the cabin roof and rowed Sam ashore.

Late in the evening, the *Salmon Eye* began to pitch in the wake of another boat in the bay. Somebody coming in very fast, judging from the height of the waves. Sam growled and dashed to the door. Liza latched the cupboard door, went up the steps to the wheelhouse, and strained to see.

A boat appeared to be anchoring beyond the islands that clogged the center of the bay. Liza had come around behind the islands. So many of the bays were too deep to anchor in—she could put out four hundred feet of anchor rode if she had to, but only in an emergency. Bigger boats generally anchored in fifteen to twenty fathoms—she liked to make it easy.

Liza turned off the cabin light, and went out on deck to try to see more clearly. In a minute, they shut down the engine. She could hear a loud generator now, operating all the internal electrical systems. Liza felt intruded upon by the noise of the generator and the steep wake that had rattled the dishes and slammed the kettle back on the gimbaled stove. She went back to the wheelhouse, pushing Sam in ahead of her, and stared out at nothing.

Liza was dozing off when she heard the rhythmic hush of water sliding from oars, She lay rigid, listening, until Sam gave a low gruff and bounded up the ladder. As she shoved the sleeping bag back, there was the dull thump of something against the hull. Sam barked sharply once, then paced rapidly back and forth in front of the cabin door, his toenails clicking on the floor above her head.

In the lights from the cabin Liza could see Jenny Andover looking up at her from an aluminum skiff. With one hand she clutched the edge of the *Salmon Eye*'s deck. Her hair, bursting from a watch cap, caught the light like a surrealistic neon halo. Liza moved toward her to take her line, and Jenny said, "Ahoy, *Salmon Eye*," softly, as though she hated to disturb the silence.

When she'd climbed aboard, Liza walked the skiff to the stern and cleated the painter. Jenny dragged her rubber boots off at the door, then went in and sank onto the bench by the table.

"Throw your jacket there—I'll make some tea," Liza told her.

Jenny took her yellow rain jacket off and tossed it down. Liza thought the pocket still bulged. Liza dragged on Sam's collar. "Lie down, Sam," she ordered. Carefully he lowered his rear end to the floor, not lying down as requested, sitting at the ready, hoping the woman was a new friend. Liza put the kettle on—she needed to wake up, though a glance at the clock showed it was just eleven—she'd dozed off early.

"Sure is dark," Jenny said. "I couldn't even tell what direction I was going after I got out there, till I saw your anchor light. I could see the name on the stern with my flashlight."

Jenny turned sideways and put her feet, encased in ragg wool socks, up on the bench, clutching her knees and huddling as if she were cold. Liza lit the diesel stove, and she nodded.

"I should have dressed warmer," she said.

"Nights are getting cold now." Had Jenny known it was the *Salmon Eye* before she started out from her own boat? It seemed odd she'd set out in the dark unless she was positive what boat was over here.

"I just needed to get off," Jenny said, "see somebody besides the people I've been locked up with all these months. I guess I'm not too social, or something. I get super tired of being around other people all the time."

So why had she headed straight over here? Wasn't Liza "people"? Liza poured water over the tea bags. "That's why this job is so nice—I love being out here by myself, nobody talking at me all the time."

"Just Sam," Jenny said, smiling slightly as she looked at him. He had taken up his position across the cabin from her, sitting straight, watching her closely as though she might be carrying beef bones in her pocket. *It's a revolver, Sam,* Liza said silently.

Jenny took the mug and wrapped her hands around it to warm them. Her eyes seemed to stray around the cabin, but Liza realized she was actually watching her face without looking at her directly. A surreptitious observation—sizing Liza up for some purpose?

Jenny's eyes, half shadowed by the lowered lids, were browny-gold. Her face was broad, with high, flat bones, a rather Slavic face, striking with no hint of prettiness. Her mouth was wide and she kept her lips tight over slightly protuberant teeth. Her nose was rather small for the rest of her face, and slightly upturned, which softened an otherwise imperious expression. It was that stiff yellow hair that conveyed the idea of a stripper in a back-alley burlesque. And Liza wasn't even sure the hair was hers. She tried to guess her age—she would have said early thirties, but there were creases in her neck that belied the smooth face. She might be two or three years younger than Liza's own forty years—no more than that.

"You owned this boat a long time?" Jenny asked.

Liza gave her an edited history, how she'd bought it two years ago and decided to provide a freight service.

Jenny frowned and pulled her shoulders up tensely. "Lot of dangers up here," she said. "Actually I'm a coward at heart. You couldn't pay me to fly in one of those little single-engine floatplane dealies. And I'm terrified out there on the water if there's even whitecaps."

Liza stared at her, puzzled. "How come you're up here,

then? I mean, if you're terrified of the seas, Alaska doesn't seem like the place to earn a living."

Jenny shrugged again, shuffling her mug nervously back and forth on the table and staring at Sam, who stared back, unblinking. "We're doing well. I can't ignore the bucks—it's super-hard work, but I'm going to pack it in maybe a year from now. If we do as well this year as last, I can go home and start the business I always wanted but never had the capital for."

"What's that?"

Jenny ducked her head as if she were embarrassed. "Yarn. Knitting and needlepoint. Classes for people, that sort of thing."

Liza laughed before she could stop herself. This huge, brassy-looking woman wanted to own a yarn shop?

Jenny read the amazement in Liza's face. "I know. I don't exactly look the type—little gray-haired ladies with prissy manners, that's what everyone pictures. But I love the colors and textures. I was raised by my aunt. In the evenings she'd let me wind up all her leftover bits of needlepoint wool, and I'd lay them out in the basket so they shaded into each other, trying to get them in exactly the right order and not being sure if one blue was a little greener or a little grayer than the next."

"Sounds like you're an artist at heart."

"I maybe should have been, but I knew I couldn't support myself with art. I studied geology in college." She stopped abruptly and changed the subject. "How long is this boat?"

"Sixty-five at the waterline. Did you work in geology when you finished school?"

She shook her head, again watching Liza from the corner of her eye as she moved her mug back and forth in zigzag patterns on the tabletop.

"You guys are longlining?" Liza asked her.

"Yeah, well, we're just looking around right now. Definitely going to longline this winter—black cod, halibut. Might crab a little, too. I don't know what Frank will decide. It'll be hard as hell, whatever it is, but there's that nice big check at the end."

"He divvy up with the crew pretty well?"

"Oh, we do well, really. And he thinks we'll do better down here."

Jenny was gripping her knees and staring off at the black window in the door. "We're headed out early, Frank says."

She looked at Liza askance, and Liza had a sudden, strong impression that Jenny was frightened. She hadn't said one word about Ellis's death, not even that he was missing. Had she come to tell Liza about it and lost her nerve?

"You heard that a man drowned?" Liza asked. "Henry Sizemore, the whale man. He was a friend of mine."

"Yeah, I heard. He was trying to find out what was happening to the whales?"

"Yes, he was. I took those hydrophones out to Point Baker for him and he didn't pick them up. I was really angry at him. I left a note on his door, and in the morning, his boat was gone. I wrote it in the log: date, time, everything. Said how angry I was. Now I'm sorry I was so annoyed."

"Wrote it in your log?"

"Yup, I did."

"Well, it happens. Boats go down in bad weather."

"But it wasn't bad weather that night. Or the next night, either. It was actually very calm."

Jenny stood and said, "I have to go. We're leaving early in the morning and it's late." She went out on deck and Liza followed her.

"Thanks for listening," Jenny said.

"Thanks for listening to me. I'm going to miss Henry a lot."

Jenny dropped over the rail to the raft and disappeared into the dark.

Sam danced nervously around, wanting to go ashore. "Oh, all right," she told him. "Once more. Five minutes, and no rolling in *anything*."

In the slack tide, the stern of the *Salmon Eye* swung no more than fifty yards from shore. Liza rowed the short distance and dragged the raft above the waterline—the tide would start falling soon, leaving the raft high and dry, except they were going back in five minutes. Sam had already bounded up the beach.

"Five, Sam," she warned him again. She aimed the flashlight where she heard him. The thin cone of light picked out one dense shadow from all the rest. Someone was standing on the rocks above her.

The rush of adrenaline that poured through her arteries caused her hand to jerk violently. The flashlight lost the figure above her. The pencil-thin light swept the rocks, catching only a tiny gleam before illuminating her own feet. But that was enough to tell her Sam was there, crouched on the rocks to her right. His throat rumbled. She called "hello" to the person above her. A brilliant, laserlike beam sliced through the night, blinding her and Sam too. He dropped down to the rocks again.

"I'm Alice," the woman said. "I rowed the skiff in. Jenny went over to your boat." The underbrush crackled. Abruptly the flashlight was aimed away from her, tracking a thin trail into the woods above the rocks.

"Stay, Sam," she whispered. Slowly she retreated along the beach till she reached the raft, dragging Sam with her. As she rowed back to the boat, she realized Alice, with her brilliant flashlight, would have had no trouble at all reading the *Salmon Eye*'s name from shore.

18

BERINGER WAS TRACKING THE *SALMON Eye* across Clarence Strait. It was a very old boat, a halibut schooner turned freighter, and maybe it leaked some type of polluting material, or perhaps the engine made some ear-piercing underwater sound in the frequencies the marine mammals heard. This might explain why the whale pods seemed so disoriented, running into boats and beaches. The Wildlife Protection office had told him about a humpback actually running into the *Salmon Eye*. That was very inter-esting.

Suddenly the radio broke in on his pondering—his office in Wrangell:

"We had another call about the whales. Report from the woman that runs that freight boat, the Salmon Eye. *She said she saw an orca stranded on the reef at Point Nesbitt."*

"An orca stranded on the reef? I'll look for it. The other orcas are up near the Rookeries feeding now. Last time I saw them they were circling an injured one—long gash in its side, maybe from running into a boat. It's damned worri-some. They may have gotten into a contaminant—some-thing in the food chain."

"The woman saw that injured one too—said it had a huge slice along its side like it might have hit something sharp."

"Maybe a propeller? I'll stay on the whales."

"Well, that's what you're there for—find out what's going on."

"Research permits take forever and usually get turned down because of the Marine Mammal Protection Act. There's no law against looking, only 'harassing.' So when is looking not harassing? Oh well. I'm clear."

He watched the *Salmon Eye* turn into Ossipee Channel. He wondered why a woman was running a freight boat. Thought she did it all alone, too. He needed hydrophones to check underwater sound.

He radioed the office back. "Can you get hold of some hydrophones so I can check for noise?" he asked.

"We sent some out to Henry Sizemore. Probably went down with his boat."

"I really need them," Beringer said. "Noise may be the most important factor if the whales are losing their sense of direction. Maybe ear bones destroyed, some huge explosive sound?"

"We'll get some to you as soon as possible."

"Gotta have them soon."

19

PAUL STOMPED INTO HIS OFFICE AND threw his cap at the hook, sitting down to shuffle through the papers on his desk.

Memo to call Lemon Creek Penitentiary.

Memo to call State Trooper office in Petersburg.

And the chief was right, as usual. They'd had no response from Ellis's boat. Paul had checked several times with the Coast Guard, and there were marine operators all along the Alaska coastline—even someone in the lower forty-eight could call a boat through an Alaska marine operator. Paul called them all from the High Mountain station down by Dixon Entrance to the Lena Point station way up on Lynn Canal. Nothing. This morning, Steve Woods stopped in Paul's office to ask if he'd heard anything.

"Fat goose egg," Paul told him.

"We can turn that homicide over to the state any time, you know. It's only because the body was on our beach that we're even included."

"I'm stubborn. I gotta find who did it."

"Don't get yourself out on a limb again." The chief walked out of Paul's tiny cubicle, leaving Paul staring at the floor. Well, he was stubborn. The chief called him 'pig-headed.' Maybe he was, at that.

He glanced up to see a tall man standing at the counter. Paul went out and asked him what he could do for him.

The man told him, "We've got a crew member missing. He's left all his clothes on the vessel, so I can't say where he would go."

"Crew member missing?" Paul said. "Come back here to my office. We need to talk."

The tall man went back to Paul's office, introduced himself as Frank Smith, skipper of a longliner. "The man's name is Barney Ellis," he said.

"Barney Ellis," Paul said. "Barney Ellis was shot dead on Petroglyph Beach in Wrangell a couple nights ago."

"Shot *dead*?" Smith said. "He had a really bad temper, but nobody I know would *shoot* him."

"Well, that's what happened to him. Lizzie Romero pointed him out to me at the Coho bar, and later he was shot at the beach and I identified him as the man from the Coho bar."

"How did she know him? We haven't been to Wrangell very much."

"She saw him fighting with somebody over at the Velvet Moose in Kashevarof. She runs a freight boat, the *Salmon Eye*. Then Jenny Anderson, Andover, whatever her name is, gave her his name."

"Yeah, that was the night that guy with the gray hair in a ponytail threatened Ellis. Shouted at him, 'You're next, you're next,' and pointed his finger at him like it was a gun."

"Most likely Tango—he's an ace short of a deck—lost his memory in Vietnam. Sorry you've lost a crew member."

Smith stood up. "We need to get going. I'm sorry, too. I didn't really like Ellis a whole lot, but he was a pretty good fisherman and knew where he wanted to go. I'll miss his knowledge, though I won't really miss him a lot."

Paul escorted Smith to the counter, told him good-bye, and went straight to the chief's office.

"Frank Smith," he said. "Skipper of a longliner. Came in and told me Barney Ellis was missing. I said he'd been shot dead on Petroglyph Beach. He shook his head over that, said Ellis had a really bad temper but he didn't think anyone would shoot him. And he told me Tango threatened the man and pointed his finger like a gun at him."

"Did you get the name of the longliner?"

"No. No I didn't. I should have, though. You'll want to question the crew."

20

THE WIND WAS WHIPPING CLARENCE Strait into a froth, and the windshield wipers barely kept a hole clear as Liza crossed toward Kashevarof. She watched carefully for whales, but didn't see any, though their spouts would be difficult to spot, with horsetails beginning to blow off the tops of the waves.

All the way over, Liza replayed the scene in the Moose, Ellis flicking out his knife and lunging at the other man, catching Mink instead. Tango's sudden angry shout. What was it he'd said? The words had faded in the confusion of the scene—something about sins, and forgiveness. But first, he'd shouted something else—what—a threat, it had been— what was it? "You're next." That was it. A curse and then, "You're next."

And then that business about the gun. Maybe Mink had dropped the gun on the bar before Janet went to work on her—she'd been behind the bar, aiming the gun at Barney, even though he was already restrained by others. But her arm was bleeding torrents—she was already sitting down, Janet winding the dish towel into a tourniquet, when Liza got to her. Had the gun been lying on the bar? There were so many people standing there in front of it, people Liza had pushed past to get to Mink.

Think about the gun. You were still standing next to Tango when Mink went behind the bar and took the gun out of the drawer. Watch Mink, now. She's hollering about Hap Farwell, and the slammer, and more muscle in the gun. Blood soaking her sleeve and streaming onto the bar. Then she . . . no, Tango's shouting . . . you're watching the bald man search for the voice . . . he sees Tango finally . . . drags the men on his arms toward the door . . . the bearded man slips out . . . you're shoving your way toward the bar now, and . . . where is the gun?

Shit, Liza, can't you remember a simple, obvious detail like that? Did you see Mink put the gun in the drawer after Janet had worked on her arm? While Jimmy was cleaning up?

You know you didn't see her put that gun away. She was so woozy Tango had to help her to her feet and support her out the door. So who's lying, Liza—you or Mink?

The radio crackled. *"Wrangell Police Department calling* Salmon Eye. *Are you on here, Lizzie?"*

"Salmon Eye. What channel, Paul?"

"Ohhh, how 'bout sixty-eight?"

She switched from the all-call channel sixteen, and repeated, "Salmon Eye."

"Yeah, Lizzie, uhhh, well, uhhh . . ."

She sighed. "Paul? Is there a message?"

"Yeah, uh, Lizzie, keep in touch, okay? I mean, the weather and all that . . . you know. If it blows up, you better not go out to Kuiu. I listened to the weather—there's a low moving in tonight—thirty knots, anyway."

"I'm only going to Kashevarof and then I'll be back."

"Yeah, well . . . keep in touch, Lizzie, okay?"

"I'll keep in touch, Paul."

"Yeah, okay, uhhh . . . oh, well. . . . Wrangell Police Department, clear."

Fix this right now, Romero. "Alone" is what you want, "Lizzie."

She took Ossipee Channel between Bushy and Shrubby Islands rather than head up through Snow Passage. When the wind blows against the tide in Snow Pass, huge standing waves build and the rips become dangerous for smaller vessels. The dock at Kashevarof was pretty empty. Liza pulled the *Salmon Eye* in ahead of the *Erin* and tied her up. She put her rain jacket on. Something in the pocket—folded-up *Wrangell-Sentinel*. She still couldn't read the story about Henry Sizemore so she just left it there.

"Lumpy out there," the skipper of the *Erin* said.

"Nobody heading into Snow Pass. It looked pretty ugly."

"You happen to see those whales?" he asked. "Big pod of orcas down there around the Blashkes. Seen 'em hanging around here for days."

"I saw them twice this week," Liza said. "And I noticed they were acting kind of odd—one of them was obviously hurt—big slice in its side—and another looked like it had gone on the rocks over at Point Nesbitt."

"That's a strange one—I didn't notice any of 'em hurt, but coulda been—I wasn't that close. Hope there's nothing wrong with 'em."

"I called the Wildlife people—they said they'd check on them. Hope it was just a fluke." Liza thought about it. "That's a joke, son," she said.

She went back to the wheelhouse to shut things down, not stopping to take off her rain gear. Large pools of water formed on the floor at her every step. She was in a hurry, though—there was something about Mink's distress and Tango's odd disappearance that roused suspicion in her own mind. She'd thought of little else since she'd left Mink weeping at the hospital. Paul was certain that the gun that killed Ellis was Mink's—that was obvious.

The wind was whistling into the bay. Liza switched the radio on and listened to the weather.

"Gale warning, inside waters, Dixon Entrance to Lynn Canal, southeast winds rising thirty-five to forty-five knots tonight, seas to twelve feet, winds easing to fifteen to twenty-five by afternoon tomorrow."

Gonna blow, gonna blow. Still, the bay was pretty protected from southeasterlies—she'd be all right tied to the dock.

Liza trudged up the hill, rain swirling into her face. As soon as she passed the steep curve below it, Liza could see Mink's elderly frame bungalow, the living room light on. Tango must be there now, wherever he'd been in the last twenty-four hours. She pictured him huddled on their bed in fetal position, waiting for Mink to return. She hurried, puffing by the time she reached the top of the long stairway to the porch. She knocked and waited, knocked again, then pushed the door open and hallooed.

It always seemed to her that emptiness announced itself. Even as she searched the rooms, she knew Tango wasn't there. But the light was on—he surely couldn't have been gone long. Their huge bed was unmade and looked as though two people had slept in it last, though of course Tango probably hadn't made it, or had tossed all night, dragging the blankets around on both sides.

There were dishes in the sink—breakfast—a hurry-up sort. For two. Most likely what Tango had fixed to get Mink going before he brought her down to the *Salmon Eye*.

Liza wondered if he'd ever come back to the house at all. A pile of books had evidently overbalanced, cascading the top volumes onto the floor, a coffee mug lay on its side by the rear leg of the table, a small puddle of coffee beside it.

Wouldn't he have picked up the mug and cleaned up the spilled coffee? Of course, Tango being Tango, maybe not.

Liza took a last look around, pulled the door shut, rattled it to make sure it was latched and wouldn't blow open, and headed down the hill. It was growing dark already, and Liza walked into several deep potholes in the road before she got as far as the Moose. Rain swirled in glazed ropes under the lone streetlight. She was wet to the knees from the muddy street, and very, very hungry.

At the Velvet Moose, Jimmy was extremely busy, wearing three hats and trying to keep up. He nodded at Liza, and when he'd worked his way down to the end of the bar, asked, "Mink? Is she better? Is she coming back soon?"

"Doctor won't let her go till that infection's gone, temp's normal," Liza said. "Any sign of Tango yet? Mink's all upset about him."

"I haven't seen him. Radio's there, same as he left it, but he's not here. I called the house—no answer. Tango doesn't do well all alone. You know."

"Jimmy, would you look in the drawer under the cash register and see if Mink's gun is there? She remembers putting it back in the drawer, but there seems to be some question about it."

Jimmy opened the drawer and looked, pulled it all the way out and peered into the back of it, shook his head before he closed it again. "It's not here. The gun's always at the front of the drawer for trouble at the bar. It's not here now."

Jimmy moved along the bar, sliding glasses along and wiping up with his towel. When he got back to Liza's end of the bar, he said, "A man called. Says you should call Paul at the office."

"Thanks. Can I use the phone in the back?"

"Sure. Storeroom's locked, though." He reached under his apron and took a bunch of keys out of his pocket. He fiddled them through his fingers. "This one," he said, holding the whole ring out to her.

Liza took it and unlocked the storeroom door, flipped the light switch, and hauled a couple of cartons over to sit on while she dialed the Wrangell Police Department.

"Yeah, yeah, Mink's gun's missing?" Paul said, when she got him. "Mink never put it in the drawer, and somebody else took it off the bar. Or somebody went back later, like Tango, for instance. Maybe Tango had a good reason to kill the guy, you know? Or, in fact, he might not have killed him. But if Tango's innocent, then where the hell is he?"

"I'm going to open the library in the morning and ask people if they saw him after we left. He was tearing back up the hill, last I saw of him." Liza said good-bye and hung up, clinging to the sound of Paul's voice, and sagged back against a row of liquor cartons, putting her face in her hands.

She didn't want to be involved in this—she'd had enough violence, enough death, to go all the way around on this damned merry-go-round. She saw Efren's face, saw him slumping to the sidewalk in a hail of bullets. Violence had ruined her life. But her debt to Tango was enormous and Tango was in trouble. What were friends for, anyway?

21

BERINGER HAD SHIFTED HIS ATTENTION to the *Sophie Marie*, a huge longliner, very old, with a black hull marked by rust. He tracked her clear out to Point Baker, where she went in and fueled up.

The crew went into the restaurant and Beringer followed them. He sat at a separate table, but close enough to hear what the crew said. Only talk about fishing prices—how bad they were—couldn't make a living at it anymore—halibut prices weren't so bad, but coho? Terrible.

Beringer asked them what they were fishing for. "Halibut," one man said. "Gonna fish for black cod next. Join us?"

Beringer moved his place to their table. "Thanks," he said. "I was getting lonely over there." He introduced himself. "Scott Beringer. Marine biologist on loan to the Fish and Wildlife Protection Agency."

"Burger and fries?" the waitress asked, setting them down in front of the man who had signaled. "Fish and chips? Clam chowder and ham sandwich?"

Finally Beringer's fish and chips arrived. He poured ketchup on the fries, and picked them up one at a time.

"Something going on with the whales, ain't there?" a man said. "Seen a couple floating around all cut up."

"Yes, there is something going on," Beringer said. "A humpback ran into that small freighter, the *Salmon Eye*, the other day. Thought the whale would have heard it coming. Something toxic in the food chain maybe, or noise. Could be noise."

"Our engine rattles," another man said. "But not real loud."

"You have toxic bottom paint?" Beringer asked.

"Nahh, haven't painted the bottom in a long time. Must be a ton 'a weeds on there, and barnacles."

"Leaking oily ballast?"

"Nahh, I don't think so."

"Well," he said to the crew, "I'm gonna track you a while, see if anything you're doing is causing trouble."

"Don't think so," one of the crew members said. "Pretty sure we'd know it if it was us."

The crew paid for their lunches, stood up, and one man shook Beringer's hand. "Ain't us," the man said. "For sure."

22

WHEN LIZA WENT BACK TO THE *SALMON Eye* late in the evening, Sam said something was wrong. He jumped over the rail, his hackles up, his tail stiff. As soon as she opened the door, he rushed through, his nose to the floor. Somebody had ransacked the boat. The cupboards were open, dishes broken, pots and pans thrown everywhere. Books everywhere. Someone had swept them off the shelves, and flung them all over, pages crumpled, spines broken.

Sam circled the cabin, the wheelhouse, then raced down the steps. She could hear him whuffing along the floor below. Sam knew who had done this, but he couldn't tell her.

She went below. Clothes had been taken out of their drawers; the things she had hung in her closet, sweatpants, wet gear, boots, were strewn all over. She looked in the head—a bottle of aspirin had been smashed in the sink and they had jammed the toilet with a roll of toilet paper. She reached in and pulled it out, wiping her hand on a towel thrown on the floor. Finally she mounted the steps again. Who could have done this?

Sam raced back and forth, now along the deck, then through the cabin, whining, giving short, sharp barks, whining again. She went out on the foredeck. She hadn't unloaded the freight when she got here—she'd do it in the morning. But something was missing. Something that had been wedged between the pallets of canned goods and the cartons of motor oil. What was it? What was it? All at once she knew. The hydrophones. Someone had taken the crate with the hydrophones.

Liza jumped over the rail to the dock and pounded on the *Erin*'s door. A very sleepy man appeared, yawning and stretching. "Did you see anyone on the *Salmon Eye* a little earlier?" she asked. "Or a lot earlier?"

"Nope," he said. "I was at the Moose till around nine. Then I sacked out." He yawned again.

"Someone's torn my boat apart."

He swung over the rail, climbed up on the *Salmon Eye*, and stood in the door. "Wow," he said. "What happened?"

Liza put her face in her hands. "I don't know," she said. She raised her head again. "And why did it happen to me? The only thing they took were the hydrophones that were out on the foredeck."

"I could help you clean up," the *Erin*'s skipper said.

"No, you don't have to do that. Go back to bed. I'll talk to you in the morning."

Slowly she began putting things back together. First she swept up the broken dishes—she'd have to get new ones. Plastic, this time. She jammed the pots and pans back in the cupboards every which way, and then started putting the books back on the shelves. They were totally mixed up—fiction, nonfiction, reference—she'd have to shelve them by number or author later on.

At last she went below. She crammed her clothes into the drawers without any order to them, and then fell into bed. But her mind was reeling—who could have done this? And why? She thought of the person with the blinding light at Kindergarten Bay. That person would obviously have seen the name *Salmon Eye* on her boat. Maybe that same person had seen Jenny rowing away from the *Salmon Eye*. And Jenny had seemed frightened to Liza. But Jenny hadn't said a word about Ellis—nothing at all.

Finally she fell into exhausted sleep, waking early, getting up to make coffee. Where was the coffeepot? She found it behind the stove and rinsed it out before she put coffee in it.

Always the first thing she did in the morning was open her log, write in the date and where she was going with freight and books. Now she couldn't find it. It was always on the chart table—she knew she'd put it back there—at least, she thought she had. She searched the shelves below the chart table—had she thrown it in the locked drawer with the freight orders and bills of lading? She unlocked the drawer, noting that someone had tried to jimmy the lock, but the log wasn't there.

Someone must have taken it. But it was right in plain sight. No one would have ransacked the boat looking for it. It was right there—right in plain sight. Now she'd have to start a new log. Suddenly she thought how she'd mentioned to Jenny about writing in her log how angry she was at Henry. But the log was there the next morning, so Jenny hadn't stolen it. Liza had written in the date and where she was going, to Kashevarof with freight. Yesterday. Now it was gone.

She searched some more. Could it have been swept to the floor and she'd reshelved it with the books? She walked into the captain's stateroom behind the wheelhouse, and tried to look along the shelves, but it was such a jumble of books she decided she'd just have to start a new log. Maybe she'd find it on the bookshelves, but she didn't want to take the time to look now.

She unloaded the freight—the pallets of canned goods and motor oil, a small generator, some rolls of wire fencing—swinging them onto a forklift, then running them to the shed at the end of the dock. Then Liza put up the "Library Open" sign in the window of the *Salmon Eye*, and half an hour later there were seven people lined up in front of the bookshelves in the former captain's stateroom.

"The books are in a muddle," Liza said. "My boat was ransacked last night, the books knocked off the shelves. I haven't reshelved them in any order yet."

"Did you catch 'em at it?" one person asked, and she shook her head.

"No, they were here and gone when I got back."

Someone else said, "Well, I like the books this way, all mixed up. Steinbeck next to a book on computers. Seems like that's how it should be."

As each of them checked out, she asked about Tango.

"Nah," Fred Heming said, "haven't seen him in a long time. Don't get into the Moose too often anymore. See, I started going to AA meetings—I mean, I was in pretty bad shape, you know, kinda like I was puttin' a lot off on Lois, woke up one day didn't know where I'd been for a couple days, made me think, you know? So I haven't been in the Moose for like twenty-six days."

Liza laughed. "So who's counting?" she said. "That's good, though, Fred. I'm glad to hear it. You can do it, I know."

Fred nodded solemnly, then grinned at her. "Yeah, I'll do it, but hell, it sure is hard to quit counting."

No one had seen Tango in the last few days. Nancy Bellamy from the grocery store checked out her books, an assortment ranging from Dick Francis to Muriel Spark, Nancy being a voracious and eclectic reader. She'd had to hunt all along the shelves to find them. Liza remembered seeing Nancy at the Moose the night of the fight—must have come in there after she closed the store.

"Seen Tango around lately?" she asked Nancy.

Nancy shrugged. "Well, funny thing. Mark said Tango was with some guy in a Zodiac heading out of the bay the other morning when Mark was coming in with his crab pots. Said he was surprised to see him—thought he'd gone over to Wrangell with Mink."

"He didn't go. I took Mink myself, and she didn't want Tango over there fussing around, making himself a nuisance. You got any idea what time that was?"

"Mark usually goes out around six, gets back, oh, maybe eight-thirty, nine. Probably must have been around eight if Mark was coming in and they were going out." She shook her head, turning to go. Then she paused and said, "Mink doing okay?"

Liza nodded. "She's still in the Wrangell hospital, though. Had some blood poisoning, so they want to keep her till that's all cleared up. But she'd like to get hold of Tango, and he isn't at home, and Jimmy hasn't seen him."

Nancy stepped toward the door, then hesitated. "I guess I should tell someone—Tango . . . when Tango was waiting for Janet to finish tying up Mink's arm, before he was talking to you, he picked up the gun Mink threw down on top of the bar. Probably he was going to put it in the drawer. But he actually didn't, not right then, anyway. I was kind of watching him—he's a weird one, that guy—what he did, he looked around like he wanted to see if anybody was watching and then he shoved it in that cargo pocket of the sweatshirt he wears, the one that says "Southeast Asian Games, 2nd Place."

This time Nancy did leave, slamming the door behind her.

After Liza closed the library, she went to talk to Mark Bellamy. Mark was sitting on the checkout counter talking to Eli Jones. Several years ago, Mark suffered severe injuries to his left arm and leg in a logging accident, and had supplemented his disability check since then by crabbing, hauling just enough to supply the grocery, the Moose, and Margie at the café. He helped his mother out at the grocery in the summer months, and filled in occasionally when she had other things to do. Mark was a Vietnam vet too, and dropped in on Tango to play chess, but they never seemed to talk about the good old days of napalm and M-16s. A shared, sealed past.

When Eli left, Liza asked Mark about Tango.

"Yeah, pretty sure it was him, you know. It was Tango all right. All hunched over on the seat, long arms and legs, skinny. Yeah, for sure it was Tango. Waved, but he didn't wave back. They was going hell for leather—he had 'a been gripping that seat like the saddle on a bronc. But sure, that's who it was."

"He was with somebody."

"Yeah, the guy steering the outboard. Big Zodiac—don't know if I've seen it in here before."

"Could you describe the other man?"

"Nahhh, they was goin' so fast I never got a good look at him."

"Describe the boat—what did it look like?"

"Ahh, just a big Zodiac—orange—console drive—really big engine—like I said, they was going like bats—huge wake it made."

"Hope he didn't try to get all the way over to Wrangell in a Zodiac—the weather turned pretty ugly after that—no visibility at all."

"Those are good boats—they could follow the shoreline and get over pretty fast, you know. He maybe wanted to check up on Mink. I heard she got knifed."

"Then where is he?"

"Yeah, that's true—he never showed up over there, hunh?

That's not so good. Maybe oughta put out an overdue on the radio."

"Well, Mink's having a cow because she can't find him. He hasn't called or anything. If you're positive you saw him, I guess we should start a search."

"Yeah," Mark said. "Yeah, I was positive."

"Well, thanks," Liza said. "Thanks a lot for the information."

"You gonna look for him?"

"I'm going to look for him. He might be in trouble in just a Zodiac. Thanks again for the help."

At least she had something to tell Mink. But Mark had said Tango might be going to Wrangell to check on Mink. And that was the morning of the day Ellis was killed on the beach with Mink's gun. She certainly wouldn't point that out to Mink. And Tango had put the gun in the cargo pocket of his sweatshirt. That made shivers go all the way down her spine.

23

LIZA TOOK THE *SALMON EYE* TO EX-change Cove and anchored there. Very peaceful, she thought. The *Salmon Eye* was the only boat there. To the south there were red banners in the sky below the heavy clouds, announcing tomorrow's weather. She pulled on her sweatpants and sweatshirt and put on her running shoes. Sam bounded about the cabin, ready to go—what was taking her so long, anyway?

She took the raft off the roof of the cabin and slung it over the side. Sam jumped in before she could cleat the line. She threw in a life jacket and let herself down from the deck, then rowed Sam ashore. He lifted his leg at each stone along the old road that came down to Exchange Cove. After that was taken care of, he trotted after Liza, then had to gallop because she was running so fast.

Liza was in a trance, soaring away from life on earth, flying through the clouds. In this trancelike state, nothing seemed impossible. She was floating above the earth; her motion made her light as a feather. She could do anything, anything at all, running as though she had wings on her heels. Sam's tongue was hanging out as he tried to keep up with her. Eventually she whistled for Sam and turned around. Sam was obviously reluctant to go back, stubbornly sitting down and hanging his head. She shouted, "Food, Sam. Dinnertime," and he leaped to his feet and raced after her.

She rowed swiftly back to the *Salmon Eye*, turning the raft around the stern to the port side so she could haul it aboard. On the port side, an aluminum skiff with a fifty-horse Evinrude was fastened to a cleat on the rail. She glanced along the deck and saw no one out there. There were no other boats anchored in Exchange Cove—who had come over here with that skiff?

Sam was out of the raft before Liza had it fastened, dashing along the deck with his nose to the planks, his tail held stiff. When Sam didn't wag that tail, he told her one of several things: "I don't know who's here"—"I don't like this person"—"this could mean trouble." But as he reached the door, his tail began to wave, moved more briskly, finally flailed the air as his dear old friend of two nights ago appeared. Jenny Andover.

Jenny strode back and dragged the raft aboard after Liza climbed out. Together they returned it to the top of the cabin and clipped it to the cap rails.

I need to get out of my sweats and take a shower," Liza said. "Can you hang on a minute while I do that?"

She dropped down the ladder, tore off her clothes and jumped in the shower. She could hear Jenny moving around up there, heard her in the stateroom looking at the books. When she'd gotten dressed, she went back up the ladder. Jenny was sitting there with *Southern Cross* by Stephen Greenleaf.

"Could I borrow this?" she asked. "I know about it and I'd love to read it."

"Sure," Liza said. "Just let me put it in a notebook with the date. I've got coffee on. Want some?"

"Coffee's fine," Jenny said.

Liza poured kibble into Sam's bowl, then got out the coffee mugs. "Where're you anchored now?"

"I left the boat the other side of Bushy Island. They were going down Clarence Strait. I didn't really want to go with them, you know?"

"No, I guess I don't know. You just left? Just climbed over and took the skiff?"

"Sort of. Yeah, Alice was eating dinner and Frank was at the helm, and I just saw my chance and got out of there."

"Have you eaten?"

"Well, yeah, I had dinner before Alice."

Liza set the coffee mugs on the table. She found Jenny's story extremely odd—how had she been able to sneak away from the boat, if that was what she'd done, without anyone seeing her go? Then she thought she knew: if the boat was towing the aluminum skiff with its outboard, Jenny could have dropped over into it, unfastened it, and the boat would have left it far behind in moments. Unlikely place to do it, though, right at the entrance to Snow Passage, where the riptides would swirl a small skiff like a feather on the water.

"So," she said. "You went A.W.O.L."

Jenny nodded. "Sort of, I guess. I got scared, is all." She shrugged and picked up her mug. "I . . . well, I just don't like being out there on the water, I guess."

Liza felt sure there was more to her anxiety than not liking ocean travel.

"I didn't actually ask you what I wanted to know," Jenny said, "and afterwards I felt stupid. Not asking, I mean. Did you ever see Barney Ellis again?"

"Isn't he still with you?" Liza said.

"Oh, yeah, sure, I mean, sure he is," Jenny said, looking out the window. "I just wondered if, you know, if you'd run into him anywhere. Like, if you'd talked to him about those medical bills, something like that."

"Jenny?" Liza laid her hands on the center of the table and waited. Finally Jenny turned her eyes away from the window and glanced quickly at Liza before looking away again.

"Yeah," she said. "I mean, no, he's not there anymore. I don't know what happened to him—he just kind of, like, disappeared. And nobody's talking about it. I kept asking for a couple days, and they just said, 'Oh, he's gone back south—good riddance.' Only, I get this feeling like, maybe he's still hanging around, or like, maybe he's going to sue us for . . . whatever. Like maybe he'll have to get his share or he'll sue. Or something. I don't know—it's just this funny feeling I get when I think about him."

Liza watched her. Should she tell Jenny that Ellis was dead? Would that reassure her, or cause her new worries? She'd had the feeling night before last that Jenny was afraid. Afraid of what?

"I do know what happened to him. The night after the fight, he was shot on the beach in Wrangell."

Her words were like a shot to Jenny. After a sharp intake of air, she jumped up and rushed through the door to the deck, leaving *Southern Cross* on the table.

"You can't know," she muttered to Liza. "You can't imagine what that means."

"Could you tell me? You're afraid of something, Jenny. Can I help you? I have a friend in Wrangell—he's a policeman. . . ."

Jenny gasped again. "No," she said, dropping over the rail into the skiff. "No, it's nothing. You can't do anything— please, please—you can't do anything." She was jerking at the engine cord now. The engine sputtered and coughed and she yanked it harder. Finally she shoved the choke in and gave it a violent pull. The skiff tore away from the *Salmon Eye*. Jenny never looked back.

24

LIZA HEADED BACK TO SHOEMAKER BAY. The forests along Chichagof Pass reflected black in the silver water, and there was snow covering the high ridge of Etolin Island.

She climbed the ramp and took the truck to the hospital. She stared at Mink's room. The bed was empty and stripped down to its plastic mattress cover; a young man was mopping the floor.

"Where is she?" she asked.

The man said, "Patient? I don't know who was in here—I just work here—nobody tells me nothin'."

She turned and went back to the nurses' station. "Minerva Michaels?" she asked.

The nurse laughed without much humor. "Checked herself out early this morning. Got herself dressed, called a taxi, charged out that front door like some army tank, thank you very much."

"Do you know where she was going?"

"Not a clue. Didn't say a word to us—just rushed out of here and got in the taxi and pointed down the road. Who knows?"

Liza heard, *Who cares?* She laughed. Mink was an awful

patient—cranky and resistant—furious at being incarcerated against her will.

Floatplanes went to Kashevarof, went everywhere, in fact, and Liza knew Mink would head straight back there. Mink was consumed by fears for Tango—she'd have gotten there by now—conned someone at the floatplane dock into flying her over. She was sure Mink was all right—she'd gone home, would track Tango down and force him to tell her where he'd been. He had not been killing people, that was all Liza could say for sure.

She went back to the *Salmon Eye* and took Sam for a walk through the forest across the road, heading up the Rainbow Falls Trail, which connected to the Institute Creek Trail, gaining fifteen hundred feet in elevation in 2.3 miles. She wouldn't go that far; that trail came out at the Shoemaker Bay Overlook.

She did go as far as Rainbow Falls, heading beyond it to the top of the falls, which had a fabulous view of Zimovia Strait, Chichagof Pass and all the islands around there. She turned around, walking down the trail and back into the forest, when she heard the crack of a rifle and a bullet whizzed past her ear. She threw herself to the ground and shouted, "Drop, Sam."

She heard him thump down in the underbrush, heard the rifle again. This time the bullet went high above her. She crawled into the salal and dense, dried-up ferns where Sam lay. Maybe the person couldn't see her in there. Someone was coming up the trail now. She tried to cover Sam, holding her breath, hoping Sam wouldn't bark at whoever it was.

Someone was going right by them. Sam made no sound. The person went on up the trail—he was running now. She peered out from the underbrush and saw that he was carrying a rifle. She heard his feet racing on the boards over the muskeg—heading higher up the trail, farther and farther away from her. She had to make a decision. Should she run for it, down the trail to Shoemaker, or should she stay hidden till the person came back and passed her by again? Go for it, she decided.

She crawled out of the bushes, Sam right behind her, and tore down the trail. The trail had a lot of wooden steps, uneven steps, and sometimes she went around them, sloshing through the muskeg, a bog where you could drown in your own footprints, gnarled pines growing from it, searching for soil beneath the water. She headed back into the forest, Sam leading the way. Finally they got to the end of the trail, raced across Zimovia Highway, tore across the parking lot and down the ramp. Sam galloped ahead of her and jumped over the rail. She was breathless by the time she got to the *Salmon Eye*. She flung herself through the door and locked it.

Throwing herself down on the bench, she tried to catch her breath. Her heart was pounding so hard she thought she'd die. She lay down on it, trying to think. Someone had been shooting at her. Could it have been a hunter, thinking she was a deer? That Sam was a deer? But that shadowy figure who had run past them wasn't dressed like a hunter. Hunters wore orange vests and camouflage. The man was dressed in dark clothes, black, she thought. The man had seen her go up the trail to Rainbow Falls, had been stalking her, shooting at her.

Why? Why was she always at the center of things? She'd call Paul, tell him someone shot at her. And her boat had been ransacked, too. She hadn't told him that, either. No, she wouldn't call, wouldn't tell him anything. He'd never let her go out again; he'd tell her, "Lizzie, somebody's trying to get you. Stay right there on the *Salmon Eye* and I'll see you don't get hurt. I'll watch the boat—anybody comes, I'll shoot him."

At five-thirty in the afternoon, Liza went to Tasha's place, thinking she might be home from work. She wanted to tell her about the shooting but she'd warn her not to tell Paul about it.

Tasha dragged her into the kitchen. "Stay for dinner," she said. "We got lots of deer stew and everybody's pretty tired of it."

Liza sank into a chair next to the kitchen table. "What's up with you?" she asked.

"Ahh, you know, just the usual. Domestic violence going right along, drugs, alcohol, ahhh, you know how it is. And what's with you? How's Mink?"

"Checked herself out of the hospital, probably got a float-plane to carry her back to Kashevarof. I think she's determined to look for Tango. Maybe he'll be at the house when she gets there, but I don't think so. He's truly disappeared. Mark Bellamy saw Tango going in a Zodiac right out of the bay at Kashevarof with someone else. Maybe the man I heard on the radio while I was writing down all those numbers. I heard him say, 'That's you for sure, you old grunt,' or something like that. Anyway, there was a man on the radio and they made an appointment to meet. I'm sure of it."

"So you think they went somewhere in a Zodiac together?"

"Could be—I don't really know that they did, but they certainly made an appointment to meet—8:00 A.M. and the coordinates for Kashevarof, but they didn't set a day, so I don't know. If they met that morning after we left I'm sure Mark saw them going out of the bay. Oh, well, I just hope Mink finds him. Now I have to tell you something else. I got shot at early this afternoon when I took Sam up the Rainbow Falls Trail."

"You! You got shot at?"

"Yup. I threw myself down in the bushes and crawled over to Sam. A man came running past carrying a rifle and went right on up the trail. Two bullets whizzed right over my head. Sam didn't bark at him, which I was afraid might happen."

"Could he have been a hunter? No, no, he wasn't because no one can hunt on the trail there. What have you done, Liza?"

"I have no idea. The guy wasn't dressed like a hunter, so he must have been shooting at me. I don't think I've done anything to warrant getting shot at." Liza shivered and Tasha put an arm around her. "I don't know what I've done, but it must be something."

"Yeah," Tasha said. "Something, all right."

"Don't tell Paul about it," Liza said. "He'll never let me out of here after he hears that."

"Oh, I certainly won't tell him," Tasha said. "He'll have to protect you all the way," she said, grinning and raising her eyebrows. "I know exactly how he'll do that."

Then she shouted, "Dinner," and all the kids came thudding through the door, giving Liza high fives, Erin hugging her. She loved each and every one of them. Family. The only family Liza had anymore.

25

SHE HAD A SLEEPLESS NIGHT THINKING about the person who had shot at her. Who could have done it? And why? She'd been peacefully going about her business, but someone wanted to kill her. She was frightened, but she wouldn't leave the boat and Sam. Sam was good—he knew when something wasn't right. He'd tell her, his hackles up, baying at her when something was wrong.

In the morning, a weary Liza went back to Kashevarof to find Mink. She'd been back and forth so many times she'd become a shuttle bus, and it would take five hours to get there, a long way to go to talk to Mink. She started the engine, and while it warmed up, took the phone line and power cord off. She steered the boat out between the markers and started through Chichagof Pass.

While she crossed Clarence Strait, she started thinking about Tango. Where had he gone? Mark had seen him in a Zodiac with someone else, flying out of the bay, but then he'd disappeared.

She tied up at the dock at Kashevarof. "Stay, Sam," she said. He hung his head, then flopped to the floor. She locked the door before she went to the Velvet Moose.

Mink was nowhere to be seen. Jimmy said, "She's gone

home—she's furious because nobody's looking for Tango. She wants a big search."

"I think there is a search going on—at least, the Wrangell Police are searching for him. But they may not know where to look. I'll take her with me—she'll know where he's gone."

She trudged up the hill and knocked on the front door of the bungalow. It was flung open before she could take her hand away.

"He'd 'a never left those books on the floor with a pool 'a coffee running around," Mink snarled. "He'd 'a picked 'em up before he went anywhere. Look at that."

Liza looked again at the spill from the coffee mug and the books spread over the floor. "So what happened?" she asked.

"So he was spooked by something. Startled, musta been—somebody came and scared him or somethin'."

"Mark Bellamy saw Tango with somebody else going out in a Zodiac at around eight in the morning when I took you over to Wrangell. They were going very fast—said the Zodiac was making a steep wake. I figured he'd decided he had to get to Wrangell to check up on you and called somebody to take him over there."

"Could be. But he'd 'a never left those books lying there. Hell, he really treasures his books."

"Well, maybe the knock on the door startled him, and then he saw who it was and just went with him."

"I suppose. Could be, I guess. So where is he? Never showed up over there, did he?"

"We'll search the shoreline—could be the Zodiac couldn't make it in that weather and they holed up someplace."

"Ain't ever showed up, though."

"So, maybe they couldn't get the engine going again, or maybe they ran out of fuel or something. Look, we just have to cruise along the shoreline and look for an orange Zodiac. They probably built a fire, put up a tarp, something like that. Maybe we'll see smoke. Anyway, we'll go tomorrow. It's too dark now—we couldn't see a thing."

They set out at first light, Mink grumbling about the hour but driven by her need to find Tango. The shoreline was curtained in mist—there would be no possibility of seeing smoke rising, but an orange Zodiac would jump out if it were hauled up on the beach. The likeliest places were the closest ones.

"If Tango could pick up Baron's transmission on the handheld radio, the range must have been fairly short and more or less line of sight," Liza said. "West coast of Zarembo, probably all the way from St. John Harbor to Point Nesbitt where we saw the whale stranded."

"Yeah," Mink said, "anything farther'd be outa range if he could pick it up."

"We can start at the southern end of the Kashevarofs and work our way north, then around the top of Zarembo. The logical jumping-off place is Coffman Cove, but if I go there, I'll have to open the library. So we won't go quite as far as Coffman Cove."

They edged the shore of Prince of Wales Island, as far south as Exchange Cove and as far north as Point Colpoys. Then they circumnavigated Zarembo Island, checking all the way into St. John Harbor, where there was a dock and former logging camp. Roosevelt Harbor, too, had a dock and logging camp—if they were in either, they would have a little shelter. Liza kept the *Salmon Eye* close to shore, Mink using the binoculars. Nothing, nothing, nothing.

"I don't know," Mink said. "He sure ain't in any of those bays. I just keep thinkin' no, he'd 'a never left those books lying there. Even if somebody came and knocked on the door and was going to take him to Wrangell, he'd never leave those books like that."

"What do you think happened, then?"

"Something made him go when he didn't want to, is what. Like, maybe somebody came and just took him away. Maybe they had a gun. Or maybe they had a knife, like that guy in the bar. I know that man, though. He'd 'a never left the books that way."

"So? Shall we head back? If you're convinced somebody made him go against his will, we won't find him till he escapes."

"Don't think he'll do that—he's such a wimp—he'd never overpower anyone. So I guess we just have to keep looking."

They checked Steamer Bay and Kindergarten Bay, circled Woronkofski Island and the islands at the head of Stikine Strait. Nothing. Finally Liza dropped a distraught, exhausted Mink off in Kashevarof, supporting her up the hill to her house.

"We will find him," she said. "We will find him, Mink."

26

BERINGER HAD ELIMINATED THE COASTAL
freighter *Ocean Pride*. It had gone all the way up to Haines
and was shuttling between Juneau and Skagway before re-
turning. That left only the *Salmon Eye*, the tugs, and the four
longliners.

The skipper of the *Salmon Eye* had reported the whale
running into the boat, as well as the injured orca and the one
stranded at Point Nesbitt. He was convinced it was noise
that was causing the trouble. The orcas used a sonar system
to understand their surroundings, and the humpbacks probably used particles of magnetite in their brains to find their direction, though the research on that wasn't finished yet.
Something, though, might dislodge those particles. And
noise might destroy the receptors in the orcas' brains that responded to the clicks.

It would take something huge, though, and very close to a
pod of whales, to do that kind of damage. They avoided engine noise, but lately had seemed as though they couldn't respond to underwater sounds. What? he asked himself. A
huge noise, close to a pod of whales. What?

Could there be some kind of secret war games going on?
Torpedoes at the ready? Submarines battling at two hundred
fathoms? Don't be stupid, Scott.

But what if it wasn't a boat? Could something be dropped from the air? Explosives? To what purpose? Ahhhhh, this was getting him nowhere. He had to have hydrophones to track noise underwater. He'd requested them but they hadn't reached the office yet. He'd go back to Wrangell to pick them up.

He'd gone back to tracking the *Salmon Eye*. First it headed toward Exchange Cove, then turned around, went north and edged Point Colpoys at some distance, the tide rips being enormous at the Point. The *Salmon Eye* went in and out of St. John Harbor, across the top of Zarembo, down Stikine Strait and into Roosevelt Harbor without ever stopping. What on earth? With his binoculars he could see a short person standing next to the skipper in the wheelhouse. Maybe they were looking for something? Waste of time with all this mist—visibility was almost zero.

He followed the *Salmon Eye* all the way back to Kashevarof, watching as it turned in and tied up at the dock.

27

WHEN SHE WENT BACK TO THE *SALMON EYE* at the dock in Kashevarof, Liza poured a cup of coffee, and took out Tango's radio log. There had to be something in that log. Though the important part would be right at the end, she'd begin at the beginning and skim quickly to get the drift of the log. And drift, she soon learned, was the operative word.

"1/1:

1500:

"Before the beginning of years

There came to the making of man

Time with a gift of tears,

Grief with a glass that ran." (Swinburne)

There were twenty-five of us. And that was all.

1547: Alpha 1—hazing from sniper. No call in.

1605: Four and twenty blackbirds, and a great horned owl to impose silence.

1632: Zulu 77 Zulu 77. Put it left of the treeline—

to the left, roger 77.'

1723: 'The Owl and the Pussy Cat went to sea.' (E. Lear)

Also the four and twenty blackbirds. And the sea became wine-dark."

This was only the first of January. Eight months of nonsense she could not even skim. She flipped the pages, noting the tiny, neat script in which he copied down his quotations and observations, the large straight-lined print in which he reported his radio contacts. She found the eighth day of November, the last entry, her own handwriting interposed in his.

"8/25:

1700: 'And she said, "It's a fact the whole world knows,
That Pobbles are happier without their toes." ' (E. Lear)
'The enemy increaseth every day;
We, at the height, are ready to decline.' (W. S.)"

She scanned the following entries, the usual mix of quotations, running commentary, and radio contacts. And then, about 1930, seven-thirty P.M. on a shore clock, there was a sharp break.

"1937: Loud and clear. Baron."

The writing started with the usual straight-line print and grew smaller and more crowded, as though Tango was writing fast, trying to keep up with the broadcast.

"Alpha 4-2 Alpha 4-2 27 yrs 27
1-0-3-1-0-2 nov 1-0-5-4-6-1-6 echo."

He had written in the margin, "That was it—that was it!" She must have come over to him somewhere in the next few minutes. He had scribbled "Baron," again, and uncharacteristically strung a row of exclamation marks after it. Then he must have turned the book over to her because he'd gone back later and put brackets around what she'd written and noted "Romeo," in the margin.

"Alpha 4-2, tomorrow. 5-6-1-8-0-2 november 1-3-3-0-9-0-9 whiskey. Roger. Alpha 4-2. 800."

That was the end of what Liza had written. The bar fight had broken out only a few moments later, while Tango was ruminating on footfalls echoing in memory and passages he did not take. The only other entry was recorded at 2109.

"The search has ended. 'He shall not live; look, with a spot I damn him . . . O Cassius! I am sick of many griefs' (W.S.)"

Liza left the notebook open on the table and went to refill her coffee cup. She sat down again and quickly reread the entire entry for November 8, thinking she might uncover a rhythm, a breath or voice or heartbeat that she'd hear in some subliminal receiver. All it did was cause great anxiety. "He shall not live." She stumbled when she came to "with a spot I damn him . . ."

Read it aloud. Concentrate on the radio conversation, not the quotations. She spoke slowly and clearly and Sam sat up, his ears turned forward, expectantly. "Repeat, five six one eight zero two november one three three zero nine zero nine whiskey. Roger. Alpha Four-two. Eight hundred."

Of course. Coordinates. Latitude 56°18'02" north, longitude 133°09'09" west. She dashed into the wheelhouse and pulled the chart that covered the whole area. #17360: "Etolin Island to Midway Islands, including Sumner Strait." She was certain those coordinates would show where he was. But they plotted exactly at Kashevarof. What use was that?

She shoved the chart aside on the table while she ran through all the bits of information floating around in her brain. "Roger. Alpha 4-2. 800." Something at eight o'clock. Something at Kashevarof. Tango had been making an appointment over the radio. Somebody real, for once. She'd heard the man herself. "Oh, that's you for sure, you old grunt."

Tango had responded, "Heh-heyyyy, Baron. Alpha Four-two, out." Excitement. Pleasure. A new look in his eyes.

Baron. Was that a name? It wasn't part of the radio alphabet. Assume it's a name, Liza. Someone named Baron met Tango in Kashevarof at eight o'clock in the morning and took him somewhere.

Wait, though. There were some other coordinates at the beginning. She went back and read the first ones. "1-0-3-1-0-2 nov 1-0-5-4-6-1-6 echo." "That was it," he'd shouted. "That was it!"

Ten degrees north, one hundred five degrees east. East? Time to get out the atlas. She pulled out the oldest of the atlases—she was certain the place was going to be something from Tango's past, and what past did he have but Vietnam? She spread it out on the galley table and found the page for Southeast Asia. She checked the latitude and longitude along the edges. The right part of the world, at least.

Heading back to the wheelhouse, she retrieved her dividers and parallel rulers from the chart cupboard so she could measure accurately. The coordinates crossed between Long Xuyen and Vinh Long, near the village of Kien Van on the Mekong River. Was it there, near Kien Van, that his platoon had been decimated in that vicious holiday celebration called Tet?

That had been a real voice on Tango's radio the other night—she'd heard it "loud and clear," as Tango said himself. And Tango must have met the man. Otherwise, where was he?

She switched the radio on, listening to requests to go to the talk channels and a Coast Guard announcement. Then, "Matanuska *passing Point Alexander heading north, all concerned traffic please contact.*" Meeting an Alaska State Ferry in shallow, tortuous Wrangell Narrows was of concern to *all* traffic, she thought.

How could she call this Baron fellow without rousing suspicion? "*Salmon Eye* calling Baron, *Salmon Eye* calling Baron," or "Tango to Baron, Tango to Baron, come in please, Baron."

Dummy. Of course you try Tango first. Why hadn't she thought of that right away? Tango didn't have his radio with him, but the man, Baron, had a radio. How else had he called?

28

LATE IN THE EVENING, BERINGER REACHED over and flipped the scanner on the radio. He hadn't picked up "the Voice of Kien Van" since the missed meeting. Ted couldn't face it, that was all. Understandable—it had taken him a week or two himself before he could answer. He ran through the channels again with the scanner. A ferry calling the tug in Snow Pass—*overtaking, port side*; on channel twenty-two, the Coast Guard weather report; on channel sixteen, . . . "Eye *calling Tango,* Salmon Eye *calling Tango, come in please, Tango.*"

Tango. Ted? Was someone actually calling him? He did know the *Salmon Eye.* He waited to see if the call would be repeated. It was.

"*This is the Motor Vessel* Salmon Eye, *calling Baron for Tango, Baron for Tango. Alpha Four-two, Baron. Come in, please.*"

Beringer watched the *Salmon Eye* come through the entrance to Exchange Cove. At the bow was a large, copper-colored dog, its front paws on the rail, long ears streaming in the wind. Nice bow watch to have, he thought, noting the lovely sleek lines of the *Salmon Eye* as she swung sideways. Long foredeck with a crane, her pilothouse aft, a narrow-beamed halibut schooner of long ago, superbly maintained, her paint and varnish pristine.

The schooner slid to the center, where the depth was close to forty feet. He heard the engine slip into neutral and the woman came out, released the anchor windlass, and the chain rattled out. When the *Salmon Eye* backed down on her anchor, the engine shut down and Beringer waited nervously for the woman to appear again. Nothing happened.

He listened for the radio, thought maybe she'd step out and shout across it—wasn't far, maybe a hundred yards— maybe he should go over there? Hell, she was probably as nervous as he was—Ted, Tango, whoever, was known to each of them as a different person, and they'd already established by radio that neither of them knew where he was. So what, if anything, did they have to discuss?

Suddenly, from the starboard side of the *Salmon Eye*, a small red raft appeared and headed toward the beach. The dog, seated in the bow, dwarfed the rower. When the raft was still a dozen feet from shore, the dog leaped over, the splash tilting the raft. The rower flung her arm up to shield her face, one oar dragging, and he could hear her shout at the dog, who stood on the beach now, waiting to shake till she got there. A comic, that dog. Somehow it made him feel better.

The dog raced along the beach, nose to the ground, pausing to lift his leg at every log and boulder—male, obviously, deep copper-colored, heavy-boned with a glossy short coat that showed off his muscles. A magnificent animal—he thought of Sarah's longing for a dog—Andrea said they were messy, though. When Sarah came to live with him, they'd have a dog—he wondered what breed that one was— what a beautiful dog.

Eventually they boarded the raft again, the woman trying to stay away from the exceedingly wet animal she was ferrying back to the *Salmon Eye*. When they were both aboard, she turned and waved to Beringer, signaling for him to come over.

He lowered himself into his own inflatable and pulled the short distance, tossing the painter up to her as she leaned over the rail. He hauled himself up onto the deck, then got to his feet. Sam, his tail stiff and his hackles raised, had never met Beringer.

She was as tall as he was, given the slight list he had from his short leg. She wore yellow rain gear over enough layers to make anyone shapeless, but her face was all bones—black eyes set deep in her skull, strands of black hair streaked with gray, pulled back under a blue cap. She looked a bit Native American, but there was something different about her face—not a Tlingit, certainly. She smiled as though she'd just made some teasing comment. "I don't know why, but this is making me really nervous," she said. "Come on in." She held the door open, gesturing for him to go first.

Beringer laughed. "Funny, isn't it? I've been uptight all day waiting for you to get here."

And you're the chief suspect—I'm very wary because you might have been involved in Tango's disappearance, she thought. "Where do you think Tango went?" she asked.

"I don't know, but he's not with me, for sure."

"I'm sorry to talk about him because Tango isn't here to defend himself. Maybe we shouldn't be . . . oh, well, I just feel like maybe we shouldn't talk about him—his past, I mean, when he isn't here."

She waved her hand at the table and Beringer slid onto the bench next to it. "Sam," she said, "Lie down." Sam looked at Beringer, clearly hoping he would reverse the order. Beringer rubbed his ears and Sam dropped to the floor next to Beringer's feet, propping his head on one boot.

Sam's owner set two mugs out and poured coffee.

Beringer shook his head at the milk carton and picked up his mug, gripping it in both his clammy hands. Why was he so tense? Because Tango was Ted Hilliard, who was dead—that was why.

She was looking at him. Waiting for him to say something? She certainly wasn't offering much herself. Serious face, something sad in her eyes—sitting there watching him as though he had answers.

"I've seen you before," she said. "At the Coho, sitting in the bar. I remember seeing you there a couple evenings ago when I was having dinner. The night Barney Ellis was shot to death. You were staring right at him."

"It's a pretty small town," he said. "How about a quick bio?"

"I run a freight service to the roadless," she said. "Logging camps, villages, fish scows. Books, too. A book-mo-boat."

"How'd you come to be here?"

"I was a librarian in my first life. After my husband was killed, I had to have a change—saw an ad for a job in Wrangell, flew up here and fell in love with the place."

"Me, too. I've only been here a week, but I hope I can find a way to stay."

"You better stay through a winter first. Wild winters, believe me—wind, sideways rain, wind, snow, wind—I mean, storm-force, hurricane winds. North Pacific monsoons. Spin off the Aleutian Low that sits out there in the Gulf of Alaska like a great green snail. It's already started." She smiled again and he noticed the odd way she had of drawing down the corners of her mouth. "Now you."

"I'm working for the State of Alaska, on loan. They made a request for a whale biologist and I got assigned."

"Oh," she said, nodding. "You're the one. I called Wildlife Protection about a couple of whale incidents, and they told me there was a biologist out there looking around. Did you know Henry Sizemore?"

"Yes, I did. Knew him very well. Went to school with him, in fact. I can't think how he drowned."

"I don't know, either. He was such a competent seaman, and a friend of mine, too—we both lived aboard at Shoemaker Bay, though he was gone a lot. Where you from?"

"San Diego."

"Not much like here, is it?"

"Well, it's the same ocean."

"You have a family there?"

"My wife lives there with my daughter, Sarah. I'm hoping Sarah will live with me. My wife and I are separated. She wants a divorce."

She was watching his face intently and he suddenly realized he couldn't remember her name. They had exchanged them over the radio, but there had been so much else—meeting place and time—the fact that neither of them knew where Tango/Ted was—what was her name? "I'm sorry," he said, "this is embarrassing, but I can't remember your name."

She laughed. "And I've forgotten yours. I'm Liza Romero. And you're . . ."

"Scott Beringer."

"And you knew Tango in his first life. Before Vietnam?"

"No, only 'in-country,' as they called it. His name was Ted Hilliard, then. And there's certainly a possibility we're talking about two different people. It seemed like I recognized the voice—he was radio operator for the platoon—but I was told—that is, somebody said—he was dead. That he actually died seventeen years ago." He didn't want to look at her in case that direct, sad focus could see into his mind and discover who had told him Ted was dead.

"I have a snapshot," she said, "but I . . . I . . ."

"You don't believe that I didn't spirit him away. Listen, I did keep the appointment, hung around the dock for half an hour, then went up the hill and asked that Japanese man in the bar and grill if he knew a man who talked on the radio using old Vietnam calls. He told me where he lived, so I went up, found the door open, went in, found books spilled on the floor and coffee, still warm. He wasn't there, though, and I haven't heard from him since."

"Yeah," she said, "that's what I found, too." She looked down at her hands, tapped her fingers rhythmically on the table, then got up and went to the wheelhouse. In a moment she was back, holding a snapshot, which she laid facedown on the table between them.

Beringer looked out the window, suddenly not ready to accept the yes or no. Either it would be a different man and he would have lost Ted twice, or he'd been lied to.

Liza was waiting for him to turn over the snapshot. He met her eyes, and she nodded. "Yeah," she said, "I can see how it is, wanting to know, but not, either."

He took a deep breath and turned the snapshot over. Ted Hilliard stared up at him. He was squinting into the sun, his arm draped across the shoulders of a very broad, short, Tlingit woman in a white dress shirt, jeans, and red suspenders. Ted's hair had receded to the crown, the sides gray and fastened back in a ponytail. He was wearing jeans and a faded flannel shirt, and he was holding his radio out toward the camera. The heavy planked door of the Velvet Moose was behind them.

Beringer had been holding his breath and it escaped now in a huge sigh. "It's him," he said. "Of course, I knew that, but it was . . . uhhh . . . hard to accept, because of the person who told me he was dead. Must have made a mistake, I guess. Maybe assumed he was dead after he didn't show up for a while, something like that. But it's him, all right. He looks okay, too—like he's all right now."

"He is all right—fine—except he's erased his first life. But you know, that's true of an awful lot of Alaskans—we come up here to escape something. To start over. Life in the bush is harsh. We have to concentrate on physical survival, which makes past errors seem trivial."

"I was pretty sure as soon as I heard his voice," Beringer said. "And then when I called him and he recognized Baron and threw a quote at me, I was certain. But it confuses my life, I have to say. I was told he was dead by somebody who should know absolutely. Actually, by his wife."

Liza gasped as he said the words. "But he's married to Mink," she said. "They're totally devoted to each other. It's like something they both need in order to survive."

Beringer suddenly heard the story spouting from his lips. He wasn't in control of his tongue. "From the day the Huey set me down in a hot zone and took out four short-timers and five body bags, I saw Ted Hilliard as hero material. I was nineteen, Ted was seven years older—Ph.D. candidate in English literature who went on a guilt trip after getting repeated student deferrals. He was married. His wife, Andrea, was only twenty-two."

Beringer's hands were trembling and he sat on them. "I visited his wife while Ted was still in the V.A. hospital. I wanted to explain what had happened to his mind. How somebody called in the Phantoms wrong—they dropped everything right on top of us. Everyone knew who'd called it wrong—both guys were stoned, in no condition to be commanding that squadron. Should have been a court-martial, but they disappeared. Maybe went north, maybe joined Charlie—nobody knew, nobody ever saw them again."

Liza was looking out the window now, her hands aimlessly scooting her coffee mug back and forth on the tabletop. Beringer watched her face, thinking again that she must be part Native, slightly almond-shaped eyes that absorbed all the light around them.

"I wonder," she said. "I was just thinking, one of the men who disappeared could have been the man Tango recognized in the bar the other night. He saw him and started shouting, "You're next, you're next," and something about "bald heads and forgiveness." The guy was bald, certainly. Short man, totally drunk. Could he . . . I mean, could Tango think he was one of the men who gave the wrong signals?"

"Short guy? Bald? One of the men who called it wrong was short—still had some hair but not a whole lot, as I remember. The other guy was tall and skinny, had a lot of short, curly hair. Could be the short guy, although I don't know if Ted would remember anything before the fire-bombing, and of course he never saw them after it."

"Maybe that would be the one thing that could knock down the wall—seeing the man responsible. I'm not much on psychology—all this lost-memory stuff seems pretty far-fetched to me, but maybe seeing the guy would bring back some association. Tango was extremely angry, that's all I know. Very unusual for him."

Beringer nodded. "I suppose it's possible," he said.

"The known facts are that the bald man, Barney Ellis, was shot dead on the beach near Wrangell the night after the fight at the Velvet Moose. Paul Howard, who's a lieutenant with the Wrangell Police Department, thinks he was shot with Mink's Colt .25. And Tango has disappeared. So of course he's the primary suspect, especially after shouting at Ellis."

"Ted wouldn't kill anyone—he'd maybe harass the man if he was certain he was one of those responsible for all those deaths—he'd maybe try to scare him—but he'd never hurt anyone."

"I know. Anyone who knows him knows he's the ultimate pacifist. But he's missing and the man he appeared to threaten is dead. Tango was seen, or possibly recognized, going somewhere in a big Zodiac right before you were supposed to meet him."

Beringer was startled. "Good lord—they passed me going about twenty knots—I had to slow down because their outboard was making such a steep wake."

"Well, that seems to confirm the report. Guess we have to call it circumstantial evidence."

Beringer picked up his coffee mug and drained it. It was as cold as he was. "He's in big trouble, isn't he? We'll have to find him. I hope he's alive."

She nodded. "I'll be out there looking," she said. "Now that I've found you, at least I know where he *isn't*."

29

PAUL HAD TO CLOSE HIS EYES AS THE
floatplane tore along the narrow channel toward the dock. It
seemed to him the wings would shear the branches of the
trees lining the shore. He had never gotten used to the
bravado with which the pilots zeroed in on a target,
skimmed the treetops, danced the plane so close to the
whitecaps it seemed bound to submerge. He liked land.
Solid earth under his feet. Air and water could not support
him. Maybe, if he lost a few pounds. . . .

The dock wove under his feet as he bent and walked
under the wing. He lifted a hand to the pilot, who was tying
the plane against the tire-studded dock. "Probably a couple
hours," he said. "I'll let you know if it'll be more."

He walked up the hill and went into the Velvet Moose.
Three women and one man were at the bar drinking coffee,
and Jimmy Matsui was scrubbing sinks. There was no one
else around at 9:35 in the morning.

Paul slid onto a stool and Jimmy wiped his hands on the
towel in his belt. "Coffee, please," Paul said, and Jimmy set
a cup in front of him, filling it from the pot, then topping off
the other cups. Paul found himself embraced in the steady
gaze of Robert Merton, the luckless steamship owner whose

vessel had provided so many appurtenances to the Velvet Moose, including his oil portrait.

When Jimmy came by again with the coffeepot, Paul said, "Wrangell Police Department—Paul Howard." He felt the instant tension in the woman next to him and laughed to himself. There was no one, no one in the whole of Alaska, who didn't have something they'd rather not have known to their friends and neighbors and authorities. At least, so it always seemed to him.

He asked Jimmy about the night of the fight. "Where were you when it happened?"

"I was standing right here," Jimmy said. "Mink took care of all the problems. I didn't."

"But you saw everything?"

"I saw that the men were angry and one had a knife. Mink got between them and he slashed her with it."

"And then she went around the bar and got the gun from the drawer. Do you know what happened to the gun?"

"No. I didn't see where it went. People were shouting and I didn't see the gun after that."

"But you know it isn't in the drawer, right? Do you mind if I look around behind the bar? Maybe it was put somewhere else in all the confusion. Mink told me I could look for the gun. But I don't have it in writing. I can get a warrant if you prefer."

"If Mink says so, you can look. Mink didn't shoot the gun, and only Mink got hurt."

Paul searched the cupboards, drawers and shelves behind the bar, turning up hundreds of rubber bands, a drawer full of bottle caps, twenty-three hoochies for salmon fishing, eleven fish hooks and a roll of nylon leader; in the lower cupboard were a pair of ancient rubber boots and a spare pair of Alaska fisherman suspenders, which he supposed were in case the strain on Mink's uniform suspenders became too great. No gun.

His audience at the bar had increased despite certain anxieties among them over his affiliation. When he was finished, he leaned on Jimmy's side of the bar and looked them over. Seven women now, ranging in age from perhaps thirty-five to one who must surely be ninety. Five men, including Hap Farwell, the Village Public Safety Officer, who hadn't been called to deal with the quarrel. He'd known Hap a long time—now and then had to take in somebody Hap had arrested, mostly for disturbing the peace or domestic violence.

Hap grinned at him. His eight missing front teeth created a rectangular black hole surrounded by grizzled beard and mustache. "I already been over that," Hap said. "Knew you wouldn't find nothin'."

"Coulda said so," Paul grunted, leaning across the bar with a high five.

"Talked to ever'body, too," Hap said. "Ain't nothin' over here anybody knows except them men was new to town."

"Well, one of 'em's dead now," Paul said. There was a general silence in the bar till one of the men said, "Which one?"

"Short, bald guy," Paul said. "I hear Tango shouted something at him, sounded like threats."

"Yeah?" Hap said, his eyes narrowing. "Tango? He ain't done nothin'. He's nothin' but a old teddy bear. He'll show up when Mink gets back. He can't show his face when she ain't around. He gets scared 'a his shadow if Mink ain't around."

The woman who'd stiffened when Paul said "Wrangell Police" suddenly said, "My son saw him. Came in from fishing and passed him." Then she clamped her mouth shut and turned her head.

"And you are . . ."

"Nancy Bellamy," she said, sliding off her stool and picking up a jacket from the back of a chair behind her. She turned to go and Paul went after her, moving quickly out from the bar and reaching the door ahead of her. He held it open for her, then walked beside her down the hill.

She said nothing more and he didn't ask questions, hoping she might be heading home, where he could find the son. Instead, she turned and walked into the grocery. "That's him," she said, tight-lipped, pointing at a man sitting on the counter talking to another man. Paul knew Bellamy slightly. He was a Vietnam vet and dropped in to play chess with Tango. When the man left, Paul asked Bellamy about Tango.

"Yeah, pretty sure it was him, you know. Had his jacket hood pulled up over his cap, but it was Tango all right."

When Paul had learned all he could from Bellamy, he said, "We've started a search. You're positive you saw him?"

"Yeah," Mark said. "Yeah, I'd say I was positive—positive as about anything, I guess."

"Positive as about anything" was all Mark Bellamy ever would be, he thought. War, injuries—everything took a toll on the human frame. But it was all he had to go on.

"I don't suppose you have any idea if the man with Tango was bald," he said.

"Head covered up with a cap and hood over it. Coulda had a whole lion mane inside it or been bald as a rock cod."

Paul nodded, thanked Bellamy for the information, and turned to leave the grocery. Nancy Bellamy was standing behind the meat counter watching him.

"Thanks for letting me know about Tango," Paul said. "Appreciate that."

She turned her back on him without a word. He wondered why she'd spoken up in the first place.

30

LIZA WAS YAWNING AS SHE ROWED SAM ashore. Sam put his nose to the ground and disappeared over the ridge of the island that divided Exchange Cove from Kashevarof Passage. She meandered along the shore, turning over a pebble with her foot, thinking about the previous evening.

She'd fixed spaghetti and a salad while Scott rowed over to his boat and brought back a bottle of red wine. They'd sat up till 11:00 talking about Tango and also their backgrounds—Liza telling him about Efren, her policeman husband who was shot to death—Beringer telling her all about Sarah, how he wanted her to live with him—he'd stay in Wrangell, get a job there, keep her in Alaska.

She guessed Beringer was a few years older than she— 45, 46? Graying curly hair, bearded, steel-rimmed glasses, hazel eyes when the glasses didn't bounce back the light. She noticed that he limped—he'd lost some of his leg when the platoon was destroyed. He described his rescue of the humpback—she wondered if it could have been the one that ran into the *Salmon Eye*. Actually quite an attractive man— pleasant and intelligent.

Beringer was trying to track boats in the area that could be polluting the water, or causing some other type of damage to them that he didn't yet understand. He asked some questions about the *Salmon Eye*—seemed to think, since the hump-back had run into her, that maybe the *Salmon Eye* was pol-luting—either something toxic or something noisy.

She'd bristled, told him there was no possibility of that; that she'd kept everything in excellent shape—the engine was old but she kept it up—had a mechanic check on it every year. He seemed a bit dubious, though.

She'd felt drawn by his compassion for the whales, but she'd learned some harsh lessons in the last year. Suspicion far exceeded trust. She'd seen Scott Beringer first at the Coho. He was sitting next to Barney Ellis. Kept staring at him. Last night, though, he hadn't said a thing about recog-nizing Ellis. Had he gone to the beach and shot him? Beringer was definitely on the suspect list.

And it would have been quite possible for Scott Beringer to take Tango away somewhere. They'd had a meeting set for eight—she was the one who'd written it down in Tango's log. Scott could easily have described the living room if he'd gone there to get him. He might have gone to the house, taken Tango—how? With the promise of a long wallow in nostalgia while Mink was in Wrangell? At gunpoint? Guns were too big a part of her life lately. Well, they were both suspicious now, one of the *Salmon Eye*, one of Scott Beringer.

She whistled for Sam—time to get going—she needed to get back to Kashevarof and tell Mink what she'd learned from the journal. He barked. Probably a seal or an otter. The seals and otters teased him, popping up to watch him on shore, disappearing instantly when he barked, only to pop up a little farther out.

Liza whistled again and shouted, "Sam, come on. Hurry up, Sam." Suddenly he bayed, a high-pitched wolf howl that ended in a yelp, a sound that invariably caused the back of her neck to prickle. Sam was on to something—he never came back if he'd found something she had to see.

She pushed through the tall grass into the trees, her feet catching in roots and vines. Climbing over a rock ledge, she dropped down onto the small mud flat, her feet sinking in at each step. She still couldn't see him. He was barking again, excited—something had gotten his attention all right. She hoped it wasn't a bear. There were plenty of black bears on Prince of Wales.

She had to climb again, get up over a rocky knob before she could see Sam. He was mostly hidden by grass, crouching and barking, now breaking into that chilling wail.

Liza pushed toward him. He jumped up as she got close and dashed over to her, circling and leading her toward whatever was hidden there at the edge of the water. Liza was shivering from the cold morning air, and fear, too. Sam had made several discoveries in the past that she definitely hadn't wanted to see.

She stopped and tried to get a grip on herself. Sam had gone quiet, waiting for her to get there. Waiting for her to take care of whatever it was, as he knew she would.

She walked ahead, feeling each step with great caution, until she could see the water racing through the narrow cut that divided the islands. Something yellow was wedged by the current against a boulder. Something that appeared to be wrapped in yellow oilcloth.

She stepped onto the boulder and bent over. She grasped the cloth, the front of a yellow rain jacket, and lifted. The submerged head rose. Salt water drained from the sagging mouth. The eyes were glazed and vacant, the skin drained of all color. The hair that streamed from the back of the head was as yellow as the jacket. Jenny Andover.

31

AT THE DOCK, PAUL STOOD AROUND
waiting for the plane to pick him up. A boat came nosing
through the channel, crane on the foredeck, narrow beam,
rails that sheered. The *Salmon Eye*. He rushed to take her
lines.

Lizzie hurled herself over the rail and stood in front of
him, her hands nervously pounding together, her eyes wide
and staring. "Paul," she said, and gasped the next words so
he had to bend to hear them.

"Body . . . found her . . . drowned body . . . oh god, I
can't stand it anymore." She was sobbing now, turning away
from him, whirling back to face him again.

"Jenny," she whispered. "It's Jenny. We have to go back
there. I couldn't . . . I could only drag her up a little way . . .
oh shit, oh Paul, I just can't stand it. Why me?" she said, her
jaw gritting over her words. "Why is it always me?" Her
words ended with a shriek and she beat at his chest with her
fists.

He grasped her by the arms. Don't sympathize or she'll
fall apart right here. "Where's the body?" he asked.

"Exchange Cove," she said, and took a deep breath. "I
dragged her up on the grass, but I couldn't lift her onto the
boat."

She was getting a grip on herself—facts always helped damp emotion, he thought. He'd rather have her collapse in his arms and weep away her years of controlled rage and sorrow, but no, it wasn't time for that—not now—not yet.

"Exchange Cove? We'll go back," he said, untying the line he'd just fastened.

Sam, seeing the boat loose, his skipper at the wheel, came racing back down the dock and made a flying leap for the stern as the boat turned out. Lizzie looked back at him as he scrambled aboard, then looked at Paul sheepishly. "I forgot him," she said. "How could I forget my first mate?"

"Brain on overload," Paul responded. "Tell me how you found her."

"I didn't," she said. "Sam did. Like the ones last spring. I should just give him to the police department. He's your perfect, all-round tracker."

"Yeah, he's good, all right. He found the woman's body?"

"He started baying—I knew I wouldn't want to see what he'd found. I was scared, Paul." She turned her head and looked at him with huge black eyes that still contained the horror of discovery.

"I thought it was just some yellow thing floating in the current—somebody's horseshoe buoy or something, but when I bent over . . ." She couldn't go on, swallowed hard, took a deep breath, and said, "It was a yellow rain jacket with somebody in it. And I lifted it, and . . . it was Jenny."

She looked at him again, shamefaced, and said, "I vomited. I couldn't . . . I simply couldn't stand it. I'd just seen her again—she came to the boat after I left Wrangell. I anchored in Kindergarten Bay—it seemed too late to go all the way across. And late in the evening I heard another boat come in. Its generator was very loud—I remember feeling intruded upon—hardly anybody anchors in Kindergarten Bay—only small boats—sportsmen, people like that, and this boat was right on the other side of the islands. And then Jenny came rowing over from it."

"Did you get a look at it?"

"No, I couldn't really see it very well—it was pitch dark by then, and it left before I did in the morning. I think it was bigger than the *Salmon Eye*, though. I'm sorry, Paul. If I'd thought about it, I could have rowed around the islands and tried to get a look at it."

She shivered suddenly and said, "No, I wouldn't have done that after what happened. After Jenny left, I took Sam ashore and someone was standing there on the rocks. Her name was Alice. She aimed an incredibly bright light in my eyes—she saw Jenny come over to the *Salmon Eye*, as well as the name on the boat. Then she went crashing off in the woods."

"So Alice has identified you and knows that Jenny came to the *Salmon Eye*. Probably wondering what Jenny told you, right? Whether she told you about Ellis?"

"No, she never said a word about Ellis, not that he was missing, even."

"But Jenny's dead. Someone killed her." He stared at Lizzie. This woman was in terrible jeopardy again. This woman he so admired. Loved. Secretly.

"The other evening, she came again when I'd anchored in Exchange Cove. She'd left the boat near Ossippee Channel. She left it in a skiff with an outboard. But I can tell you that Jenny was scared to death when I told her Ellis had been shot. When I told her Ellis was dead she jumped up and flung herself back in the skiff and took off like a shot herself. I have no idea where she went."

He thought back over the course of events that had led him here—how his life seemed constantly tangled with Lizzie's—why the hell did she always seem to be caught in some hideous crime she had nothing to do with? Last spring, three of them. First Ellis, then Andover. Jenny knew something, that was for sure. Then . . . who? The "who" next time would not be Lizzie. Over his dead body.

Anchoring off the small island in Exchange Cove, Lizzie unclipped the raft from the top of the cabin, and Paul dropped it over the side. They rowed to the island, and between them, dragged the body into the raft. Water poured from Jenny's boots.

"Shot in the back," Paul said, pointing to a burn hole in the back of her jacket, which had leaked a pinkish fluid after they'd dragged her body up on the bank. "And there's a big exit hole in front."

Lizzie began shuddering, her face gray-green. Paul thought she might vomit again—she turned and faced away from him and he could see her swallowing.

They rowed back to the *Salmon Eye* and Lizzie climbed aboard, shutting Sam in the wheelhouse before they tried to lift the body. But she was too heavy for them—waterlogged dead weight.

Lizzie started up the crane and Paul shifted the straps till they were supporting the body in three places. Lizzie shoved the gears and Jenny hung suspended in air, her arms dangling loose, her head tilted back so the yellow hair streamed down. Lizzie maneuvered the crane to lower the body to the deck. Then she turned toward Paul and fainted.

32

BERINGER GRABBED A DISH TOWEL AND wiped the inside of the boat. The walls were sweating moisture—fiberglass did that—one of the only things he didn't like about the boat. He was going to look around at wooden boats for his own use—maybe one of those old double-enders. Wood boats were warmer and the planking wouldn't sweat like this. Maybe he'd get a bigger one— something he and Sarah could live aboard after she finally got to move up here. He wrung out the towel and hung it above the tiny sink.

If his office reassigned him, he'd just . . . the radio interrupted, announcing a tug and barge entering Snow Passage from the north, *all concerned traffic,* et cetera, et cetera. The radio burst forth again. *"Manly Marine operator calling the Keltie, Scott Beringer on the Keltie. Switch and answer twenty-four, Keltie."*

He reached over and grabbed the transmitter, switching to channel twenty-four. Andrea.

"Scott? Could you take Sarah back for a couple weeks? I have this chance to take the place of one of the other partners at a meeting in Florence, Italy. It's week after next, though. So I just wondered . . ."

He knew that Sarah was more inconvenience for Andrea than joy. So would he take Sarah? "Delighted," he said.

"As long as I'm over there, I'd like to do a little traveling, too. So maybe three weeks?"

"I want her, I want her," he said. "You know I want her permanently. Share, Andrea, even if you're not ready to give her up full-time."

"Scott, this isn't the time to discuss it. You know I don't want shared custody—she'd spend half the time roaming around the ocean with you and half the time in a perfectly stable home with me. You know it wouldn't work. She'd go crazy with a life like that."

"So why don't you just take her to Europe with you? She'd acquire the culture like a sponge." He was self-inflicting pain now, bracing himself for the permanent loss of his only child.

"It wouldn't work, Scott. I'll be very busy and then I'll be traveling with others, who probably wouldn't want a youngster with them."

"Somebody else in the picture already?"

"Scott, this call can be heard by others, you know."

"You trade in your exes pretty often, Andrea."

"What do you mean by that, Scott?" Her voice was ice-cold now. *"Maybe I shouldn't send Sarah after all. You're sounding rather hostile."*

"Not to Sarah. Sarah's mine. No matter what you do or say, she'll always be mine. We're a team. You send her. What day will she come?"

"I thought the Wednesday before Thanksgiving. I know that's a little soon, but I'll need to pack and get organized, and I won't have a lot of time, what with this case I'm on now."

"Wednesday's fine. I'll meet the morning plane in Wrangell. I'll look forward to it." He paused, thinking over a sudden new idea. Maybe, just maybe, he'd have a little something to tell her next time they talked. "Andrea?" he said, "I'll be waiting. So long."

A long shot. But still possible. Definitely possible. He just had to find the guy.

33

PAUL CALLED THE WRANGELL POLICE
dispatcher.

"You got a body aboard?" Norma asked.

"That's right. Aboard the *Salmon Eye*."

"Where are you?"

"In Exchange Cove."

"Well, just bring it back to Wrangell on the boat. Time we get a plane mobilized and sent out there, you'll be here."

"All right, we'll be there around one. Paul Howard, clear."

Paul felt awkward at the wheel, but determined that Lizzie should lie down until she was fully recovered. He had caught her just before she hit the deck, had held her till she opened her eyes, her legs twitching uncontrollably. Slowly they'd made their way to the cabin, where she sank down on the bench by the table and cradled her head in her arms. He'd made hot tea, having to ask everything—how to light the stove, where to find the tea bags—embarrassed that he knew so little about her boat when he felt as though she'd been part of his life forever.

He'd found a tarp and covered the body, first dragging it to the stern so it wasn't visible to the skipper. He'd felt horrified himself at the sight of the body lifted by the crane—the streaming of arms and legs and yellow hair and water—he couldn't imagine how Lizzie had managed to get those levers in gear, raise and lower a dead woman she'd actually known. It was one more scene that would live with her forever.

He turned the boat slowly out of Exchange Cove and up around Fire Island, watching the depth till he got well north of it. He wouldn't try Ossipee Channel with the tide half out and so little knowledge of this boat. He headed north—he'd go around Zarembo and straight across to Wrangell.

Paul turned as Sam preceded Lizzie through the door of the wheelhouse, wagging and circling Paul, bashing himself against Paul's legs. Paul looked at Lizzie where she leaned against the doorjamb. Her face was still white, her eyes staring at the pictures in her mind. He held out his hand and she took it and moved toward him, pausing as Sam wedged himself between them.

"Jealous," Paul said. "He doesn't want you paying attention to anyone else."

She nodded, her mouth quirking at the corner, and bent to rub Sam's ears. "I can take over now," she said.

"Nahh, I need the exercise. Oughta know more about the waters around here than I do anyway. You can be lookout if you're feeling up to it."

"Stupid," Lizzie said, staring out the window, "I don't know why I did that—I mean, all I had to do was get the hoist going and set her down, but . . . well, she looked so . . . you know."

"I know—yes. I do know. I had some trouble with it, too. But I've been trying to sort out a few of the whys and the whats. And the whos, too. And it doesn't seem to make a lot of sense, to tell the truth. Money or love, most murders. Someone killed both Ellis and Jenny. Frank Smith, skipper of the longliner, came in to say he had a crewman missing—

said Tango had threatened Ellis after the fight. You said it, too."

"Paul. I'll keep telling you till I die that Tango would not kill anyone. He absolutely would not do it."

Paul turned and looked at her. Her eyes were boring into his face with the intensity of a hot poker. He couldn't withstand that gaze, and looked away. "So," he said, "we'll have to see."

"You don't understand," she said. "There is no . . . Paul, look. There are the whales we saw when I took Mink to Wrangell. See? They're still circling the injured one. Look— it's doing better, I think—it looks like it might be feeding."

Paul peered through the window. A series of tall dorsal fins rose and vanished and he saw two spouts, then one from the center. "That one in the center? That the one you thought was hurt?"

"I saw its side. It has a huge gash in it. But it seems more active today, like it might be getting better."

"Lot of whale damage lately. That humpback that ran into you? Really odd. Wonder what's going on."

"There's a marine biologist out here trying to find out what's happening. That guy we saw in the Coho that night? The one with the limp? I hope he does find out. I feel like those whales are my best friends."

"Right after me?" He turned to grin at her but she was staring at the floor.

"It's so hard, Paul. You're a policeman first and always. That's how it was with Efren, too. Policeman first, then friend, and if push comes to shove . . ."

He felt his feet caught in a tar pit. "You have to defend your friends from me, right?"

"It seems that I do."

He couldn't look at her. He shrugged and pushed the throttle up. "I'm sorry," he said.

* * *

Paul had radioed ahead. They went into Reliance Harbor, and at the dock, the EMTs carried the body up the ramp on a stretcher and headed for the hospital. Paul walked to his car in front of the harbor master's office where he'd left it about two eons ago. Something mourned the impending separation. He wasn't going to have her—she shied from all policemen—he could tell that from the mention of her husband, how he'd had to be a policeman first. Paul could separate job from love. He knew he could do that. But in this small community, often divided against itself, there would have to be sides taken, friends lost in the fray. And Lizzie wasn't up for that. Not anymore.

He went to the police station. The chief was waiting.

"Now what?" he said. "My god, Howard, can't you stay out of trouble for a day?"

"Lizzie found her," Paul said. "I didn't have anything to do with it."

"That woman. She's always coming up with bodies. How come she's always on the spot?"

Paul shrugged. "I think maybe . . . oh, maybe it's something to do with the dog. It's usually the dog who finds them."

"Yeah, well, you hang around with both of them way too much." The chief turned his back and stalked off.

Paul threw his jacket at the coat hook in his office and flopped down in his chair. He did hang around Lizzie—he knew that. And it wasn't going to work. Sheesh. What the hell had gone wrong with his life? Five years ago he'd had the original lock on it—then Carolyn took Joey and nothing had ever worked again. And now Lizzie was telling him: "Reject." Well, if no one else pitied him, he'd do it himself. Wallow, Paul Howard.

34

JAKE WAS STANDING ON THE DOCK WHEN Liza returned to Shoemaker Bay with the *Salmon Eye*, setting down a white plastic bucket to take her lines, cleating them while she shut down the engine.

"Want some fish?" he asked. "Ling cod."

"Love it, Jake," she said, "if you can spare some."

He reached in the pail, lifted out a long filet the color of pale willow, and handed it to her.

"Gorgeous," she said, trying futilely to hold it so the drip didn't run up her sleeve. "It's an awful lot for just me."

"Sam can have leftovers," he said. "Yuh, Sam dog," as Sam bounded over the rail to greet him. "You want to go fishing with me?"

Liza laughed. "He's a great fisherman, Jake. He loves to roll on them. For the perfume."

Sam was a very glad dog—glad to be alive, glad to be the owner of a person and a boat, glad there were fish in the sea and on the beach for eating and rolling in. Whenever Liza left him for an hour or two, he knew deep in his heart he'd never see her again. Not only had she returned this time, contrary to his worst fears, but she was bearing gifts that dripped deliciously onto his nose and ears and the dock all around him.

"You been out a while," Jake said. "Thought you'd 'a been back yesterday."

"I've been over in Kashevarof a couple days trying to sort out some things to do with Mink and Tango." She glanced at Jake and looked away again. "And I found someone dead, Jake." She shuddered when he stared at her open-mouthed. "Sam found her, actually."

"Oh, Sam's a tracker, all right. Finds all sorts of things. Funny you always get caught by some deader, hey?" He stared at her, obviously remembering the events of the previous spring.

"I guess it's what happens when I roam around these waters so much."

"Fishermen—we get around, but I don't see no dead people. Funny how you get caught every time."

"Well, it's over and done with now. I'm just going to get on with my business and forget I ever found anyone."

"Where was it you found it?"

"Over at Exchange Cove. Somebody I'd met before, too. A woman named Jenny Andover. Paul Howard helped me bring her back to Wrangell. He was over there in town asking about the man killed on the beach in Wrangell."

"You sure do collect 'em, honey. Man, I don't know how you do it but I sure wouldn't want to wear your boots."

She looked down at Jake's boots—must be about a size 14 wide, she thought. She grinned at him and said, "Don't think your feet would fit in my boots, Jake."

He looked down and nodded. "Lucky for that," he said solemnly.

Her discovery in the morning had caused her immense anguish; she imagined the crane with Jenny hanging from it, her yellow hair streaming, her arms hanging—uuugh. She shivered and tried to force the picture from her mind.

She put the ling cod into the refrigerator and wiped her

arm. She was exhausted, and threw herself down on the bench beside the table, trying to catch her breath, trying to relax her mind and body. Instantly she fell asleep, waking around two in the morning—pitch dark, and Sam jigging around needing to go out. She was still fully dressed, so she took Sam up the ramp and walked around the parking lot with him.

She didn't want to let him go into the woods across Zimovia Highway—she still remembered the crack of the rifle, the bullet whizzing past her ear. She shuddered, whistling for Sam, who was a long way away from her now. He raced back to her, and she put her hand through his collar before she walked down the ramp. When they got back, she poured some kibble in his bowl, climbed into her bunk and fell into a black hole.

Liza woke a little after six. The *Keltie* had come in during the night—she saw the stern over on the next finger, and Scott Beringer was walking along the dock. She walked over to meet him.

"How're you doing?" he asked.

"Not so good," she said. "Sam found Jenny Andover's body when I took him to that little island that cuts off Exchange Cove from Kashevarof Passage. She'd been shot in the back. I'd met her a couple of times—she was the one who told me about Barney Ellis before he was shot. Said he had a very bad temper and would never pay a cent for Mink's medical bills."

"I can't believe it—two people shot?"

She shivered, and he put an arm around her. "Up early," she said. "Where are you going?"

"To Archie's for breakfast," he said. "Want to come?"

"Sure," she said. "Just let me get my purse."

They took Liza's truck to town so Sam could go. Liza put

the tailgate down and Sam jumped in. Beringer drove an elderly Datsun, streaked with rust. "Got this car in Wrangell when I got here," he said.

"Looks like a clone of most of the cars in town," Liza said.

They sat at a table at Archie's, and Liza ordered pancakes; Beringer had two eggs easy over, hash browns and toast. They made small talk for a while, about the weather, the wind and rain, about the town of Wrangell—Beringer was going to stay here—he loved it.

Liza looked at Sam through the window. He was yearning over the tailgate at a small, nondescript black dog. Finally she asked him about the whales.

Beringer leaned back in his chair and put his arms behind his head. "I went to Robson Bight about a year ago, in late August and September. You know where that is? Johnstone Strait, in British Columbia. The whales were there, a huge pod of orcas. And what they love to do is rub themselves on the smooth stones at the bottom of the bight. We used underwater cameras to watch them. It was grand to see them— I loved it."

Maggie brought their eggs and pancakes and poured some more coffee. "Anything else you need?" she asked.

They shook their heads, eating a while in silence. Beringer went on then, talking about the whales in Sumner Strait. "I think it's noise that's doing it, some enormous explosion."

Liza said, "My boat doesn't make some huge explosion. I'd hear it. I'd know it if it did that, and Sam certainly would."

Beringer nodded. "You know, the journal *Nature* had an article in it about beaked whales washing ashore in the Mediterranean Sea after a NATO operation that involved sound waves of two hundred and thirty decibels. That's just a *huge* noise. Wave frequencies of two hundred and fifty to three thousand cycles per second, a very low frequency in our hearing range. Those deep-diving whales are especially affected by those frequencies. And they're related to the orcas.

"Then the Navy conducted a series of tests in the Bahamas involving sonobuoys that generate sound waves underwater, sounds of about two hundred decibels at 6,600 to 9,500 cycles per second. And twelve beaked whales beached themselves right after those tests. Two of them had bleeding eyes, suggesting acute shock trauma. A bunch of volunteers pushed seven of the whales off the beach, but five died."

"Oh, I'm certain it was those tests," Liza said. "Something tells me the humpbacks and orcas in Sumner Strait have lost their hearing. That humpback ran into my boat, and an orca was stranded on Nesbitt Reef. I saw it when I was bringing Mink over."

"The orcas use a sonar system to figure out their environment, a series of clicks," Beringer said. "They have receptors in their brains that respond to the clicks, and the clicks bounce off things differently. Kelp is differentiated from rocks or sand, and they feed themselves that way, too, search for schools of salmon, herring, seals. The humpbacks use particles of magnetite for direction-finding and those particles might be dislodged by an explosion or some huge noise underwater."

"But what could be making such an enormous noise underwater in Sumner Strait?" Liza asked.

"Might not be a boat at all. Might be something dropped from the air. I just don't know what it could be. I've asked for hydrophones so I can listen underwater."

"I delivered hydrophones to Henry Sizemore out at Point Baker and he never picked them up, and the next morning his boat was gone. I was furious at him—I left a note on his boat when I got there, and he just went off and never picked them up. But then he drowned, so I was sorry I was so annoyed at him."

"Do you still have them?"

"No. No, I don't. Someone stole them off the foredeck when my boat was ransacked."

"Your *boat* was ransacked?"

"Yup. Someone broke in and tore everything up and stole the hydrophones, and my log is missing. I've started a new one—I write down everything in it, where I go, what I'm passing, where I anchor, everything. I still have no idea who could have done it. And then I was shot at when I took Sam up to Rainbow Falls."

"*Shot* at?"

"Yes. I turned around at Rainbow Falls and went back into the woods, and someone shot at me. I crawled into the bushes when I heard the first shot. There was a second shot, and then a man ran past me on those planks, carrying a rifle. I lay there with Sam till he'd gone by, and then raced back to the boat."

"Who could be after you?" Beringer asked. "Why would anyone want to kill you? Or maybe just scare you?"

"I have no idea," Liza said. "None. But I'll be out on the water and it's safe out there. I'll be okay."

"Really sorry to hear about that," Beringer said.

They finished eating and argued over the bill, finally deciding to split it. They drove back to Shoemaker and parted at the foot of the ramp, Beringer still shaking his head at someone shooting at Liza.

When Liza got back to the *Salmon Eye*, Sam raced down the ladder to the lower deck and started barking. Liza dropped down the ladder and looked. He was barking at the engine-room door. She jerked it open, and Sam rushed in, his nose to the floor. He pushed his way along, went behind the engine and started barking again. Liza moved forward, looked over the big old diesel engine and couldn't tell what he was barking at.

"Come on, Sam," she said. "Let's get out of here and go up."

He barked once more, then pointed his nose at the ceiling and bayed. Liza knew then that he'd found something—he bayed like that whenever he found something she didn't want to see.

She jammed herself behind the engine. A small box was attached to the ignition wire with wires running from it, wrapped around the starter. She tried to uncoil the wires; she poked at the box. Finally she pulled Sam away and got herself out from behind the engine.

Staring over the engine at the box, she finally accepted it. What had made Sam bay was a bomb attached to the starter. When she started the engine, the bomb would go off and she and Sam would be blown to bits. She had to call Paul Howard.

She dragged herself up the steps, called the Wrangell police station, and asked for Lieutenant Howard. For once he was there.

"*Lizzie,*" he said. "*How are you?*"

"Not so good, Paul. A few days ago, when I walked up the trail to Rainbow Falls, somebody shot at me. And when I got back to the boat this morning after having breakfast with Scott Beringer, Sam was barking at the engine-room door, and I went and discovered a bomb attached to the starter. If I'd started the engine, I'd have been blown to bits."

There was a long silence at the other end of the line. "*Jesus, Lizzie,*" he whispered. Then he said, in a louder voice, "*I'll be there. We don't have a bomb squad, but Luke was in the army—maybe he'll know how to get it off.*"

"I'll be waiting at the top of the ramp," she said. "I don't want to stay on the boat in case it goes off by itself."

"Yeah," Paul said. *"Shouldn't wait on the boat. I'll be right there."*

The Blazer came with siren blaring; Chief Woods was in the Blazer with Paul and Luke. There was a fire engine behind it. Liza was waiting at the top of the ramp.

"Keep away from the boat," Paul told her. "Stay here. Keep Sam with you."

She watched as they all rushed down to the *Salmon Eye*. Sam tried to run with them, but she grabbed his collar and told him, "Sit. Stay."

She watched the boat, hoping it wouldn't be blown to bits, taking all those men with it. The firemen had a hose that went all the way out to the *Salmon Eye's* slip, and they were standing there, holding it on the *Salmon Eye*. They had left one man there to turn the fire hydrant on should there be a huge blaze.

Beringer came running over when he saw the fire engine and the hoses, then dashed up the ramp when he saw Liza sitting at the top. "What's going on," he asked. "Fire somewhere?"

"No," she said. "I found a bomb. Sam was barking at the engine-room door, and when he rushed in he bayed, so I knew something was wrong, and I found that box with wires running to the starter."

"Liza, you gotta get out of here. Absolutely, you have to go."

"I don't want to do it yet. And anyway, who would take Sam?"

Beringer shook his head angrily.

It had started to rain and the wind was blowing. She went to the truck, put Sam in, and climbed in herself. Beringer climbed in on the passenger side. She felt sorry for the man waiting at the hydrant, but he was dressed better than she was—he had rain gear and a helmet. They sat in the truck for an hour, talking about the bomb and the shooting, before anyone came out on deck. Then all of them were there. She could see Chief Woods bending over something—Luke was there, and Paul. The firemen came up, took the hose off the hydrant, put it on the truck and began reeling it in.

Paul came up the ramp, carrying something in his hands. He handed it to her. "That's the bomb," he said. "Luke did something to defuse it."

"So it won't go off?"

"No. It took him a long time—he had to do it very, very carefully so the bomb wouldn't explode."

"And you stood right there watching him. Paul . . ."

"Yeah, I did. And the chief was there, too. We both stayed. Probably been blown up if the bomb had gone off, but Luke did it."

He turned away as Luke was coming up the ramp, clapped him on the shoulder and shook his hand. "Super job," Paul said. "Super job."

"Ahh, wasn't much to it," Luke said. "Just had to get that fuse out."

The chief came up and said, "Somebody's after you. Paul tells me you were shot at. And there was a bomb on your boat just waiting to go off. You gotta go away for a while. Get outa town. Go on the ferry somewhere, or fly to Anchorage or Seattle. You gotta go."

"No, I won't do that. I'll stay right here on the *Salmon Eye*. If somebody thinks they can scare me off by wiring a bomb to the starter switch, they're wrong. If I go, maybe they'll try it again. I'll stay right here. Sam's a good protector."

Paul said, "You go somewhere. Somebody shooting at you—maybe he'll hit you next time."

Beringer repeated his own urgent request that she go.

"I'll be out on the boat for a while. I'll be all right."

Beringer stomped down the ramp, and the chief frowned and shook his head.

Paul said, "You can't leave the *Salmon Eye* alone, then—somebody might get aboard and do it again."

"Liza, something's going on," Chief Woods said. "Somebody's after you. You gotta get out of town."

"I'll be out on the boat—nobody will get me when I'm out on the boat. I'm not going, so there. *I am not going away.*"

Chief Woods shook his head and Paul turned and stormed over to the Blazer, his shoulders angry.

She had to go to the freight dock to pick up freight and go out to Point Baker to deliver it. She'd promised Avery she'd get his boat transmission to him that very day. Cartons of canned goods and motor oil, three bundled rugs, four spools of electric cable, an air compressor, two kegs of nails, a crated sink, the boat transmission, two troller poles and three spools of gill net. When the hoist lowered them to the foredeck, she strung a cable around the heavy items and secured them to the rail and deck. The smaller cartons she covered tightly with a net to keep them from shifting in heavy seas. Blue tarps held down by shock cords topped everything.

The rugs, the sink, the boat transmission, troller poles and gill net were going to Point Baker. Everything else went to Labouchere Bay. As she jogged the boat up, Sam dropped to the deck, the wind of their speed more than he enjoyed. He came in and made his usual circular round, checking to be sure everything was as it should be, then dropped heavily onto his cushion forward of the binnacle.

The poached-egg sun had vanished and the wind was rising now, probably twenty-five knots with higher gusts. Liza switched to the weather channel and heard "storm warning inside waters, Dixon Entrance to Lynn Canal." The wind swept up these broad straits as though sucked by a giant vacuum cleaner, and in a gale, you needed to get on the lee shore of a substantial land mass if you didn't like green water breaking over the roof. She didn't really want to set out along Sumner Strait in a storm.

She grabbed the chart and looked at it and nothing looked good at all. The bays on the north shore of Prince of Wales Island don't offer much protection. She'd be better off getting out to Point Baker before it got worse. The north side of Sumner Strait wasn't even visible through the rain squalls. It could be as far away as Japan. She pulled the throttle back slightly to keep the *Salmon Eye* from slamming the waves so hard.

Wind swept the rain upward for an instant, making an alley of visibility toward the west. She could see a boat in the distance, little more than a gray lump on a gray horizon. Through the binoculars, she thought it might be a longliner, but even with the glasses it was only an outline before the rain closed over it again.

The shore of Prince of Wales Island loomed now and then out of the sweeping mist, its dark silhouette too close at one moment, gone the next, an invisible, rock-infested coastline she had to maneuver past. She turned out a little more. She didn't want the current to set them on Pine Point, but as soon as she headed due west, the *Salmon Eye* began pitching steeply, seas breaking high and crashing into the windshield. The heavy wind and flood tide had reduced the speed to 4.3 knots. It was going to be a very long day.

At a little after five in the afternoon—pitch dark—she pulled up to the dock in front of the Point Baker store. Liza threw her lines to Avery, who was working on his gillnetter.

"You bring my transmission?" he asked. When she nodded, he said, "Can't make it anymore with prices what they are—salmon fishing's dead in the water with those prices. Gonna fix this damn thing and sell it, but there's no market for fishing boats anymore."

She nodded again, and set the crane over to lift the transmission. She adjusted the levers and swung the transmission over the other boat, Avery maneuvering it above his deck before she lowered it.

"Well, thanks for bringing it," he said. "What do I owe you?"

"Seventy-eight seventy-five," she said, and he peeled off exactly seventy-nine dollars from a wad of cash.

"Keep the change," he said, grinning up at her, his grizzled beard quirked sideways and his eyes squinting beneath the bill of his Norquest cap.

"Many thanks," she said solemnly. "You'll make me a rich old lady at this rate."

When she got back from the store, Avery was invisible but the air was blue with muffled curses. She swung aboard the *Salmon Eye* and secured the crane, folded the tarps and stowed them in the hold. It was after six and she still had a delivery for Labouchere Bay. Two dozen cases of canned goods and an air compressor, two kegs of nails and the spools of electric cable for the people who were wintering over. She'd leave them a bunch of books, too. The logging camp had shut down and most people had left. She'd leave Labouchere Bay early the next morning and catch the slack in Sumner Strait.

35

THE CHOP IN SUMNER STRAIT WAS fierce—short, steep waves that forced the *Keltie* sideways— it wasn't a heavy boat, despite its speed. A slight drizzle was changing to steady rain, and Beringer turned his windshield wipers up. It was a slow trip—he had to set a speed that didn't slam the boat into the steep chop.

Whales out there now. Their towering spouts said humpbacks, though he couldn't see their short dorsal fins because the waves were so steep. He turned out, trying to get a better look at them. He thought there were two, possibly three. It was very difficult to tell with such poor visibility, and they didn't come up to spout simultaneously. Usually they fed in pairs. He had anchored once in a large bay where two of them were feeding. He thought of them weaving the bubble net, enclosing the krill and shrimp and herring in air, one rising in the center of the net to feed. He had gone to sleep listening to the great sighs of their breath.

He didn't want to chase these whales, but he did want to see if they showed any sign of injury, any sign that they had lost their sense of direction. Staying back was hard to do with a following sea. He tried to zigzag back and forth but was frequently caught in the troughs of the waves and had to turn out. The *Keltie* kept gaining on the whales—they could swim much faster than the *Keltie* could go, but they were just lazing along, feeding as they went, storing up for the winter.

After they left Alaska, humpbacks wouldn't eat for five months. The mothers gave birth in the warm waters around Hawaii, nursed the newborns, and never ate again till they returned to the waters of the North Pacific.

He was chasing them now. Harassing them? Getting too close, anyway. And suddenly they disappeared. Their tail flukes rose in a vigorous wave, signaling a dive—they could swim for miles underwater before spouting—they were gone.

Later he caught a glimpse of a longliner in the growing murk. He scanned her closely. What, he wondered, was a longliner fishing for at this time of year? Halibut, he supposed. There'd been a change in fishing regulations for halibut—you could buy up somebody else's halibut quotas and fish much of the year, compared to the old days when there were a few two-day openings and you went no matter what the weather. This plan was probably better—but he wasn't sure exactly when the current season ended, or had ended?

He heard rifle shots. A whole series of them. What was going on out there? Someone hunting on the water? Shooting sea lions? Seals? Nobody would do that, would they? Endangered species, they were.

The wind was rising—he didn't want to go back out into the middle of Sumner Strait. He'd anchor in Port Protection, tie up to the dock in Wooden Wheel Cove, where all those fancy houses would be closed up for the winter, the windows shuttered, the roofs green with mold.

He swung the *Keltie* along the edge of Joe Mace Island north of the entrance to Port Protection. Beyond it he could see the reef with the blinker on it. He rounded the south tip of Joe Mace Island. Someone was lying motionless on the rocks, his head only a few inches from the rising tide.

36

SHE DELIVERED THE FREIGHT TO THE now-defunct logging camp at Labouchere Bay. Both of the people who were wintering over were there—caretakers for the logging camp.

"Can you open the library so we can pick out a bunch of books?" the woman asked.

"Sure," Liza said. "I was going to leave you some books anyway."

The man and woman came aboard and looked along the shelves in the stateroom. They chose a huge number of books, the woman going for mysteries and biographies, the man looking for books on the Second World War, the Civil War, and books on boat repair. Liza put all the titles in a notebook under the name Labouchere Bay.

"I don't know when I'll get back here," she said, "probably not for a while. When I do come in, you can return them and check out some more." She gave them a crate to put their books in, and they carried it between them up to the bunkhouse.

She left the *Salmon Eye* tied to the dock and took Sam for a walk along the beach. When they got back, she said, "Suppertime, Sam." His tail beat the stove in wild percussion while she filled his dish. "Sit," she told him, and he did so, quivering with anticipation till she said, "Okay, go for it."

She threw Jake's ling cod into a skillet, added onions and celery and a can of tomatoes, turned the stove down and got out a third of a bottle of red wine, left over from the evening with Scott Beringer. She poured half a glass, put the fish on her plate, and sat at the table. Finally she got out her book, *A Thousand Acres*, the Jane Smiley book she'd never gotten around to reading.

She sipped her wine and ate while she kept the page open with the salt shaker. Their mother was dead, that was the whole trouble. A mother kept your head straight, kept you from making dumb mistakes; you laughed at her while secretly wishing you were just like her.

Abruptly she is sitting at the kitchen table, doing her sixth-grade math homework—something about two trains heading toward each other. She crumbles an oatmeal cookie while she watches her mother's blue Plymouth turn the corner. She looks down at the book, picks up her pencil, glances out the window again. There is no car coming in the drive. Was there ever a car? She isn't sure. She tells the police when they come hours later that she isn't sure, she can't remember. Guilt. The black wolf on her shoulder.

Liza stood up and ran water into the sink, sliding her plate and fork into it. Then she poured the rest of the wine in her glass and flipped the VHF radio on, stretching her legs out along the bench when she sat down again, leaning against the end cushion. Rain drummed and poured off the corners of the cabin roof, splashing onto the deck. Even in the bay, the boat rocked from the heavy chop that rolled in, the wind in the strait still rising. Though it was only eight-thirty, she fell asleep.

A voice inserts Tango's name into Liza's brain. She is trying to follow him along a narrow trail that becomes a cliff, calls to him to wait but he is too far away, he can't hear her; she shouts his name. Her shrieking mumble wakes her.

The voice on the radio was staticky and frantic. . . . *unconcious . . . soaked . . . hypothermic . . .*

. . . floatplane . . . eta 2050 . . . medics . . .

She glanced at the clock. 8:35 P.M.

. . . try to warm . . . don't know . . . will make it. . . .

Keltie . . . stand by . . . out.

. . . standing by.

The *Keltie*. Scott Beringer's boat. Where was he? Why did she think she'd heard Tango's name in her dream? Had Scott been referring to him?

"*Salmon Eye* calling *Keltie*, *Salmon Eye* calling *Keltie* . . . come in, Scott."

There was no answer. She tried again and got a different voice.

"*Wrangell police . . . Salmon . . . Tango . . . Port . . .*"

"You're breaking up," she said. "Repeat."

"*Tango . . . Port Protect . . . where . . . ?*"

"Labouchere Bay," she said. "I'm going over there right now."

"*Stand by.*"

"*Salmon Eye*, standing by," she said, and hung up the transmitter. She started the engine, then flung herself out on deck to release the anchor brake. Visibility was nil—she'd have to watch the radar—set a course with the GPS. She switched on the running lights and headed toward the rock-strewn entrance of the bay.

Could it be Tango who was unconscious and hypothermic? No, not likely. She'd simply had a dream about him, and waked to hear Scott's voice talking about someone else. It couldn't be Tango—why on earth would he be here?

With her eyes glued to the radar screen, she picked her way between the two islands at the center of the bay, and turned north past the string of islands that protected the bay from Sumner Strait. The wind was creating mountainous seas now, and it was so dark in the strait she could see nothing at all—no light—it was like being a mile underground.

Northwest of Protection Head a boat showed up on the radar screen headed south, moving almost as fast as she was going north. By the time she had reached the entrance to Port Protection it was a mile south of her. Maybe a tug or a small coastal freighter, though this time of year there weren't many boats in the area.

As she headed into Port Protection, a floatplane was revving its engine for takeoff. This time of year, and in the dark, and in this huge wind, it shouldn't be out here. Visible Flying Requirements were in effect for all the bush planes—they weren't allowed to fly on instruments, and the wind was fierce. But it was here and taking off and she wondered where it would go.

She watched as the plane bounced on the whitecaps; the pontoons made a steep white rooster tail before it lifted from the water, twisting in the wind as the sea let loose of it. She could see a small boat over there by Joe Mace Island with its cabin lit up, and she headed toward it. When she got close enough she could make out the name on the stern: *Keltie*. Beringer was standing on the deck waving. She turned the *Salmon Eye* toward Wooden Wheel Cove, went all the way in and tied up at the dock. The *Keltie* followed. She went out and took his bowline.

"Was it Tango?" she asked.

He nodded. "He was nearly frozen. I don't know if he'll make it."

37

BERINGER CALLED THE MARINE OPERATOR to ask for the Wrangell hospital number. She connected him and he asked for Tango's condition.

"Critical," the nurse said. *"Hasn't regained consciousness."*

He had to get back to Wrangell. Somehow, before Ted/Tango disappeared from the earth, he, Scott Beringer, needed to make contact with him, even if it was just to hold his hand, hold him in his arms as Ted had held him when his leg was blown away.

He'd chance it—if the boat was swamped, well, he had his survival suit. He'd float. He zipped on the exposure suit he'd worn when he rescued the whale—it was insulated and would protect him from the elements. If the boat became too hazardous, he'd take it off and put on the survival suit. At least the exposure suit kept his hands and feet free.

He checked the lines that held the raft on top of the cabin. They seemed secure—he'd need that raft if the boat went down. He started the engine, then went to the bow to lift the anchor hand over hand. Sharp needles of rain drove into his face, sideways rain that Liza Romero had warned him about. "Wind," she'd said, "sideways rain, wind, snow, wind. . . ." Yeah, it was like that. Exhilarating, though. He loved fierce weather, loved being out in it. "Let it snow, let it snow, let it snow," he chanted aloud, as he headed away from Wooden Wheel Cove.

And it did. The snow swirled against the windshield in pinwheel patterns. In half an hour he knew he couldn't make it. There was green water over the cabin—he pitched into the troughs between waves and the next wave broke over the boat. He couldn't control the steering—he was being carried west by the seas and the southeast storm-force wind. He tried to turn, but was caught in the trough, the waves coming at him from the side.

The boat was underwater. He felt it lifting, slamming down again on its side, lifting again. He was pinned to the wall of the cabin, desperately trying to hold the wheel, turn out of the trough. A towering wave rolled the boat over—he was upside down, tumbling over and over—couldn't reach the radio—couldn't shout "Mayday."

Charts and books flew around him—a cupboard he hadn't hooked threw pots and pans at him. His head slammed the steering post—he was dazed—tumbled like clothes in a dryer—he tried to grab the rail that ran around the cabin but was thrown on his face. His forehead hit the corner of the cupboard and blood trickled into his left eye. He tried to raise his hand but was spun into the wall with such force he saw and heard nothing more.

38

A LOW-PRESSURE SYSTEM, SPINNING OUT of the Gulf of Alaska with sixty-knot winds and heavy rain, had churned Sumner Strait into a stew. Liza would not tackle it in the dark. She hoped the tiny plane had made it back—they'd left several hours ago, before the wind rose this high. She tossed in her bunk, wondering how Tango had come to be washed up on Joe Mace Island—how incredible that Beringer had found him, how doubtful Scott was that he would survive. He had to, that was all. Mink's life would be ruined if Tango didn't survive. Why had he washed up on that beach?

In the darkness that morning brought, she thought the wind had subsided a little though the seas were still enormous. She ran with Sam along the fronts of the boarded-up houses, fixed oatmeal though she wasn't hungry—needing desperately to return to Wrangell. She called the Wrangell Police Department on the radio—no, Paul Howard wasn't there—yes, the dispatcher would tell Howard, when he got back, that she had called.

"Tell him Tango's been found," she said. "He was washed up on the beach on Joe Mace Island. I hope he's still alive."

Daylight, at least enough to see Sumner Strait, came around eight-thirty. She secured everything in the cabin, checked to see that the crane was tightly fastened, then headed out. Sometime in the early morning, the *Keltie* had left. She hoped he'd make it back. It wasn't a heavy boat and the seas were still enormous.

The southeasterly was driving across Sumner Strait, so she could quarter the waves coming at her—she tried to stay away from the coastline of Prince of Wales Island. Waves slashed against the windshield, and she had the wipers on their highest speed. Snowing, too, virtually a whiteout by the time she passed Point Baker. The *Salmon Eye* pitched through a trough, made a slow roll, then pitched through another trough. Sam curled on his mat under the binnacle, bracing himself against it, eventually lying flat on his side to go with the roll. Liza stood with her feet wide apart, trying to relax her knees so she wouldn't be thrown by the waves.

The *Salmon Eye* rounded Point Baker at a distance and skirted Merrifield Bay. The wind swept the snow upward now, swirling it into ropes. She could see through the side windows over the doors, the odd updraft making the shoreline visible. She passed Merrifield Bay, looking back at the rocks that edged the northeast point. Then she grabbed the binoculars and stared. A small boat lay wrecked on those rocks. It looked like—oh, surely it couldn't be—but it did look like the *Keltie*. She'd have to go back, turn into Merrifield, maybe tie up at the little dock below the house.

She turned the boat around, taking the full brunt of the waves as she turned, the *Salmon Eye* rolling steeply in the troughs, green water slamming over the wheelhouse. She clutched the wheel, trying to drag it over. Finally the boat came around and began pitching and yawing in the following sea, white horsetails blowing off every crest.

A long reef ran out on the west side of Merrifield Bay, and a rock that bared at half tide sat near the center of the entrance. The rock wouldn't show up on radar, but she had her charts—stay toward the east side of the entrance and she'd be fine. After a very long time, or perhaps only minutes, she turned in to Merrifield Bay. The bay was on the lee shore of Prince of Wales Island, cut off from the southeast wind that shrieked across Sumner Strait.

There was a notch in the east side of the bay with a house sitting above it and a dock below the house. The dock was too small to accommodate the *Salmon Eye* so she released the anchor and listened to it rattle down. She threw the raft over and tried to grab Sam before he launched himself into it, but was just too late. She grabbed a flashlight, tossed in a life preserver, hung her legs from the deck and slid into the raft. Grabbing the oars, she pulled for the dock.

Sam, in the bow, whined and then bayed, a sound that sent a chill down her back. He leaped out ahead of her and raced up the hill past the house. She whistled for him but he had disappeared. With her flashlight she scanned the snow for his tracks. In the distance she heard him bay again.

It was hard to follow Sam but she plodded on, using the flashlight to look for his tracks. She came to the high ridge behind the house. Below it was a narrow strip of water and a rocky extension beyond that. Sam's tracks went over to the other side of those rocks. She trudged on, her feet making larger tracks over Sam's. Skirting the water, she dragged herself up on the rocky point. Looking down, she saw the wreckage of the *Keltie*.

39

BERINGER'S HEAD HURT. HE TRIED TO raise his hand to touch it but something was pinning his arms. He struggled, trying to get loose from whatever was holding him. A blinding stab of pain in his head brought instant darkness. Time became some peculiar kind of whirring motion. He was floating in time—the day before, the day after, the now—all of them were one.

He roused again and every bone seemed damaged, every nerve and muscle. Something had pinned him to the floor. He lay still. He imagined he might be dead. But if he were dead, he wouldn't hurt so much, would he? The pain was a message: he was alive. He tried to listen. He thought he could hear water, waves hitting rock? Something scraping on rock, grinding.

Where was he? It was so black—he could make out nothing in the absolute darkness—this was some kind of nightmare—he'd try to sleep again—everything would be different when he woke up—he would be fine, he'd fix breakfast, take the boat from Port Protection . . . no, no, he'd already done that. Knowledge washed over him like those waves that had tumbled the boat—the terror when he knew he was going to drown.

But he hadn't, had he? Was he underwater now? The boat

on the bottom, could he be sealed in a tiny air pocket? He struggled to sit, forcing up what felt like a table that had collapsed on top of him. He got to his knees but his head hurt so much he had to lower himself to the floor from pain and dizziness. Everything revolved even though he could see nothing. Where was he? Why could he hear waves and grinding of rocks?

This time he sat up slowly, gripping his head with both hands, finally getting back to his knees again. The floor, or possibly a wall or ceiling, angled upward, and he felt his way sideways along it. Under his knee there was a Plexiglas window. He must be inching his way along the side wall of the cabin, the boat turned so that the wall was now the floor. He lay down again, trying to get his bearings, the pain in his head too intense to think very hard.

With his ear against the floor—wall—he could hear grinding. The boat was being pushed farther onto the rocks by the waves; the tide must be carrying it, jamming it higher on whatever rocks these were. He lay there listening to the noise of the pounding surf, floating again on a raft of time—hours or minutes, he knew not which.

After the hours or minutes had passed, he reached out with his arms, feeling for whatever was close to him. Above him was the wheel—he tried to turn it but the rudder must have been jammed against the rocks—he couldn't do it—maybe he was just too weak. He felt along the crack between the side wall and what must be the ceiling. There was a pan lid, a screwdriver, and . . . a *flashlight*. Please, god, let it work.

He switched it on and it pierced the cabin with a single thread of light. His maneuvering along the wall had informed him correctly. The windows weren't broken, the ceiling was beside him, the wall angled up to the floor, and the floor—the floor was splintered. He set his feet at the angle between the wall and ceiling and tried to look through the splintered floor, aiming the narrow light between the cracks. The hull was overhead now. He tried to examine it but the light was weak and dispersed before it reached the outer shell.

He tried to scramble higher up the wall, tried to put his eye to the cracks in the floor and look upward. He thought he saw a crack in the hull itself, but couldn't be sure. The hull was still above water, but maybe not for long. He thought the tide was rising—he could feel the boat shudder under him. Maybe the boat would fill. He was too weak, in too much pain, to get out of it. Well, he'd have to anyway. He could do it if he had to, gather strength while he waited for whatever happened next. He switched the flashlight off, put his head down, and was instantly asleep.

Nightmare: he is sledding in a blizzard. It is terribly cold, the wind howling, snow driving into his face. At the bottom of the hill are trees, dense trees, trees he will crash into. He is going faster and faster now, brush clawing at his face as he plunges downhill, heading toward that impenetrable forest. He is lying flat on the sled, racing down the hill headfirst, the trees coming at him much too fast. He can't stop himself. He tries to drag his feet but his legs are strangely doubled under him.

Now he reaches the edge of the forest. The trees are huge and make a roof above him. The sled hurtles through the tree trunks; the forest is on such a steep slope it is almost a cliff. He hears wolves howling and looks for their tracks in the snow but he is going so fast now his sled has become airborne. He is flying among the tree trunk's—flying over the cliff.

He flings his arms out, trying to grab something, grab branches, hold himself back with a trunk. He strikes something with his hands and opens his eyes. Above him the wolf stares down, his teeth in an awful grin. The wolf is looking at him through a little window in the roof. The wolf throws his head back and howls.

40

SAM HAD JUMPED TO THE SIDE OF THE
boat, which was actually now the roof, and was staring
down at the interior. He whined and wagged his tail, crouching with his front legs, pushing his nose against the window.
Liza moved forward and tried to scramble up next to Sam,
but the boat quivered and shook. She didn't want to dislodge
it. If someone was in there, she'd have to find some other
way to get him out.

The lower part of the boat was in the water, the windshield turned sideways. Maybe she could edge herself along
the rocks and peer through the windshield. Holding on to the
narrow keel, she picked her way along until she could look
in through the windshield.

Beringer was stretched out on what was once the wall but
had become the floor now, more or less standing up, feet
braced in the corner, arms extended. "Get out," she shouted.
"Crawl toward me."

She waited a moment, then shouted again. This time she
heard a groan. "I'll try to get you out of there," she called.

Sam had jumped down from the roof and was circling the
upper part of the boat, his nose to the ground. If Scott was
alive in there, she couldn't dislodge the boat from the rocks,
but she couldn't get at him without breaking something,

which might send the boat sliding into the water. Her mind wasn't functioning—she'd found Scott but he was hurt, maybe dying—she had to help him—her brain was blurred by panic. Snow was falling; she could hear the surf pounding the rocks—the tide had turned again and would soon lap the wrecked boat.

Think, Liza. Go back and get a crowbar and a hammer. Break the windshield and climb through it.

But Sam had discovered the crack in the hull. He jammed his nose against it, then clawed at it. That was the solution. She would get the crowbar and force it into the crack, tearing away the hull until she had a hole big enough to let her through. She ran back to her raft and rowed to the *Salmon Eye*, grabbed the crowbar and hammer and rowed back to the dock. Sam was waiting for her and together they hurried back over the high ridge and down onto the rocks.

The boat had slipped farther down the rocks, half of it in the water now. The crack in the hull was still above water, but it wouldn't be for long with the tide rising fast and the waves breaking over the lower part of the boat. She forced the crowbar into the crack and pried.

In a minute she knew she couldn't get through the hull— it wouldn't splinter or break in pieces—she'd have to smash the windshield. With a mighty swing of the crowbar she made a glorious sunflower burst in the window, swung again and again and finally the windshield cracked. With another blow it broke inward, but the boat was sliding, sliding, only the upper part now above water.

Scott Beringer was crawling toward her. She could see him dragging himself along between the ceiling and the wall—she stretched her arm through the hole to help him out before the whole boat sank. She was bending over now, the boat almost underwater. It had started to fill from the crack in the hull—water pouring in, the lower part now with a foot or two of water. Desperately she reached through the broken window again, struggling to drag him toward her.

He crawled over the steering post and slid between the now upright shelf in front of the windshield and the ceiling, then put one leg through the hole in the window. Liza braced his arms and slowly he pulled himself through, sinking to the rocks and holding his head in his hands. Sam was consumed with joy and danced around him, leaping and barking, licking his ear.

"You're hurt," Liza said.

"Banged my head," Beringer said, his voice muffled by his hands. "Thought Sam was a wolf."

"We have to get you back to the *Salmon Eye*. Can you lean on me? Or I could go back and get a tarp and try to pull you, but it might be a pretty jarring ride."

"Give me a minute. I can crawl anyway."

Liza crouched beside him, holding his elbow. His forehead was bloody—something had made a deep gash in it. At least he was dressed warmly—the orange exposure suit was zipped up and he had gloves on and boots, but no hat. The snow, falling heavily, was already clinging to his hair.

Finally he got to his knees, putting his hands down on the rocks, and pushed himself to his feet. He lurched sideways and Liza tried to hold him up. Very slowly, Beringer leaning heavily on Liza, they made their way up the rocks, slipping in the snow. Once Beringer went to his knees and Liza waited till he pulled himself up on her. Sam led the way, dashing forward, then turning back to make sure they were coming.

From the top of the rocks they heard a grinding noise and turned to watch the wrecked boat sink out of sight.

Somehow Liza managed to get Beringer aboard the *Salmon Eye*. The raft was a very shaky platform—he leaned against the side of the big boat, then tried to drag himself onto the deck using the cleats on the deck, Liza pushing from below. Halfway up, his waist at deck level, his toes propped on the inflated air tube, he had to rest, laying his head on the deck, panting and coughing.

Liza climbed over him. She crouched and simply pulled him onto the deck by throwing herself backward, bracing her feet on the rail. He lay on the deck for a while, then gathered enough strength to get to his knees. Slowly he pulled himself up on the bulkhead and went in the door to the cabin, dropping immediately to the bench by the table.

"That was an ordeal," he muttered. "Sorry."

"I'm just glad you're safe," she said. "That boat wasn't going to last much longer, though it might not have gone so fast if I hadn't slammed it with the crowbar. I'm going to make some tea—you need to get warm. Then we'll head back to Wrangell. You need to get that gash sewed up."

He leaned over and put his head in his hands again. "Not much help, I'm afraid."

"You don't need to be—let's get something hot into you and then we'll set out."

41

BERINGER LAY ON THE BENCH IN A CO-
coon of strange ideas. He moved slightly but continuously
inside the sleeping bag. Sometime in the past he was sledding and there were wolves howling. When had that been?
He couldn't remember when he had done that. Now the
Keltie was pitching in the wake of some huge ship that had
come into Exchange Cove—he stretched out his arm to hold
the charts on the table. They were charts of where the whales
were. He was following the whales and a humpback had
risen up under the *Keltie* and caused it to swamp.

No, that wasn't it. A storm. That was it, a storm and he
couldn't get through the waves—the wind was driving him
back, the tide. His boat had swamped and been carried onto
the rocks. He was rescued from the sinking boat. His head
ached. He stretched his legs out straight, then raised his
knees and turned on his side. With his fingers he felt the
rough fabric cover of the cushion on the back of the bench.

He dreamed about Ted Hilliard. He was following Ted
through elephant grass along a river, and a land mine went
off and he was hurt. No, it wasn't that way. Something else
happened. But his leg was hurt, and Ted's brain.

Ted was quoting something to him. He remembered it
clearly: *Humankind cannot bear very much reality*. That was

true—he knew that was true because his leg hurt and his head hurt and he needed to get away from both things, but he couldn't because both of them were real and true.

He turned again, lying on his back, making his head swim. Andrea was Ted's wife and Sarah's mother. How could that be? If Andrea were Ted's wife she couldn't be Sarah's mother because Sarah belonged to him. He shook his head and a sharp pain tore through his skull. He couldn't think anymore.

His hand rubbed the fabric of the cushion again, and the other hand reached out to the table, feeling along the edge of it. He must be sick. He hadn't been ill for a long time, but he was having fever dreams. He was lying on the bench behind the table of the *Keltie* and not able to think straight. He was sick.

Sarah. Two years old, pushing the buttons on the answering machine, erasing every message. He caught her up in his arms too late. Two years old. No, wait, she wasn't two anymore. She had been here—when was it—she was twelve now—tears ran down his face. How had he missed all that time in between? Why was she two years old and then twelve and the years between had all escaped him?

Sarah. He loved her so dearly and all those years had gone by and now she was grown up. She loved baseball the way he did, and animals, the way he did, and she was coming here to see him. He sat bolt upright, terrible pain jolting through his head. Wednesday Sarah was coming. Wednesday. What day was it? Why couldn't he think what day it was? He had to go, he had to get to Wrangell and meet her on Wednesday. He got to his feet, the pain in his head like a torch burning him up. This wasn't the *Keltie*. Somebody else's boat, much larger, much older.

His feet were tangled in the sleeping bag and he sat on the bench and lifted them out, slowly and one at a time, the pain in his head causing him to lean back on the bench. A big dog was standing in front of him now, wagging his tail. Sam. The name came to him from outer space. Sam. He held his hand out and the dog came toward him so he could rub his head. Why was he on this boat? Where was he going? He had to get to Wrangell. He had to meet Sarah. Wednesday. Sarah was coming on Wednesday.

Someone must be in the wheelhouse steering this boat. He put his hands on the table and pushed himself to his feet, lurching as the boat pitched into a trough, almost going down. Hand over hand, holding the table, then the rail along the bulkhead, he made his way up the three steps to the wheelhouse. There was a woman steering the boat. Liza. Again the name came to him abruptly.

"What day is this?" he asked her. He startled her and she jumped, swinging around to look at him.

"Friday," she said.

"Is that the Friday before or after my daughter is coming?" he asked, tears streaming.

"What day was she supposed to get here?"

"Wednesday. But I've forgotten the week. I can't think. I can't remember anything."

"I think you've had a concussion, Scott. You need to lie down while we're traveling, otherwise you'll be thrown around and it will make things worse."

"I know it's Wednesday she's coming. What day is today? I mean, what date?"

"November fifteenth."

"Maybe it's next Wednesday. God, I hope so. She wouldn't know anyone—she wouldn't know where to call." The tears started again. "Where are we going?"

"To Wrangell. We need to get you to the hospital, get that gash sewed up and find out if you've had a concussion."

"Wrangell. That's good. I'll be there when Sarah comes."

"Let me help you back to the table. You need to stay warm and you need to lie down."

She put her hands under his arms while he went back down the steps, holding him as he crossed the floor to the table and sank down on the bench. She waited while he shoved his feet into the sleeping bag and pulled it up around him.

"I can't think anymore," he said, drawing a shaky breath. "All these strange ideas float around."

"We'll be there soon," she said. "You'll be fine in a day or two, when the effects of banging your head wear off. Go to sleep, and when you wake up we'll be in Wrangell."

He nodded. His brain was floating on a sea of pain. He sank into the sea and disappeared.

42

SHOULD SHE TRY TO PICK UP MINK AND take her to the hospital? Mink would be a wild woman to have on board, demanding that the *Salmon Eye* speed up, get her there in record time despite what would surely be terrible conditions in the strait. Still, Liza wanted to take her if no one else had. She called the Manley marine operator at Petersburg and gave her Mink's home number. There was no answer.

She changed the number to the Velvet Moose and Jimmy Matsui answered. "She's going crazy—you talk to her."

"He's terrible, terrible—critical condition—I gotta get there—he won't . . . if I'm not . . ."

"Mink, I'll pick you up and take you over. I'm about an hour away."

"Shit, Liza, he's critical—I gotta get there sooner than that."

"You could take the mail plane if it comes today."

"Won't be no plane in this wind."

"Well, I'll stop by and see if you're there."

"I gotta get there right now!"

"Calm down—you live on an island with a moat around it. You'll get there when you can."

"Sheeee-it, Liza—I gotta go!"

* * *

It was a hellish trip to Wrangell, Mink lurching into the walls of the cabin as she tried to pace, Liza trying to keep the boat at a speed that didn't slam into the mountains of water coming at her. Fortunately Beringer slept the whole way. Liza had become somewhat attached to him. She thought of his compassion for the whales, how he'd rescued the humpback in Port Beauclerc—an intelligent and attractive man, she thought.

Liza decided to go to Shoemaker Bay. Her truck was there, and if Beringer couldn't make it up the ramp, she could call the aid car. Mink could help him on one side and she could support him on the other. But Jake was there and took her lines.

"I've got someone injured on board," she told him. "Maybe you could help me get him up the ramp."

She went back to the cabin and looked down at Scott Beringer. He was curled on his side, breathing quietly, sleeping soundly, she thought. She reached down and took his hand and he opened his eyes immediately.

"We're here," she said. "We need to get you to the truck. Jake from the *Aquila* across the dock from us can help us up the ramp."

He propped himself up and swung his legs to the floor, then pushed himself to his feet using the table as a prop. Jake was there and took his arm.

"Head hurts," Beringer said.

"See you got a sliced-up forehead," Jake said. "How'd that happen?"

"I found him inside a wrecked boat out by Merrifield Bay," Liza said. "He must have slammed his head pretty hard—I think he has a concussion."

They moved slowly out of the cabin, waiting for Beringer to lift one foot at a time over the high threshold, then supporting him across the deck. The steps were in place on the dock, and Jake helped him down them. One on each side, they moved him along the dock to the ramp, Mink leading the way impatiently. At half tide, the ramp was fairly steep. A few feet up, Beringer had to stop to rest.

Liza looked over at Jake and shook her head. "Maybe we should get the aid car," she said. "I could call—they'll have EMTs who could handle this better than we can."

"I can make it," Beringer said, pulling himself along on the railing. Jake and Liza pushed him from behind, Mink supporting his side. Eventually they reached the top.

"My truck is old and has a high step, but it does have a running board," Liza said. They made their way toward the ancient lime-green truck. She opened the door on the passenger side and Jake all but lifted Beringer onto the seat. He sank back and put his head in his hands. "My god, I can't think," he said. "Where am I?"

"In Wrangell," Jake said. "Liza here'll drive you to the hospital and they'll fix you up. Gonna be okay."

Mink jammed in on the far side, forcing Scott to slide to the center, where he leaned against Liza's shoulder.

"The boat," Beringer mumbled. "It's wrecked, isn't it?"

"'Fraid so, Scott," Liza said. "They'll have insurance on it, though. It belongs to Wildlife, doesn't it?"

"I'm so sorry. I have to tell them. I'm so sorry."

"It's all going to be all right now," Liza said soothingly. She started the truck, waved to Jake and shouted, "Thank you," over the deep-throated rumble of the engine. She tried to avoid the muddy potholes in the parking lot, but hit a couple and Beringer clutched his head each time.

"I was trying to get back—I needed to . . . touch him, hold him . . . he held me when my leg . . ."

Four miles to the hospital. She drove slowly, trying not to jar his head more than she had to. At the emergency entrance, she went in and asked for help. Mink disappeared down the hall. A nurse and an orderly came out, took one look at Beringer and went for a gurney. One braced it while the other slid him onto it; they fastened the straps and wheeled him into the emergency room. Liza followed.

"I found him inside a wrecked boat up on the rocks. I think he hit his head very hard—seems like he has a concussion at the very least."

"We'll x-ray it—could have a skull fracture. And that cut needs some stitches. Do you want to wait?"

"I have a friend in here—I'll go see him and check back later." She patted Beringer's hand and he looked up at her. "Thanks," he mumbled. "Thanks for everything."

She smiled at him. "You're going to be fine," she said.

Liza sat down in the waiting area and wondered why Tango had been on that beach. She picked up a magazine, *Sports Illustrated*, and idly thumbed through it, then a *Road and Track*, *People*, *Better Homes and Gardens*, *Reader's Digest*, *Good Housekeeping*, *Family Circle*. She was down to the religious tracts before Mink came back.

"He ain't so good," she said. "They're tryin' to thaw him out, but he ain't lookin' so good." She turned her head and blinked. "Shit, I wouldn't know how to live without . . ." She broke down then, her tears coming in huge, muffled gasps.

Liza stood and put her arms around her. "He survived Vietnam. So there's hope. We have to have hope."

Mink nodded and wiped her eyes on Liza's shoulder. "I'm gonna stay—I'll just sit with him till . . . whatever."

"All right. That's good. He'll know you're there. I'll go back to Shoemaker now. Call me when he wakes up." She hugged Mink again and whispered, "Hang on."

Liza drove down the hill to the police station. A modern, gray-sided building, two stories tall, it housed the fire department as well. She walked through the entryway and went into the police department.

"I'd like to speak to Lieutenant Howard," she said to the clerk at the counter. And he was there. He came out and pulled her into his little cubicle, carefully closing the door. He held her arm tightly with one hand.

"Lizzie," he said, "Lizzie. Uhh, how are you?"

He sat across the desk from her. She smiled as she looked at his hands crumpling the papers on it to keep himself from reaching toward her hands.

"You called to tell me Tango's been found, Lizzie. He's unconscious, though, extremely hypothermic. They're trying to get him warm."

"Yes, I did call. I was out there at Labouchere Bay when Scott Beringer, the marine biologist, found him. He called for a medevac—they sent a small plane out in the dark in all that wind. I don't know how they could have done it."

Paul nodded. "Bush pilot knows how to do it, but yeah, there sure was a lot of wind last night."

"Beringer tried to get back here in that huge storm but his boat couldn't handle it and was wrecked out by Merrifield Bay. He has a concussion and a big split on his forehead. I was passing out there and found him and got him out just before the boat sank."

"What the hell were you doing out there in that storm?"

"I was taking freight to Point Baker and Labouchere Bay. The storm hit early last night. I went to Port Protection after I heard about Tango on the radio."

"Lizzie . . . you shouldn't be out . . . sheesh . . . I don't want you to go out . . . you can't . . ."

"Listen, this is my livelihood now. I'm cautious and I take care of myself. I didn't leave the next morning till the seas had come down some and the wind had dropped. But Scott Beringer left long before I did, and he couldn't make it."

Paul put his head in his hands, muttering something under his breath. He looked shaken, his forehead in deep furrows, his eyelids at half-mast.

"I'll be fine," she said. "I look after myself and, of course, I have to look after my first mate, Sam, so we're always safe."

Paul shook his head. "Don't like it," he grumbled. "I hope Tango makes it, though. I need to talk to him."

"Question him?"

"Sure, question him. How did he come to be washed up way out there? He was evading the law, going off somewhere on a boat. Who knows what he was doing?"

She drew a deep breath. She wasn't going to argue with this man any more. She said it anyway: "He did not kill that man. Tango would not kill anyone."

Paul raised his head and stared her in the eye. "Hmmph," he grunted. "You never know, do you?"

They glared at each other. Then Liza burst out laughing. "Paul Howard—make my day."

He stretched his hands forward, took hers and grinned sheepishly. "At least I'm good for a laugh," he said.

43

Liza drove the truck back to Shoe-maker. At the slip, she poked the phone and electric lines through the forward hawsehole and climbed over, plugging both lines into the boxes on the dock. The *Nereia*, next to her, was put to bed for the winter, her green covers flapping in the wind like small sails. Jake emerged, standing on the bow of the *Aquila*, asking after Beringer.

"I took him to the emergency room and left him there," she said. "They'll admit him overnight, at least."

"Might need to stay longer if he's got a concussion. Took a pretty bad hit, I'd say."

"Well, they'll keep him as long as they have to, I guess. I'll call his office and let them know what's happened. And Tango was found washed up on Joe Mace Island."

"Hunh," Jake said. "Old Sam, here—he find him?"

"No, it was Scott, who actually knew Tango when they were in Vietnam together. Scott called for a medevac that came and flew him in to the hospital. Tango has to survive—he just has to." She felt her eyes fill and turned away. Exhaustion was taking a toll—she'd had little sleep last night worrying about Tango, then finding the *Keltie*, and that horrendous trip back to Wrangell, the wait at the hospital,

Mink's collapse. "Scott was coming back in that huge storm just to see him. That's when his boat got wrecked."

"What was Tango doing out there?" Jake asked. "Musta been on some boat that got sunk or something."

"I don't know—I can't even imagine what he was doing out there. I heard Scott calling on the radio and went over there, but the plane was just taking off. The wind was fierce and I worried all night that the plane might not make it. Didn't think a plane would come out in those conditions. Dark, too."

"Some floatplane jock—fly even when they can't see nothin'."

"Well, thank goodness they picked him up and got back to the hospital. He might make it—at least they're doing everything they can to warm him up. I have to go—I need to make some calls and then go back to the hospital to be with Mink. Hideous trip, Mink pacing and hurtling into the walls because the seas were so steep, Scott rolling around on the bench asleep."

"Yeah," Jake said, "It sure was awful out there. See yuh, Sam." He held his hand up to Liza and ambled back into the *Aquila*.

On the way to town, Liza saw Tasha's little yellow Rabbit outside the building next to the police station and turned in, parking beside it. Tasha and Paul were neighbors—she worked at the Wrangell Alcohol Program, counseling those who abused alcohol, abused drugs; counseling those who had lost their jobs, those who were involved in domestic violence. Paul worked next door, dealing with the spin-offs from the same drugs, alcohol and domestic violence.

Liza knocked on the door of Tasha's office and Tasha shouted, "Client." Liza sat down in the outer office to wait, though she needed to get going, stay with Mink—be there when Tango roused from his coma—was it a coma or was it just that he was too cold for his brain to function?

A woman came out of Tasha's office. She had a bruise on her face that she'd tried unsuccessfully to cover with makeup. Tasha followed, put her arm around the woman, whispered something in her ear that Liza couldn't hear. The woman nodded, pulled away from Tasha's arm, and went out the main door, her shoulders sagging and her feet finding the curb by feel only.

"You again," Tasha said. "What's up?"

"Well, Scott Beringer—he's the new whale expert after Henry Sizemore was drowned, found Tango washed up on the beach on Joe Mace Island last night. He called for a medevac—got him flown to Wrangell. I don't know if he'll make it. I picked Mink up on my way back today and brought her over. She says he's not too good. Hospital says 'critical.' He hasn't regained consciousness."

"Shee-it, Liza. She won't make it if he doesn't. What can we do?"

"Not much. Either he'll survive or he won't."

"What the hell was he doing out there?"

"I have no idea—we might never know what he was doing out there if he doesn't live."

"Shit, he has to. He owes it to Mink. He owes her one for picking him up off the beach."

"I gotta go—I just wanted to let you know. Actually, I just brought Scott Beringer into the hospital too. His boat got wrecked in that storm. Banged his head pretty hard—probably has a concussion."

"My god, something wrong with everyone—I'll stop by after work and see what's happening."

"They're warming him much too slow," Mink said. "They coulda got him thawed out a lot faster."

"I think they know what they're doing. Anyone who's been in that frigid water takes a long time to warm up. And he's wiggling his fingers—look, Mink—he's moving his whole arm."

"Jesus, I ain't seen nothing like that before. Hey, look, he's raising his hand. Gimme that hand," she said, taking it in hers and squeezing it. "He's squeezing back," she said, tears streaming down her face. Liza nodded, putting one arm around Mink before she turned away. This was reunion time.

Liza went to the nurses' station to ask about Beringer.

"Concussion and hairline fracture," the nurse told her. "If there's any evidence of a sub-dural, we'll send him to Ketchikan for a CT scan, but he's not showing symptoms of that yet."

Liza nodded and went down the hall to room 110 to look in on him. He was sound asleep, drugged, she thought, by painkillers. He looked very peaceful lying there—she'd become fond of him—she remembered how he'd dragged himself out of the boat through the window, how he'd asked her what day it was. When he woke up, he'd know what day it was.

She drove the truck back to Shoemaker. She was exhausted. She fed Sam, threw some hamburger into a skillet and chopped a few onions to go with it. She'd take Sam for a walk and turn in as soon as she got back. While she ate, the phone rang. Tasha's familiar voice said, "He made it. He's actually talking to Mink."

"When I left he was squeezing her hand. He's talking?"

"He's talking. Well, quoting."

"That'll let me sleep tonight. I'm so tired. It's been an in-credible few days—I'm so glad you called."

"Go to bed—I'll talk to you tomorrow."

Liza dragged herself up the steep ramp to the parking lot

and let Sam run through the woods on the R.V. campsite next to the Shoemaker parking lot for a few minutes. She could hear his tags jingle, now and then see his shoulders moving, his tail wagging the brush. She wanted to keep him close. She still remembered those shots. The forest seemed darker than usual, filled with the creak and groan of ancient trees bowing to the wind. Sam plunged across her path and she slipped her hand under his collar. "We're going home," she said firmly, and he pranced at her side till she released him at the top of the ramp.

When she got to the boat, Paul Howard was there, seated on a stack of motor oil cartons.

"Figured you were running Sam," he said. "Thought I'd wait a little, see if you came back pretty soon."

She flung the door open and held it for him. She thought he looked strained and tired—he'd had a very long day, too. Why was he here? She wanted to go to bed—he looked as though bed would be the first thing on his agenda, too. But not together—there would be no more policemen in her life, ever.

He put one hand on her arm. "Lizzie, I know you think Tango is pure as driven snow, but . . ."

She pulled away from his hand and glared at him. "Yes," she said. "I do think that. Or at least, I know he would never kill."

"Well, I came to apologize for suspecting him. There are lots of other suspects, too. And I'd like to take your word for him—I mean, I hope you're right."

"Listen, Paul, I will not, repeat, not, allow you to divide me from my friends. You've assumed a rather large role in my life at the moment, but I am not going to give up all my friends just because one or another of them is on your suspect list."

"Well, I didn't come here to fight with you over this—I

just . . . uhhh . . . well, I just wanted to talk, I guess. I mean, we could talk about something else . . . how your freight business is doing, things like that . . . I hear Mink's at the hospital with Tango."

"Which brings us right back to the same old thing. Which is what we'll always come back to when we try to talk about something else."

He met her eyes and shrugged. "I guess," he said, and opened the door. "I just wanted to apologize for having Tango at the top of the suspect list."

He stepped over the sill onto the deck. Then he turned back and stared at her again, his face dark and taciturn, his eyes only slits under the heavy lids. "But that's right where he is."

She watched him swing over the rail and let himself down onto the dock. Then she went out on deck, leaned on the rail and murmured, "Well, take your suspect list and shove it."

44

PAUL TURNED OVER, DOUBLED THE PIL-
low under his head, threw the blanket back, then got cold
and pulled it up again. Why had he gone to the *Salmon Eye*?
He hated himself, hated his words, hated hers. Somehow
he'd wanted to reassure himself that they could stay close,
stay in touch despite their differences, and then he'd said all
the wrong things and she'd responded angrily and it had become a lost cause. They'd pass on the street like strangers.

He'd go back and apologize. He sat up, turned the light on
and looked at the clock. 11:45. He threw himself down again
without turning off the light. Too late to go back. Too late to
apologize. He sat up again and threw the blanket back,
swung his feet to the floor and stood up. Numbly he went
through the motions of getting dressed. He had to do something—he'd go back to the boat and make some sort of fee-
ble apology—it wouldn't do, but at least she would
understand how much he hated his words.

He clomped down the stairs and turned the kitchen light
on. Maybe some coffee—if he took time to make coffee,
maybe that would help him think how to say what he needed
to say. He ran water in the kettle, turned the stove on, turned
it off. It was too late to go out there already. If he was going

to do it, he better go, but it was much too late. Too late in all ways—the hour too late, the apology too late.

He slammed the kitchen door and forced his feet into the damp boots he left on the back porch. The Blazer was in the drive—his garage was full of junk—he'd been meaning to clear it out but hadn't gotten around to it. He climbed in and stuck the keys in the ignition, then sat there with his arms propped on the steering wheel. Too late. It was much, much too late to go there and to say anything at all. He'd lost everything he wanted in a fit of frustration, talking about Tango being at the top of his suspect list.

He muttered aloud and twisted the key, listening to the engine turn over. He'd drive out to Shoemaker, but he wouldn't go down to the boat—he'd just look at it lying there in the black water, sit there and look at it, wait a while, think about the things he'd said, then turn around and come home. He put the car in reverse and backed down the drive.

At Shoemaker he inched his way down the steep ramp. Must be a minus tide—ramp was almost straight up and down. A heron at the end of the grid squawked hoarsely, disturbed by his presence. At the bottom he turned to the right, heading for the last finger. At the corner he made a left. He was moving slower and slower now. The southeasterly made the rigging on the boats clank against the metal masts and poles. He stopped fifty feet away from the *Salmon Eye* and stared at it. There were lights showing through the curtains in the cabin. She must be up, then. Why would she be up so late? He turned around. He couldn't think of anything to say—it was too late to say anything. He walked back to the corner of the dock, then stopped and looked again. He had to try, anyway. He walked toward the boat, forcing himself to go there, to climb over the rail, to knock on the door. What would he say?

Sam barked and Paul could hear him scramble toward the

door. Lizzie pushed the curtain aside and peered out, then unlocked the door and opened it. Sam, as usual, was over-joyed to see him, bounding in circles and beating his tail against the table and benches. Lizzie pulled him in and shut the door.

"I couldn't sleep," she said.

"Me either."

She put her hand on his arm and he pulled her close.

"I didn't want to say those things," he said. "I'm just so . . . well, you know. I didn't want to say that."

"I know. I shouldn't have answered like that."

Suddenly Sam wedged himself between them and she laughed. "Trying to protect me from you. Your place, Sam," she said. "Your place."

Sam lowered his head, then reluctantly went over and curled on his mat.

"I hated my words," Paul said. "You have to know . . . well, I hated those words."

"And you hated mine. And so did I."

He had his mouth against her hair, rubbing his mouth along her skull, pressing hard, feeling the bones like a blind man. She turned her face up and his mouth was on hers and he was holding her so tight he could feel every curve of her body, every muscle, every bone. He ran his hands down her back and below, pressing her into him so she could feel how hard he'd become. "Lizzie," he muttered.

"Are we there?" she said. "Is it going to happen? I didn't want another policeman, but it seems to be my lot."

Paul stumbled down the steep steps to the level below. She pulled him into the narrow bunkroom, slamming the door behind him to keep Sam out. It was dark in there, though a small amount of light came through a porthole from a sodium light on the dock. He reached out for her and pulled her against him, his fingers clumsy as he pulled her sweatshirt over her head, pushed her sweatpants down, braced her as she slid them over her feet. There were too many clothes—he was still fully dressed—he started on his own clothing and she helped him, unfastening his shirt, his belt buckle, sliding her hands down and down. And then they were on the bunk, and his hands remembered everything and they were lost in each other.

Later he returned to consciousness. He was still lying mostly on top of her—the bunk was very small for two people, and the zipper of the sleeping bag was digging into one hip. He tried to pull it out from under him, pushing down on her as he lifted the other hip, and she woke. She pulled his face down to hers, then slipped her hands down, massaging as she went. He laughed, rolling onto her, then a joyous surging into her again and again.

When at last it was over, he put his head beside hers on the pillow. His heart pounded wildly—he thought he might die, die in ecstasy. Breathless, he said, "I love you."

He felt her nod. "I know. Since we met on the trail I've wanted you."

"That long?"

"That long. Why do we always end up fighting?"

"Because you don't want another policeman."

"Yes," she said. "I mean, no, I don't want to be involved with a cop. But I seem to go for them. Something about . . . maybe it was the cops who came when my mother disappeared. Maybe it's been going on for thirty years. Oh, I don't know . . . I just know . . . well, I guess I've fallen for another one."

"I'm ugly and fat and old. How could you?"

"Prickly on the outside, soft inside."

He rolled off, then had to flip one leg off the bunk to keep from falling on the floor. "This bed's way too small," he grumbled. "Next time at my house."

"Is that an invitation?"

He hurled himself over on top of her again. "You bet," he whispered. "You bet it is."

45

GRAY LIGHT CAME THROUGH THE PORT-
hole. Liza glanced at the clock. 8:45. Paul had left two hours
ago—she had felt him slip away from her, watched as he
dressed, sitting on the bunk to put his thick wool socks on,
leaning over to kiss her. She could still feel the lingering
warmth of his mouth on hers. She had turned over and gone
back to sleep, exhausted by the rapid shift in her emotions.
Last night she had been furious with the man, too angry to
sleep, then too frustrated to sleep, then too sad to sleep. He
had come to say he was sorry for his words and she had
thrown her arms around him and made love to him. And did,
in fact, love him.

Sam was whining at the door—he'd be frantic by now,
desperate to go out. She sat up, pulled her sweatpants on and
her shirt over her head, grabbed her socks and running shoes
and carried them up the steep steps. She tried to call Paul,
needing to hear his grumbly voice, but he wasn't at home
and she didn't want to call the office—he wouldn't be free to
talk.

Sam was jigging back and forth to the door and, when she
opened it, dashed through and over the rail. She raced after
him, waiting patiently while he disappeared into the wooded
strip around the parking lot, then setting out to jog along Zi-

movia Highway, past the Wrangell Institute. It was filled with asbestos and the ancient buildings were collapsing further each day, the roofs falling in on themselves, the windows stark without glass.

She pushed herself, running with joy. She'd made a commitment—had joined with Paul and put the past behind her. Her first life was over. Efren was long dead and buried. Her mother was gone forever. The black wolf on Liza's shoulder stirred, shifting its weight. She's dead, Liza. She never would have left you. Now "Lizzie" was free to go forward with Paul. Her feet felt light and springy and she raced Sam all the way back to the boat.

Driving to town for groceries, she noticed Tasha's car in the drive and turned in, braking as she discovered a pile of bicycles lying in the center of the muddy river the driveway had become. She turned the old truck to the side and jounced through the ruts, coming to a halt in a half circle of blue oil buckets and paint cans with assorted colors running down their sides. She made her way through the extraordinary number of boots on the back steps and pounded on the door.

"Say what?" Tasha said, as she opened the door and pulled Liza in. The house resounded with heavy metal on somebody's stereo. Marge, Andy and Erin were playing Monopoly on the kitchen table and gave her high fives when she came in, Erin adding a big hug.

"What's this?" Liza asked. "I thought they'd all be in school."

"Teachers' inservice," Tasha said. "I suppose they deserve a day off once in a while—they get the little buggers all the rest of the time."

"So you're home running the show?"

"Yeah, I had to take a personal day, but hell, why not?

These kids, they're all I got left anymore—I gotta try to keep their heads straight."

She poured two mugs of coffee and they went out on the old sunporch, never sunny at this time of year. "Turn that down," Tasha shouted, as they passed the foot of the stairs. "Shit, they crank that up so loud you can hear the boom from the highway." Heavy footsteps sounded overhead, and in a minute there was a very slight reduction in the volume. "More," Tasha shouted, "keep going."

"So what's happening with you?"

"Well, not much, actually. And you?"

"I heard kind of an odd story from Scott Beringer, the marine biologist. He came to the *Salmon Eye* and told me about Tango, who was named Ted Hilliard when he met him in Vietnam. Thought he was dead till he heard him on the radio. Then he went to meet him, but Ted/Tango never showed up."

"That *is* peculiar—was that when Tango disappeared?"

"Yeah, exactly. Scott said he'd seen the Zodiac going out of the bay right past him, making a huge wake so he had to slow down. It's all very odd. Paul Howard is sure that Tango killed the man on the beach for hurting Mink. We fought about it, but then we, uhhh, sort of made up."

"Sort of made up?"

Liza felt her face growing warm. "Well, yeah, last night he came to the boat to apologize for the words we'd had earlier. And, uhhhh, things went on from there."

"He's a good man, Liza. I know he was harsh about some things last spring, but he's a good man."

Liza nodded and rubbed her hands over her face, trying to cool it off.

"I know you didn't want to take on another cop after Efren, but you're probably the only one who understands how it is with cops."

"Cop first and always, Tash. That's how it is. I'm always the second-class citizen. But, well, I'm in love again."

"So love him. He's a good man." ·

The music suddenly hit a new decibel high, thudding drums and electric guitar. Tasha leaped up and rushed to the stairs. Liza shouted over the booming noise that she had to go. Tasha waved as she raced up the steps, then clapped her hands over her ears and disappeared down the hall. Liza went out the back door laughing, knowing as she'd always known, despite the angry words, that Paul Howard was "a good man."

46

TWO DAYS LATER, EARLY IN THE MORN-
ing, Beringer was following the RTO along a trail by a river.
The RTO turned his head and it was Ted. He reached out, he
opened his eyes, Ted was bending over him, holding him in
his arms. "What," he said. "I'm dreaming."

"'Tis I," Ted said. "'You see me, Lord Bassanio, where I
stand, such as I am . . . ,' Baron, Baron. 'If I should meet
thee after long years, How should I greet thee?' It's been so
long . . ." There were tears running down Ted's face and he
was gripping him, hugging him, holding him tightly the way
he had done when his leg was so damaged.

Beringer struggled to sit up. He held on to Ted, pulling
himself forward, wrapping his arms tightly around Ted,
burying his face against Ted's shoulder, sobbing into it. Ted
sank down on the bed, still holding him. They sat that way
for a long time—Time: minutes, hours, days, weeks, had
somehow escaped from Beringer's brain—he had no idea
how long they sat entwined. Finally he raised his head and
looked Ted in the eye. "There's only one of you, not two."

"Fortunate, that," Ted answered. "Indeed the fact that
there is only one of me is a blessing to the world."

"I was seeing double. At least there's been a little

progress." His head didn't hurt as much either, though that might have been the painkiller the nurse kept feeding him.

"How did you get here? When did you . . . wait . . . it's coming back—I found you. I actually found you. You were lying on rocks . . . you weren't moving . . . where was it? Why can't I remember that?"

Suddenly the man in the other bed sat up and tore off his oxygen tube, swinging his emaciated legs over the side, struggling to get to his feet. "Go home," he whimpered. "My wife is sick. I gotta go home."

The room seemed to be full of people. Beringer tried to focus on them—a short, heavyset woman behind Ted, a tall woman behind her. The tall woman moved over to the other bed and punched the call button for the nurse, stroking the man's arm and speaking quietly to him. "Someone will come right away and help you," she said. "If your wife is ill, perhaps she should be here in the hospital with you."

Liza. That was her name. She had brought him here, hadn't she? Several days ago—he couldn't really remember when it was, but he thought she had brought him here. He swung his head around to the others, but the nurse came in and they moved back against the wall.

"Wife is sick," the old man said, sliding forward till his feet touched the floor. "Home . . . gotta go home."

The nurse put her arms around him, trying to push him back onto the bed. "Your wife died four years ago, Gus," she said. "I'm sorry. You need to be here now so we can get you better."

He fell back onto the bed, curled his knees up and fell into great gusts of weeping. "I didn't know that," he gasped. "I didn't know she died. Martha," he cried, "Martha, come back."

"I'm sorry," the nurse said to Beringer and the others.

"This has happened before—sometimes he remembers and sometimes not."

" 'Were it not better to forget, than but remember and regret?' " Ted said.

"If you want, we could give you a different room," the nurse said.

"No," said Beringer, "I'll stay here. Maybe he needs company. And I'll be going soon, anyway."

"Martha," the man sobbed. "Martha, Martha, Martha . . ."

"I'll wait till he's calmer to put the oxygen tube back," the nurse said. "I'll leave you to your company."

"This is my wife, Mink," Ted said. " 'A rose, by any other name . . .' "

Beringer smiled and held his hand out. She responded with a hard grip.

"Lookin' okay," she said, " 'cept for that embroid'ry. Look, I got my arm stitched up like Mabel Anderson's tea towels." She pushed her sleeve up and showed him the long red scar on her upper arm.

"Very recent, wasn't it?"

"Yeah, two guys in the bar, one with a knife. Got between 'em. Totally dumb thing to do, wouldn't you know?"

Beringer looked at her hard. She was so different from Andrea, who was tall and blonde with gray eyes and a lovely wide smile—when she smiled, which was not very often of late. This woman was Indian, black eyes, with grizzled hair clipped close to her head, short and very wide. Unsmiling, her eyes pierced into him like scalpels. They made him uncomfortable and he looked away, but was drawn back, finding her gaze unyielding.

This was the woman Ted had married. But he'd never been divorced from Andrea. Which made Beringer's marriage to Andrea invalid.

"You know I married Andrea? I thought you were dead.

She told me that, that you were dead, had died on the freeway. She even told me she'd scattered your ashes in the Mississippi River."

"I did not die on the freeway. I have not died anywhere at all," Ted said.

What a confounding of their relationships. And Sarah? What was she, the child of a non-marriage? When you can think better you will have to puzzle this out.

Tasha George appeared in the doorway. "This is where you are. Looked in Tango's room—nobody—asked where he was—nurse said, 'Room 110.'" Ted introduced her to Beringer. "My god, what happened to you?" she asked, looking at the bandage.

"Banged my head and cut it open. Hard to remember how it happened—something on the boat. Liza brought me here."

"You don't remember? Musta banged it pretty damn hard."

"I remember finding Ted, I mean Tango, then not much after that. So what were you doing out there washed up on those rocks?"

"'Not that the story need be long, but it will take a long while to make it short,'" Tango said. "I eluded my captors when we were leaving a bay. I took the current and I floated to shore, or I would have lost my life. '. . . And we must take the current when it serves, or lose our ventures.'"

"You were on a boat?" Beringer asked.

"Indeed, on a boat, 'a beautiful pea-green boat.' Only I don't think it was pea-green, I think it was black."

"And how came you to be on a boat?"

"On the morning we were to meet, someone came to the door rather early with a gun. And he took me away, 'for a year and a day,' to the 'beautiful pea-green boat.' Unfortunately it was Pete Walstrom. I'd recognized him the night before. A lot of things came back to me that night. He was one of the pilots who blew away our platoon."

"You recognized him after all those years?"

" 'His identity presses upon me.' Yes, I did recognize him—he looked much the same as twenty years before."

"So you got your memory back," Mink said.

"I believe I have," Ted said. "I remember the other pilot also—I saw him many years ago in St. Louis—they were the ones that destroyed the platoon."

"Well, thank god for memories," Mink said. "Remember your previous life?"

"Only in shadows. '. . . that I could forget what I have been, or not remember what I must be now.' "

"Still talks in quotes," Mink said.

"He was an English professor before he went to war," Beringer told her, and Ted nodded.

"Walstrom took me away and sped me from the harbor to a waiting boat. And I was 'imprisoned in the viewless winds, and blown with restless violence round about.' I never saw Pete Walstrom again."

A huge bear of a man leaned against the door frame. Now he walked over to stand right next to Ted. "You sure about that?" he asked.

"Indeed, his face never again passed before my eyes, Lieutenant."

Beringer watched the big man. Indian man, he thought. Ted had called him "Lieutenant." Was he something with the police? His expression was an odd mix of distrust and recognition.

"Didn't you see him on the beach in Wrangell? Didn't you, in fact, shoot him with the gun you took away after the bar fight?"

" 'When you shall these unlucky deeds relate, speak of me as I am.' I did remove the gun from the bar, fearing I might need to defend myself from Mr. Walstrom. When he appeared at my door, he acquired that gun, which I had left on a stack of books on the table."

"That's how the books got thrown all over," Mink said. "Coffee spilled. Didn't think you'd 'a gone off and left those books in a puddle of coffee. Hunh."

"No, I would never have left them had I not had a gun at my back. But to answer your question, Lieutenant, I did not shoot Mr. Walstrom because I was incarcerated on the boat. He took me there, and perhaps left again, I do not know. I only know I did not see him after my imprisonment."

"Short guy? Bald?"

"I believe we are describing the same man, but who can tell?"

"His name was Barney Ellis—anyway, that's what he was going under."

"I believe Pete Walstrom had a small scar next to his eyebrow. And did the man called Barney Ellis show the same ancient wound?"

"Yeah. He did. Had a scar right next to his eyebrow. So if you didn't shoot the guy, you got any idea who coulda done it?"

"'Truth will come to light; murder cannot be hid long.' I do not know who could have killed the man, but it will be revealed."

The man stared at Ted a while. "You did not kill Ellis/Walstrom, whoever he is?"

"I did not. I will swear to that. I could not have because Walstrom took me to the boat and I was imprisoned on it. I kept asking to use the bathroom. A few days later, when I heard the anchor being raised, I demanded to use the bathroom again. I locked the door from the inside and opened the porthole. I am very thin these days, and I went through it and fell into the water."

"Walstrom took you to the boat in a Zodiac?"

"We went by raft to the boat, traveling at a rather high speed."

"Describe the boat."

"I believe it was black and seemed to me very large. I have no knowledge of boats so I do not know what type of boat it was. I'm sorry I cannot give you a better description."

"See anything on deck?"

"You will find me very unobservant, but I noticed nothing because I had a gun held to my head as I clambered aboard."

"Where were you held?"

"In a tiny room with two bunk beds. A lovely blonde lady attended my every wish and told me stories, though after many days—I don't know how long—she vanished. I missed her. I grieved."

"Jenny Andover," Liza said. "I'm sure it was Jenny."

"Indeed, her name was Jenny. 'A wretch, a villain . . . can betray sweet Jenny's unsuspecting youth.' Perhaps she was betrayed by Walstrom. I do not know; I know only that she disappeared."

"Tango, I found her body," Liza said.

"'Give sorrow words.' She tended to me with such kindness. 'Yet she must die, else she'll betray more men . . .' She told me stories, told me about the boat. They were searching for gold. I have no idea how they were searching for it, over the bounding main, as it were. But they were geologists looking for gold."

"Jenny came to the *Salmon Eye* and told me she had a degree in geology," Liza told him. "I never thought about it— she said they were longlining."

"Good identification," Beringer said. "We'll go out there and look for a longliner."

"Not you," said Mink. "Not Tango. No way."

The lieutenant, or whoever he was, turned and looked

over his shoulder. There were so many people in the room, Beringer wasn't sure who he looked at—it could have been Liza or Tasha or even Mink. But Liza looked at the big man angrily and shook her head.

The lieutenant stood before Ted, his eyes narrowed. Finally he nodded, turned, and left the room.

47

.

WHY HAD HE QUESTIONED TANGO IN front of everybody? Lizzie had turned her back on him when he left. Pay attention to your job, Howard. He had to find that boat. Find out if Tango had been imprisoned on it or was working with them; could he have gone that night to Wrangell and shot Ellis or Walstrom or whatever his name was? Think, Paul. Who could help you find that boat?

When he got back to his office, he called the helicopter service. They could fly him out along Sumner Strait—that must be where the boat had gone—Tango was washed up on Joe Mace Island out by Port Protection. Maybe the boat had gone south from there. Or west. Wherever it had gone, he had to find it.

They were looking for gold. How the hell could they do that from a boat? You had to go up the Stikine for that, pan or dig into the earth, something like that. You couldn't do it from a boat.

How could he distinguish one boat from another from the air? Probably have a big Zodiac on it was all, if what Mark Bellamy and Tango had told him was true. Might be the only distinguishing feature. He groaned aloud.

The pilot headed along Sumner Strait, over Five Mile Island and Vank, then split the distance between Mitkof Island

and Zarembo. From that altitude, it was difficult to make out a lot of detail on boats—there was a tug with two barges in tow heading for the entrance to Wrangell Narrows. The helicopter continued west along Sumner Strait and from the air Paul could see the dock at Kashevarof, a couple of small boats tied up.

"Thought we'd go out as far as Point Baker and back on the other side," the pilot shouted. "Couple sport boats is all I see."

Paul nodded and slid his earphones back over his ears—the noise was giving him a headache. Or maybe it was the big zero he was getting searching for the boat.

At Point Baker there was one boat tied up at the float. It had a Zodiac swung on davits. How the hell could he tell if Tango had been aboard? All he had was Mark Bellamy's dubious report that Tango had gone out with somebody in a Zodiac with a big outboard. Gone tearing past, outboard throwing up a huge wake. And Tango's report that it was a raft, going very fast.

The pilot swung down over Port Protection and Labouchere Bay before he turned back, At the west end of Sumner Strait, close to Strait Island, Paul noticed a large black-and-gray boat. He pointed at it and the pilot dropped down toward it.

"Longliner," the pilot mouthed, and Paul nodded. He remembered seeing a black-and-gray longliner at the fuel dock the other day, the strange gear it had on deck. He tried to look back at it. The pilot turned again and passed closer to it and Paul could see blue oil drums and the shiny coils wedged between them.

"Think they're something to do with spill recovery, something like that," Paul shouted. "I saw them in at the fuel dock the other day. Let's not buzz them again. I don't want to scare them off."

He pressed against the side window and looked back at the longliner once more, trying to pick up her numbers. Started with 647, but he couldn't get the rest. This time, though, he noticed a large orange inflatable with a big outboard swung on davits. He remembered now that he'd seen that the other day at the fuel dock.

He tried to remember what day he'd seen that boat at the fuel dock. Seemed like it might have been the day Lizzie had called him about the whale. Then next time he saw Lizzie was the night they had dinner at the Coho. His thoughts reached a sudden block. He was holding her in his arms again, pressing his mouth to hers. The stirrings were growing urgent now—he shifted in his seat, pulled at his pants, adjusted things—he had to get a grip on himself

Think, Paul. That woman, Jenny, had told Lizzie she was on the same boat as Ellis. And right after that, Ellis was shot. And a few days later, the woman was shot. Of course, this boat might not be Ellis's. Most boats had inflatables. But that was a big outboard for a Zodiac. He was sure going to check on that longliner. First lead in the whole damn thing.

From his office Paul called as many agencies as he could think of, Coast Guard, Alaska Fisheries, even the Wrangell fuel dock. Yes, the attendant remembered the huge gray-and-black longliner—no, the guy had paid cash so there wasn't a check or credit-card receipt—been in at least three times. No idea where they were headed. Yeah, they'd had a console-drive Zodiac on davits—towing an aluminum skiff with an outboard. Noticed they seemed to have a lot of extra equipment—maybe they were headed offshore?

Paul thanked him and hung up. Not very far offshore right now. In fact, they were right there by Point Baker and he was going to check them out. Where to get a boat, though? He knew he shouldn't try to do it—he should get the state guys in—but he was the one who identified the dead guy on

Petroglyph Beach, wasn't he? And he was absolutely certain, well, pretty sure, that that longliner was the one Barney Ellis had been a crew member on. Frank Smith, skipper of a longliner, had told him Barney Ellis was missing, and the big Zodiac identified it.

How could he do it? One idea—he dialed the phone. "Hey, Arnie," he said. "Listen, I was wondering if I could borrow your boat."

48

BERINGER LAY ON HIS BACK AND STARED at the ceiling. His head had recovered pretty well—if he didn't move too abruptly, it just had a dull ache, no sharp pain. The man in the next bed was asleep, snoring gently. The nurse had restored his oxygen after he'd dozed off. Beringer needed to call the office and find out when he could get another boat.

He sat up and picked up the phone.

"Gonna be a while," the director said. *"First gotta get the insurance payment on the* Keltie. *Then we gotta find another boat. Maybe the first of the year."*

Beringer tried to argue.

"Can't do anything till we get that insurance—most likely be January before we can get a boat. January for sure, or could be a little sooner if we get the insurance and find a boat."

Beringer slammed the receiver down and swung his legs over the side of the bed. Taking great care not to jar his head, he got himself dressed in the clothes he'd worn when he'd been wrecked. He pulled on his wool socks. He was dizzy after bending over and clutched the bedside table for support. Last he crammed his feet into his rubber boots. The exposure suit wasn't there—he thought Liza might have it on the *Salmon Eye*. It would probably have a lot of blood on it from the gash on his head, but he'd take it back anyway.

He'd go out to Shoemaker and find the *Salmon Eye*. Maybe she'd take him to track the longliner. Now he discovered he had no wallet and no wristwatch. Someone must have put them into the hospital's safe. The clock on the wall said 7:20. He should wait for the doctor, but who knew when he'd get in. Could he go ahead and check himself out of the hospital? Pick up his wallet and watch? Yes. He could. He would. He needed to find the *Salmon Eye* and track that longliner.

He was comfortable sitting on the edge of the bed, nothing to make his head hurt, but he had to get going. He tried to gather his energy. Get moving, Beringer—you need to track that boat. He put his hands on the edge of the bed to push himself up and raised his head and there was Ted standing in the door.

He pointed at Beringer and said, "'The day's disasters in his morning face,'" then asked, "How are you?"

"Ready to go," Beringer said.

"And I, also. And where shall we go together?"

"To the *Salmon Eye*. Liza said she'd take you home and I hope after that she'll go tracking that longliner."

"Ahhh, my lady saith not. But perhaps I shall elude my lady fair and accompany you on your search."

"Come along. Have you been checked out yet?"

"The doctor has appeared and allowed me to leave my current prison. I am still fatigued, but improved."

". . . and here he is for me."

The doctor examined Beringer's stitches and asked him how he was feeling.

"Fine," said Beringer. "Very well indeed."

"That hairline fracture will heal with nothing done to it, but don't bang your head again. No pain?"

Beringer shook his head, regretting it immediately, but allowed that he had no pain.

"Okay," the doctor said. "You can go. Tango here can go, too. Everyone's free. I got twins coming in the next couple 'a hours, so get out of here."

Beringer stopped at the office to pick up his wallet and watch and give them his insurance card. Yes, they'd bill directly. No, nothing to pay right now. They'd get hold of him if the insurance didn't cover everything.

He called a taxi to go out to Shoemaker and Ted went too, right past Tasha's place, where Mink was staying. An icy rain with a few flakes of snow blew into their faces as they went down the steep ramp. The *Salmon Eye* wasn't in her slip. Jake ambled over and asked Beringer how he was.

"Pretty good," he said. "Dizzy when I bend over, but it's going away."

Jake turned to Ted. "Hey, Tango," he said. "Heard you got washed up on some beach. Whatcha doing way out there?"

"I eluded my captors and fell into the sea off a boat."

"Hunh," Jake said. "Fell? Off a boat? What were you doing on the boat?"

"'Imprisoned in the viewless winds.'"

"Hunh," Jake said again.

"Where's the *Salmon Eye*?" Beringer asked.

"Left early this morning to pick up freight."

"We need to track down a longliner and follow it for a while. Would you be for hire?"

"What'd the pay be?"

"How about two hundred dollars a day?"

"Plus fuel?"

"Oh, sure."

"Yeah, I could do that. Okay, sure, I'll do it. Climb on— take me a little to warm the engine up, but we'll go pretty soon. What boat we looking for?"

"Just a longliner. Probably pulling a big Zodiac. Black-hulled. At least Tango describes it that way," Beringer said.

"Hunh," Jake said, which seemed to be his answer to everything.

They climbed aboard and Jake started the engine. "Ain't got nothin' with ya?" he asked. "No rain gear?"

"These clothes are what we came in," Ted said. 'Then he rose, and donn'd his clothes.' These are all we have."

"I got extra. Beringer's got boots—you need some. Boots'll be kinda big on you, but I got extra. And I got rain gear for both 'a ya.

A pounding on the hull of the boat made them all look down. Mink stood there, her hands on her hips, her face furious.

"Standing there at the end of the drive waiting for Tasha when you guys went by in the taxi. Shitheads. You planning to go somewhere without me?"

Simultaneously all three men said, "Uhhhh. . . ."

"Yeah," Mink said. "Sneakin' out on me. Well I'm comin' along. And we're goin' home, me and Tango. That's our desti-tudi-nation. Help me up."

Beringer and Ted swung to the dock, each taking one of Mink's elbows. She braced herself, a hand on each shoulder, and they pushed her up onto the deck. She lumbered through the door into the wheelhouse and sank down on the bench. "Phee-ew," she grumbled. "Ain't in much shape to climb. So, now what? Take us home is what."

"Gonna look for the longliner," Jake said.

"Over my dead body," Mink said. "These guys are hurt and sick and no way are they gonna go after that longliner. Sheee-it."

" 'There were three sailors of Bristol City who took a boat and went to sea.' "

"Not on your life. Where's Liza? She'd give you hell for even thinkin' of it."

"Went to pick up freight," Jake said.

"Said she'd take us home," Mink said. "So she'll be back. We're goin' back to Tasha's and wait for her."

"'I can't do't, 'tis more than impossible,'" Ted said. "We shall search and then cease."

Mink tried to stare him down but he stood his ground, and finally she had to concede. "Shit, go ahead. Make fools of yourselves, do your damage. I don't wanta watch. Go on, get outa here."

She went back on deck and scrambled over the edge. Her legs were too short to reach the dock but she jumped for it and stalked off without looking back. Ted watched her go, his face pressed against the window, his hands clenched at his sides.

49

TODAY LIZA WOULD PICK UP FREIGHT and new books, some of which would go to Kashevarof. But where would Beringer go till he got a new boat? Well, that wasn't her problem. But his daughter was coming a week from tomorrow. He'd just have to rent a room till they found him a new boat. Anyway, he wasn't in shape yet to go back on the water.

She took the *Salmon Eye* to the freight dock. There she acquired seventy cases of canned goods, an eighteen-cubic-foot refrigerator, a spool of baling wire, one generator, three cases of motor oil, two chain saws, and a laundry sink. Then she went to the fuel dock and chatted with Richard while the tank filled.

"What's the gossip?" she asked.

"Ain't much—saw that policeman friend of yours early this morning."

"You did? What was he doing at the fuel dock?"

"Came in with some little boat, big outboard, filled a couple 'a tanks with gas."

"A skiff?"

"Nahhh, had a cabin on it, but it was kinda small. Maybe a police-department boat. Didn't say nothin' on the side, though."

"I don't know if they even have a boat. Did he head out of the harbor, or tie up across the way?"

"Oh, he took off, went right out of the harbor. Yeah, going somewhere for sure."

The handle clicked off and she paid Richard, puzzling over where Paul could have gone. Oh well, it wasn't her problem. Wow, she was getting pretty good at dismissing those things that had always weighed on her in her first life. "Not my problem" had become her motto now. She wouldn't worry about anyone else anymore. The joy of it.

She whistled for Sam and started the engine, then made a broken U-turn in the inner harbor and drove back along the transient dock, trying to see if the boat Richard had described was tied up there. Nothing like it appeared. Where had Paul gone?

She moored the *Salmon Eye* at the transient dock and trudged uphill to the police station. She had to know where Paul had gone. The woman at the counter shook her head and started to say something when Chief Woods appeared and waved her into his office.

"Howard's gone off in some little boat," he said. "I don't know what he's thinking about—he says he's looking for that longliner that might have had Tango on board. Howard knows that boat isn't in our jurisdiction—god, I can't believe he'd go off in this weather chasing some dumb boat."

"He's pretty independent, I guess."

"Yeah. He's stubborn as they come."

"What's the name of the boat?" she asked. "And the call numbers?"

"Don't know either one," the chief said. "I think he borrowed a boat from somebody he knew. He's pretty important to you, isn't he?"

"Well, uhhh, yes, actually he is. I was married to a cop

down south who was killed in a drug bust. But Paul is so . . . comforting."

"You were married to a cop? At least you'll be able to deal with Howard. He's stubborn as six donkeys and flat out pig-headed. I'd fire him tomorrow if I didn't like him so much."

"Well, so do I. And he lost Joey—I think that's what makes him so stubborn—he can't give up anything else."

"He has to figure out what he's doing out there—he's in bad trouble here, I can tell you. He needs a desk job, is what. And he'll get it, if he keeps this up."

50

ARNIE'S BOAT WAS A CHUGGER THAT didn't work too well—the outboard engine kept missing. Paul tried to set the choke up and it smoothed out a little, but it was still rough, the speed way less than he'd expect from a 150 Evinrude.

He wove his way past McArthur Reef and the Eye Opener, then dropped down toward Buster Bay. He'd turn past Point Baker, maybe anchor in Port Protection. By the time he got out there it would be dark—he needed to check out that boat and get back before the chief threw him out for insubordination. This was definitely not Wrangell's territory—Wrangell's boundary went right down the center of Zimovia Strait, about two miles offshore of Wrangell Island.

Continuously he thought about Lizzie—how he'd held her in the bunk, what she'd said about him, "prickly on the outside, soft inside," Well, he was, actually—he had to be to keep up his policeman image, and anyway, losing Joey had made him pretty bitter. But then she'd turned her back on him after he'd questioned Tango. He was on a slippery slope, for sure.

It seemed to Paul that the engine had slowed again— seemed to be sputtering a bit. He fiddled with the choke and throttle, trying to get it to settle down. He should be able to see the longliner now, if it was still there.

But it wasn't. He searched the gray water, the clouds halfway down the dark islands now, the visibility growing poorer by the minute. The storm had subsided but the waves were still high for such a little boat. At least it was a following sea. If he'd had to plow into it, the boat would never have made it.

He took the glasses and scanned the west end of Sumner Strait. Maybe the longliner had gone around to Port Protection or Labouchere—they'd been close enough to head for either one. Or maybe they'd headed farther south. Or across the strait.

Further on, he saw a canoe with a lot of men in it. Looked like a war canoe. He was hallucinating. He closed his eyes, then opened them. The canoe had pulled away from him, but he was going pretty fast—the canoe couldn't paddle as fast as he was going. He thought he heard a faint sound of drumming. What *was* it out there? He must have gone crazy.

Later he wondered what had distracted him. Some tiny thing, it must have been, some imperceptible detail caught from the corner of his eye. He'd turned his head, one split second only, then back, too late—much, much too late to avoid the collision. Two immovable forces sliding into each other before he could spin the wheel the other way.

He was thrown forward across the wheel, sliding down it, spinning it hard to port. Possibly that had reduced the force of the collision. The whale arched over before it dove. Maybe he'd been going too slow to cause it great injury, but he could still feel the moment of impact shuddering down his spine. He must have hurt that whale. A humpback— huge, lying there just under the surface—he should have seen it, if he hadn't had that momentary distraction.

Why was the whale lying there in the path of his small

boat? And what had caused his sudden distraction? He wracked his brain—a glimmer of something—what was it? Something moving, he thought—something orange. He massaged the back of his neck. He was going to regret this accident by tomorrow.

The canoe had vanished. There was a story he'd heard that a whale had gobbled up a canoe and taken the men to live at the bottom of the sea. In the story it was Killer Whale who had done that; Killer Whale was the one who would not release the men until they told him where their salmon traps were. Killer Whale was the one, but this was a humpback whale. He just didn't know about that.

The engine had quit altogether after the crash, and the boat was drifting rapidly in the outgoing tide and the fierce wind. He choked it and pushed the starter button, and it whirred futilely. A hundred yards away the whale breached and he stared at it, grabbing the binoculars just too late. There didn't seem to be any visible wound, but he hadn't seen the other side. On the other hand, he thought he'd hit this side of the whale—he hoped he hadn't caused it permanent harm.

The engine. Shit. He tried it again. Maybe it was flooded. He pushed the choke in, waited while he drifted farther down the strait, then tried again. Nothing. He had the little Honda ten-horse kicker—maybe he could get back with that, but he couldn't overtake the longliner without speed. He might need to make a quick escape, too.

He made his way to the transom, lowered the Honda and gave it a pull. Three more tries and it started. He had to sit out there on the transom, though, to steer with the smaller engine, and it was starting to rain, the clouds gathering in an ominous way, the wind rising. He'd have to go into Merrifield Bay east of Point Baker—he couldn't see anything in this rain. But somewhere out in the strait he thought he'd seen something orange.

He could work on the big engine and sleep over. It would be a long, long trip back to Wrangell with the kicker engine—and he certainly didn't want to be chugging along Sumner Strait in the dark. He had a sandwich—some crackers and cheese he'd jammed in his pack when he left to pick up Arnie's boat. A bottle of water. Rather have bourbon, but water would do. He turned into Merrifield and called the marine radio operator. "Get me the Wrangell Police Department.

"I'm out here looking for that boat that Tango said he was a prisoner on. Collided with a whale," he said to the dispatcher. "Some damn thing wrong with it. I'm staying here in Merrifield till morning—my engine quit and I don't want to have to go back in the dark with the small one. Yeah, I know the boat isn't in our jurisdiction—yeah, yeah, I'll call the state troopers, get them to take over. Okay—this is Paul Howard, clear."

After I find the boat. He called the marine operator again. "Patch me in to Wildlife, would you?"

"We're getting reports from all over," the woman at Wildlife said. *"Seems like some kind of epidemic or something. The biologist thinks it's noise. Biologist is in the hospital, though. Banged his head when his boat got wrecked up."*

"Noise? Like engines? They always keep out of the way of engine noise."

"He isn't sure what. Could be some kind of explosion or something like that. He thinks it destroys their direction-finding."

"Hunh. Haven't seen anything like that happening. I mean, somebody'd report blasting, you'd think."

"Well, we aren't sure what it is. Could be something else that affects them—but he's pretty sure it's got something to do with how they direction-find—how they visualize their

environment, distinguish food, things like that. Anyway, I'll let him know where you are."

Paul tied up at the little dock below the only house on the bay, then dragged the inflatable down from the roof of Arnie's boat and tossed it over. Gingerly hooking it with one foot, he let himself down into it, put the oars in the oarlocks and began to pull along the shore of the bay. Now he wasn't sure he'd seen anything. Probably just a boat. What else could have distracted him? Motion, and something orange. He glanced out at the strait. The rain had turned to light snow and visibility was almost nil, the wind creating a steep chop on the water, but he saw it again. Motion and something orange. Quietly he rowed toward it.

51

LIZA RETURNED THE *SALMON EYE* TO HER
slip around eleven in the morning, noting that the *Aquila*
was gone. She put the "old" new books into milk crates,
hoisted them over the rail and stacked the crates on the hand
truck, Sam dashing ahead of her up the ramp. At the top of
the ramp she found Mink. And Mink was furious, stomping
and kicking at the logs that rimmed the parking lot, her
speech incoherent. Eventually Liza made out that Tango had
gone off with Beringer, "looking for that stupid longliner,"
Mink said, raging aloud.

"Who did they go with?" Liza asked.

"That dumb ding-dong on the gillnetter across from you."

"Jake? I can't imagine Jake going out in this weather."

"Probably paid him. Anyway, that's who they went with."

"Well, I'll take you home, but first I have to go to the library."

Mink folded her arms across her chest and stormed over
to the truck. Liza put the crates and hand truck and Sam in
the truck bed and started the truck. Mink climbed in and
muttered to herself, some of it loud enough for Liza to hear.
"Shouldn't be doin' it," Mink grumbled, "one sick, one
hurt." Her voice fell to a low rumble, but she carried on all
the way to town.

The Irene Ingle Library was another modern building, having been remodeled and updated, tall cedar boards for the siding with huge glass windows in the front. Mary Stanton was working the desk. Mary's flesh was composed of patience, her bones filled with kindness. The Library Board could scarcely contain its glee when Liza took over the book-mo-boat/freighter and stopped meeting the Wrangell public as head librarian.

Well, she just didn't like whining, that was all. It seemed to her that people who had real problems never whined. And the whining at the library was almost always related to pages that had offended the eye of the reader. "I don't think the library ought to allow this book on their shelves," went the melody, and the works concerned sex or profanity or, god forbid, humanism.

Liza liked to be certain of the nature of the complaint before she took the matter to the board. "Show me the pages," she demanded, politely, of course. "This? Right here? This paragraph where it says . . ." And she'd read it slowly and in a clear voice and rather loudly to be absolutely certain there could be no mistake: that those were indeed the words causing the reader's distress. And complaints dwindled, though Liza Romero's name came up now and then in small gatherings and anonymous letters to the board.

Mink sat in one of the chairs at the table, her arms folded. Her expression was fierce and black. Finally she put her elbows on the table and her head in her hands.

"Trade some?" Liza asked Mary.

"Sure—whatever you want. Just don't take the ones on the new-book shelf—they're the latest to come in. I'll help you, till somebody comes to the desk."

Liza knew most people loved suspense and mystery so she took dozens of them. Tom Clancy, Danielle Steel, Maeve Binchy, Stephen King, John Grisham—everyone loved to read those. Took a bunch of biographies, too—books on Vietnam, the Second World War, the Civil War—men liked to read about those things, men who'd never even been in those wars liked to read about them.

Finally she had refilled the crates. Mary had had to go back to the desk, answering a question for one patron, checking out books for several others, showing one how to get on the Internet.

Several people spoke to Liza, one haranguing her about taking the boat out in the winter, how dangerous it was to be out there, ". . . and you all alone, too."

"Oh, but I'm not," she said. "I always have my dog, Sam."

"You don't wanta go out there in the winter. Unnhh-unnh," he said. "You gotta stay on shore in winter—way too much wind out there."

"Well, I'm careful—I don't go when there's a gale warning." Only she had—right into the teeth of that storm. Well, she'd handled it all right, but she'd been pretty scared out there with those seas coming over the boat.

She waved to Mary and trundled the crates out to the truck, Mink trudging along far behind. Sam was yearning over the tailgate at a small black-and-white dog with one flop ear, one erect. She shooed him back and hoisted the crates over, then backed out of the parking lot and went over to the post office, the social gathering spot in Wrangell. Lots of people greeted her as they trudged up the steps of the vintage granite and marble edifice built in the late '30s.

She grabbed the mail from her box—mostly junk mail—no, not everything—a letter from Paul with an apology—he regretted his words—he hated for her to be angry with him—he'd signed it, love. . . . The letter made her sad—he'd thought so much about his words when she'd dismissed them, dismissed him from her mind—no . . . no, she hadn't—she could never dismiss Paul Howard, not since the very first time she'd met him.

Liza drove the truck back along Zimovia Highway, noting that the wind was rising again, whitecaps along Zimovia Strait, clouds halfway down Woronkofski Island across from Wrangell, a few tall spruce nailing the clouds to earth. She parked the truck at Shoemaker and she and Mink got out. Liza listened to a pair of bald eagles shriek in the stand of spruce around the campground to the north. She tried to see where they were—finally found them near the very top of the tallest tree. They nested up near Rainbow Falls— she'd seen their nest in an old snag, but today they were here fishing. They'd add to their nest in March and lay their eggs in late April, the fledglings' first flight near the Fourth of July.

Sam raced up and down the ramp. Liza moved the crates of books down, gripping the railing with one hand and the hand truck with the other, the ramp steep at low tide. Mink dragged back on the other side of the hand truck, her weight sufficient to keep it from zipping down the ramp.

It was beginning to rain—she had plastic over the books but the wind was tearing it off. Liza stopped to tuck it in more firmly. Mink set the crates of books up on deck and Liza piled them in the cabin. Then Liza said, "Mink, I'll take you home, but you've gotta get rid of that ugly mood."

"Hunh," Mink said, "shouldn'a gone off like that," her tears streaming.

Liza put her arms around her. "Jake's a fine sailor. They'll be all right," she said.

52

"Visibility's pretty poor," Jake said. "Don't think we're likely to find that longliner. And the wind's blowing, too. Whitecaps out here."

"Maybe you don't want to do it," Beringer said.

"Ahh, heck, for two hundred bucks a day, I'll do anything. But I doubt we can pick up the longliner—she'll be hiding in the rain." Jake steered the *Aquila* around Elephant's Nose and past the upper end of Zarembo Island. "Wanta go into St. John and look for her?" he asked.

"Last time I saw her," Beringer said, "she was way out by Point Baker. Let's head out there, and if we can't find her, we'll check Port Protection, Labouchere Bay, go across to Port Beauclerc. She's a big boat so I think we can find her."

Jake turned to the weather station. *"Gale warning, inside waters,"* the announcer said. *"Seas to twelve feet."* "Hunh," Jake said. "We can do it, but it'll be hard. Gotta sit down on that bench, the two of you, not go pacin' around like you're doin'."

Beringer and Tango sat down on the small bench behind the captain's chair, crammed against each other, and braced themselves with their feet. The boat pitched and rolled and Jake tried to quarter the waves to decrease the motion. Beringer and Tango were too low now to be able to look out the window. Beringer stood up and braced his legs far apart, grabbing the shelf under the window and looking out. His head hurt and the motion of the boat made his stomach queasy. He'd never been seasick on the *Keltie*—he thought the motion that made his head hurt also made his stomach sick.

Tango stayed on the bench and said, "The boat was black. We went extremely fast."

"Where was the boat at the time?" Beringer asked.

"Among islands. I saw whales there among the islands. They scattered when we went by so fast."

Beringer said, "They must have taken the raft to the Velvet Moose that night of the fight. And then Walstrom came back the next morning and took you away."

"I believe that is what happened."

There was silence after that in the wheelhouse. The boat was rolling fiercely. "You better sit down," Jake told Beringer. Jake was clinging hard to the wheel, still quartering the waves that were getting higher and higher. Spindrift was blowing off the crests now, and the *Aquila* plunged down the side of one wave and rose on the next.

"Might hafta go in to Red Bay," Jake said. "Can't take a lot more 'a this."

Beringer nodded, grabbed the rail behind him and lowered himself onto the bench next to Tango. Jake steered the boat past McArthur Reef and turned down. The waves came now from the side so he had to tack back and forth, trying to make his way to the entrance of Red Bay.

"High-water slack is the only time I'll go in—kelp markers then, but they go under in the current. 'Bout five knots current in the entrance between tides," Jake said. He grabbed the tide table and looked at it. "We'll prob'ly get there before high slack—right time to go in, but the slack is very short."

Beringer said, "I went in once at mid-current and got turned all the way around."

"Sure. That's what happens."

Jake made his way into the narrow entrance between Bell Island and Danger Island, then he went along the Danger Island shore till he got halfway through the entrance, then turned across to the Bell Island side to avoid a rock at the southeast point of Danger Island. The current was still swift and little whirlpools formed, but he steered the boat steadily, going around Flat Island to a little bay east of it. He signaled for Beringer to go out on deck to release the anchor.

Beringer grabbed Jake's rain jacket and climbed out. He released the brake and the anchor went down with a clank. Jake backed down on it and turned the engine off. Beringer stood there a moment, savoring the silence. The rain beat down on him, but this place was protected from the wind, whatever direction it came from. It had taken them six hours to get just this far—they'd left at ten that morning, and it was already dark. Jake had turned the floodlight on in order to see where the entrance was. Reluctantly, Beringer returned to the wheelhouse.

"Beer," Jake said. "Plenty of it."

Beringer took off his rain jacket and they all went below. Jake screwed the caps off three beer bottles, raised his bottle and said, "Safe harbors."

Beringer and Tango toasted that and Tango set his beer down. "'I'm only a beer teetotaller, not a champagne teetotaller,'" he said. "That's from Shaw's play *Candida*. You can have my beer. In fact, I don't like champagne, either. You got any Coke?"

Jake brought out a can of Pepsi.

"Cheers," Tango said.

Beringer's stomach was still unsettled. He set his bottle

down on the table and leaned back. His head ached, too. But he'd be entirely well by the time Sarah came.

Tango started talking and he listened, the words passing his ears but not really entering his brain.

". . . rifle shots in the night, a lot of them. Why would they need so many shots? I, for one, wondered who would be hunting on the water."

"Could be shooting geese," Jake said, "or ducks."

"At night?"

"Well, I guess if you could see anything, maybe geese floating on the water, something like that? Maybe turned their flood on and blinded 'em."

Slowly the words began to penetrate Beringer's brain. He'd heard those shots, too. When he was following the whales. "Rifle shots?" he asked.

"I do believe they were rifle shots."

"At regular intervals?"

"Yes, they were at regular intervals."

"I heard them, too. I was following the whales, and the shots might have been coming from the longliner, but I don't know. It was too murky to see much."

Beringer thought about it for a while. Then he said, "You know, those might have been seismic airguns."

"Seismic airguns? Do they sound like rifles?"

"Yes—like the crack of a rifle. They're towed behind a boat to explore the ocean bottom for oil or minerals. Then they're recorded by hydrophones and a tracing is made showing where there might be hard minerals below the bottom surface. Maybe that's how that longliner was looking for gold. You said they had geologists on board.

"Glaciers, like those up the Stikine, grind gold away from the earth's crust and the gold flows into undersea rivers. If you've been looking at seismic scans a while you can make a pretty good guess at where the gold lies. But seismic airguns are illegal in southeast Alaska waters. No private company could do it."

There was a long silence. Then Beringer said, "That's it! If the airguns were towed through a pod of whales, they'd damage the whales' ears or maybe dislodge the magnetite particles in their brains. Those airguns release high-pressure air into the water—a pressure pulse of several hundred pounds per square inch. And they make a huge noise, which is transmitted through water for hundreds of miles—some of them operate at acoustic frequencies of more than one thousand hertz. *That's* what's happening to the whales!"

"Canned spaghetti or baked beans?" Jake said.

53

IT WAS DARK WHEN LIZA AND MINK GOT to Kashevarof. The wind had risen, churning Clarence Strait into a mighty froth. Mink was silent the whole way across, a sullen silence, Liza thought.

Mink dragged Liza up the hill to the Velvet Moose. "Feed her something," she told Jimmy. "Steak, somethin' like that. And me, too." Then Mink went up the hill to her house to see if Tango was home.

"Not there," she said when she got back. "Still lookin'. Don't know how long he'll keep lookin'—till he finds it, I guess. Well, good luck to him, I don't think."

"Mink, calm down. Either they'll find it or they won't. And he'll be back sooner or later."

"Hunh," said Mink.

Liza took Sam for a walk, then threw herself into her bunk when she got back. She was exhausted, on overload, but sleep didn't come. She turned on her back and stared into the dark. What if Paul hadn't found that longliner? What if the wind and the waves had been too much for the outboard?

She'd better go out there and look for him. Not now, though. It was too dark to see a small boat carried by the waves, the waves huge, the wind still rising. She sat up and put her feet on the floor and Sam leaped up from the cushion where he slept. There could be no further sleep with such anxiety about Paul. The night was going to be endless.

She mounted the steps, turned the cabin lights on and looked at the clock. 1:53 A.M. She would go and look for Paul.

The lights at the Kashevarof dock were dim against the black sky, and snow twisted slowly under them. Liza went through the entrance and turned the *Salmon Eye* north. She felt swallowed up by the dark. Waves crested and broke, shooting spindrift behind them. She crept along the edge of Prince of Wales Island, a huge land mass that seemed to have no end. The wind was still rising and the seas steep. Following seas, this time, and the *Salmon Eye* was pushed along a lot faster than when she'd made the trip a few days ago with the tide against her. The tide had gone slack now, would turn and ebb soon.

Liza checked the floodlight on the roof—she might need to use it. She'd have to steer close to shore, aim the light onto the rocks and beaches—he'd be there, somewhere he'd be—she'd shout, wake him up, listen to his voice grumbling at being woken up, then he'd see her, he'd climb out of the boat, stand on the deck, hold his arms out. That's how it would be. She shivered, thinking it might not be like that.

She tried to follow the shoreline, not too closely though—there were rocks and shallows—Pine Point protruded—the surf pounding over it. She went into Red Bay. The slack was gone and there were whirlpools everywhere. She turned the floodlight on and scanned the shore. Nothing. Making her way back through the entrance, the *Salmon Eye* yawing in the whirlpools, she turned west again. There was a boat far ahead of her on the radar screen, right at the edge of it. Who would be out on a night like this?

She dipped down along the edge of Buster Bay, turning the floodlight along the shore, picking up no small boat—nothing but a rocky beach. The *Salmon Eye* was tearing along now with a following sea and an outgoing tide. Must be the dark and the howling wind that made it seem so long, as well as her worries about Paul.

Merrifield Bay: there was a notch in the east side of the bay with a house sitting above it, a dock below the house, and a small boat tied to the dock. Maybe Paul's boat? She couldn't get the *Salmon Eye* in close enough to tie up to the dock. She released the anchor and listened to it rattle down. She thought he might have heard it too, but no one appeared. She threw the raft over and tried to grab Sam before he launched himself into it, but was just too late. Oh, well, maybe essence of wet dog would have to be Paul's alarm clock.

She grabbed a flashlight, tossed in a life preserver, hung her legs from the deck and slid into the raft. Grabbing the oars, she pulled for the dock. Sam, in the bow, whined, then barked. Surely Paul would have heard that bark. Where was he?

Tying the raft behind the little boat, she switched the flashlight on and noted the name on the stern: *McDuff*. Sam had bounded over and was sniffing along the side of the boat. Liza climbed onto the dock and went over to the boat, bending to look in. There wasn't much to see—a wheel, some electronics, a tiny V-berth ahead of the wheel that was empty. No one aboard. Where was he? There were a few tracks in the snow along the dock but they didn't seem to go anywhere.

Surely this was the boat he'd borrowed. An outboard, Woods had said. There was a big outboard, raised, a small one in the water—where was Paul now?

She paced the dock, then went up to look in the windows

of the house—a big deck, the windows shuttered. She pounded on the door, waited, pounded again. Nothing. And anyway, there were no tracks in the snow up to it, although the snow might have covered them up by now. Maybe he'd gone over to Point Baker just as she'd imagined, hanging out at the restaurant, sleeping on the floor. She looked at the small boat again—there was no raft on it, no skiff tied to it. That must be where he'd gone, although the weather was so bad she didn't think he would have set out last night to row all that way. Shit, where was he?

She returned to the boat and found the door was unlocked. Before she could restrain him, Sam leaped into the well and forced his way through the door. Liza recognized Paul's backpack, an old one, the leather on it worn. Sam sniffed everything, obviously hoping Liza would share the sandwich Paul had in his backpack, then plunged through the door and bayed. She shuddered. Sam never sounded like that unless he sensed that something was wrong. The way he'd bayed when he found James on that rock—when he found Jenny Andover.

Maybe Paul had gone ashore and set up camp. She'd go back to the *Salmon Eye* and turn the floodlight on, scanning the shore with it. But a faint light had appeared in the sky—a dawn so leaden she could make out no features of the land. She glanced at her watch. Seven o'clock. She had wasted the entire night coming out here to find Paul, and he was nowhere.

She whistled to Sam but he had disappeared. From a long distance she heard him bay again. No, she wouldn't go and look. Yes, she would—maybe he'd found Paul. A terrible convulsion rattled her bones. If he'd found Paul, Paul must be . . . She couldn't say it.

With her flashlight she scanned the snow for Sam's tracks and began to follow them, her eyes blinded by tears. At last she found him where the wreckage of the *Keltie* had lain. She glanced down, at last forcing herself to look at what lay there now. A small red inflatable had been driven onto the rocks by the tide and wind. One tube was collapsed. The name on the little raft was *McDuff.*

54

BERINGER LAY AWAKE FOR A TIME,
thinking about the seismic airguns. If the crew of the longliner was searching for gold, and Tango had said that's what
they were doing, then probably they were dragging the strait
with airguns. And that would account for the disorientation
of the whales.

He turned on his side, then rolled onto his back again,
staring into the darkness. He was terribly tired and his head
ached steadily. His bunk was narrow. He'd had a V-berth all
to himself on the *Keltie*. He thought about Sarah, how she'd
be coming up the day before Thanksgiving. He knew now
what day that was—not this week, but the one after it. He'd
be able to keep her, since Andrea had lied to him about Ted's
death.

He turned on his side again. Jenny had told Tango all
about their search for gold, and now Jenny was dead. And
Ellis was dead, too. Ellis, or whatever his name was. Who
had killed Jenny and Ellis? And why had they been killed?
Because they were talking too much? Because they knew
too much? To throw suspicion on Tango? That seemed the
likeliest explanation. Tango had recognized Ellis as one of
the pilots who had blown away his platoon, so he could have

murdered the man. But he hadn't. Puzzling over this, Beringer fell asleep.

He awoke to the roar of the engine. He heard Jake stomping around on deck, heard the rattle of the anchor chain. It was dark below. He threw himself from the borrowed sleeping bag and mounted the ladder to the wheelhouse. It was dark up here, too. Tango was sitting on the bench and Jake came through the door of the wheelhouse and put the engine in gear. "Gotta go out on high slack," he said. "Only time to go because of the current."

Beringer nodded and looked at his watch. 4:15. In the morning? Sure. They'd spent the whole night here, and high slack had been 3:45 yesterday afternoon. His head still ached, and he was still extremely tired, but his stomach seemed better. Jake steered the *Aquila* through the long entrance to Red Bay, and they were out in the strait again. The wind had died down a bit and the seas were less, too.

"You guys fix breakfast," Jake said. "There's cereal, bread, might be eggs, but I dunno. I'll eat later. But I need coffee. Fix coffee first."

Beringer brought coffee to the skipper. "Where're we going?" he asked.

"Said the boat was out around Point Baker last you saw it," Jake said. "We'll head there first."

"Really dark," Beringer said. "We could miss her along the shore."

"She's got running lights. Or an anchor light if she's anchored. We'll catch her."

Eventually the *Aquila* rounded Point Baker. Nothing at all in sight, no fishing boat, no tug and barge, no freighter, no longliner. It was growing light and the sun poked a single ray beneath the low black clouds.

"Whatcha wanta do?" Jake asked.

"Try Port Protection," Beringer said. "Then Labouchere Bay. Hole in the Wall."

"No longliner could get in there. Too deep a draft."

Beringer grabbed the chart. "Says here, one fathom two feet at low tide. That's eight feet. If they went in at the high, they could make it safely."

"Hunh," said Jake.

They circumnavigated Port Protection, checking behind the small islands, checking Wooden Wheel Cove, finding nothing. "Gotta go back to Point Baker for lunch," Jake said. "They got great lunches. And we gotta get more food at the grocery, and fuel up."

At Point Baker, they asked the restaurant owner/cook/ waitress if she had ever seen a black-hulled longliner come in.

"Been a couple in here," she said. "Both of 'em took on diesel, and one crew bellied up to the bar, drank like there was no tomorrow. Short woman, tall man. Seemed to be all there were."

Tango said, "There were more, once upon a time."

"And what happened to them?"

"The rest are dead."

"Yow," she said. "They died?"

Tango nodded solemnly.

55

LIZA DRAGGED THE LITTLE INFLATABLE over the rocky ridge. Why had Paul set out in that inflatable when the seas were so high and the winds so strong? Where could he have been going?. He hadn't drowned, though. He'd swum to shore, made a fire—she'd see the smoke and rescue him.

Sam ran back and forth, wanting her to follow him, looking back over his shoulder to be sure she was. Her footsteps were slow, her eyes blind. Finally she dragged the inflatable to the dock and fastened it to her own. Sam jumped in and she rowed back to the *Salmon Eye*. The other raft flopped sideways because one tube was deflated.

She cleated the smaller raft to the stern of the *Salmon Eye* and put her raft next to it. Then she went in and threw herself facedown on the bench, crying out at a world gone wrong. Later she fell asleep. When she woke, the sky was growing dark and the wind was rising again. She sat up on the bench and rubbed her eyes. Sam sat by her knee and she bent over and hugged him.

She rowed Sam to shore in her own raft. A light snow was falling, veiling the shore. The branches of the spruces and cedars were covered with snow. Liza found it lovely and peaceful. When she came back, she rounded the stern of the *Salmon*

Eye. One of the tubes was totally flat on the raft named *McDuff*. She felt along the tube, There was a tiny round hole in it. She felt along underwater and came across another little hole. Something had gone all the way through it and come out the other side. No rock would puncture both sides of the tube. She puzzled over it. What had Paul done that could have caused that little hole? It must be a bullet hole. No, Paul had not been shot, either. He *wasn't* dead.

Sam had jumped onto the deck, and Liza pulled herself up and cleated the raft on the stern cleat next to the *McDuff*. She would stay here tonight—Sam would need to go ashore again late in the evening and in the morning, too. She wouldn't look at Paul's boat tied up at the dock, refused to look.

Finally she took down the radio transmitter. What could she say? Talk to Chief Woods.

"*Salmon Eye* calling the Wrangell Police Department. Please get me Chief Woods."

"*Chief Woods here.*"

"This is the *Salmon Eye*. Shift to sixty-eight. I think it was Paul's boat at the dock in Merrifield Bay—I'm sure it was— I recognized his pack, but he wasn't on it. The name on it was *McDuff*. And I found an inflatable blown up on the rocks on the point, and the name on it was *McDuff* too, but I refuse to think he drowned."

There was a long silence. Then the chief said, "*No. I won't believe that either. We'll find him. We'll send someone out to look for him. We'll do everything we can to find him.*"

"I'm staying here in Merrifield tonight. Maybe he'll come back here. I think he rowed somewhere. At least, the inflatable blew up on the point, no oars in it, and one of the tubes was collapsed. It probably has a bullet hole through it. But I refuse to think he was shot, either."

"*We'll find him, Liza.*"

"Yes. We *will* find him. I'm clear."

56

THE *AQUILA* WENT TO THE FUEL DOCK
at Point Baker, then out again through the rocky entrance.
Beringer asked Jake if he'd like him to take over the wheel
for a while. Jake shrugged, then nodded. "Take a nap after
lunch," Jake said. "Always do when I'm home." He went
below and Beringer took over the wheel. Tango had
stretched out on the bench. "I would like to have my radio,"
he said. Beringer turned the volume up on the *Aquila*'s radio
and poked the scanner.

Beringer made his way south through the reefs till he got
to Labouchere Bay. There was no longliner in there, only a
gillnetter, its net still wound on the drum. A woman waved
to them from the shore, then turned and walked up the road
to the abandoned logging camp.

Beringer turned the *Aquila* back through the entrance,
then turned south. He didn't know where to go next. He didn't
think the longliner would have gone into Hole in the Wall—
it was such a narrow entrance, shallow too, and there wasn't
a lot of swinging room in the little bay. He passed the Bar-
rier Islands, went into Shakan Bay, nothing there, went into
Shipley Bay, nothing there. Where had that boat gone? He'd
better look on the other side of the strait, along Kuiu Island.
He'd been in Port Beauclerc when he'd rescued that

whale—maybe that's where they were. Or Affleck Canal? Too many bays, too many places to look.

He went a little farther south, then turned north again, heading toward Kuiu Island. Where the hell were they? Had they abandoned their project, quit and gone home? Or had they located gold on the bottom of the ocean and were going to drill for it? They couldn't do that; drilling wasn't allowed in southeast. Some sort of clandestine operation, maybe.

He headed for Port Beauclerc. Maybe they were in there. Probably not. A wild-goose chase this was. And all for nought. They should get in the state troopers, let them find the boat and see if they were dragging airguns. He reached for the radio transmitter. Then he heard a familiar voice.

"... rowed somewhere. At least, the inflatable blew up on the point, no oars in it, and one of the tubes was collapsed. It probably has a bullet hole through it. But I refuse to think he was shot, either."

"We'll find him, Liza."

"Yes. We will find him. I'm clear."

Liza's voice over the radio. He was sure of it.

He'd call her on channel sixteen, the all-call channel, and then switch if she answered. "This is the Aquila calling the Salmon Eye, Aquila calling the Salmon Eye. Come in, please."

She came right back. "This is the Salmon Eye."

"Switch to channel seventy," Beringer said. "Where are you?"

"In Merrifield Bay," she said. "Is this Jake?"

"No, Scott Beringer," he said. "We're searching for that longliner that had Tango imprisoned on board. Tango said the boat was black, and I've been tracking a black longliner called the Sophie Marie."

"Is Tango with you?"

"Yes."

"Mink's furious. I took her home, and then came out here to search for Paul Howard. His boat's tied up here at the dock in Merrifield but he's not here and I found an inflatable washed up on the point with the same name on it. But I refuse to believe he's drowned." He heard her take a deep breath before she let off the transmitter button.

"We're out near Port Beauclerc," Beringer said. "Shall we come over there? We could search for him—maybe he's just made camp somewhere along the shore."

"Come if you want," she said, *"I'm clear."*

"Who's Paul Howard?" he asked Tango.

"A lieutenant with the Wrangell police," Tango told him. "Liza had some relationship with him last spring, after the first death."

"Who died?"

Tango said, "A multiplicity of deaths there were, some necessary, some not," and he fell into silence from which Beringer could not rouse him.

They'd go to Merrifield, look for Paul Howard along the way, and maybe they could comfort Liza. Jake came up from below, yawning and stretching, and told Beringer he'd take the wheel again. They exchanged places in the captain's chair. "Where we going?" Jake asked.

"Merrifield Bay," Beringer said. "The *Salmon Eye* is in there. We'll look for Paul Howard along the way, though— he might have gone to shore and set up camp. His inflatable may have floated away and been driven up on the rocks."

"Paul Howard. Wears a badge. Gover'ment. Hate the gover'ment."

"Why is that?"

"Makes laws, regulations, can't go fishing except when they say, can't crab except when they say—hunh."

Snow was falling heavily by the time they reached Merrifield Bay and the sky was pitch dark. "Don't know this bay," Jake said.

Beringer grabbed the chart and noted a rock awash. "Stay to the east side of the entrance," he said.

The *Salmon Eye* was anchored in the center of the bay and they rafted to it, Tango going out and dropping fenders over the side of the *Aquila*. Liza came out on deck and took their lines, cleating them down before Jake shut the engine down. The three men climbed over and went into the cabin and Tango took Liza in his arms.

" 'Make dust our paper, and with rainy eyes, write sorrow on the bosom of the earth,' " he said.

57

AT MIDNIGHT LIZA SAT UP, TURNED ON
the light, and picked up her book. She turned the pages without reading them. She was numb to all feeling, her mind a
blank. At four in the morning, she went up and put the kettle
on. She'd make herself some tea, then head back to
Wrangell, looking for a fire, any sign of life, along the shore.
But the *Aquila* was rafted to the *Salmon Eye*. Well, they'd
just have to put down an anchor when she left.

She looked over at the *Aquila*. Scott Beringer was in the
wheelhouse and waved to her. She went out on deck and
called to him. "Want some tea?"

He nodded and climbed over both rails. "I couldn't
sleep," he said. "I just don't know what to do. I'd like to find
that longliner, but maybe we should just get the state troopers to look for it."

"Whatever," Liza said. "My mind's a blank—I can't think
anymore."

"You had some kind of relationship with Paul Howard?"

"I . . . yes . . . yes, I did. He was kind to me after . . . after
the events of last spring. Death and destruction."

"Maybe he's safe somewhere."

"I found that little raft blown up on the rocks and I think
he rowed somewhere. But I'm determined not to think he's

dead. He must have swum to shore and made a fire. I'll cruise the shoreline looking for smoke."

"Maybe you'll find that longliner somewhere before I do," Beringer said.

"You were thinking of getting the state troopers to look for it."

"Oh, I don't know. The problem is, I don't have a boat to use. If I had a boat I'd hunt for it, never mind the state troopers. If they're dragging seismic airguns through pods of whales, then I'll get the state troopers in. It seems to me that's how they must be looking for gold."

"Seismic airguns? What are those?"

"They're towed behind a boat to look for oil or hard minerals. The high energy blasts from them look at the sediments all the way down to the basaltic rock bottom. Hydrophones are towed also, and transmit the echoes from the various strata. Then, from the tracings on the charts, you can differentiate oil from hard minerals, gold from magnesium, or tin. They operate at hundreds of pounds of air pressure per square inch, and they make an explosive noise, sometimes above one thousand hertz."

"I might have heard those shots when I was anchored in Labouchere Bay," Liza said. "I thought someone was hunting over on Protection Head, but it might have come from the water beyond it. A lot of shots. They might have been, what do you call it?"

"Seismic airguns."

"Yes. Seismic airguns. Shots at regular intervals?"

"Right. Sounds like a rifle far away, but at regular intervals, and when you get up close, they're way louder than a rifle. I think that's how the longliner is looking for gold," Beringer said. "You said Andover had a degree in geology, and Tango said the crew was looking for gold. So that must be what's going wrong with the whales. A huge explosive noise, and enormous air pressure would destroy the whales' hearing."

"Oh, I'm sure that's what's doing the damage," Liza said. "Tango said, 'at night.' They wouldn't see the whale spouts if it was dark, and they might just go through the pod anyway. Yes, yes, you've found it—I'm sure of it."

"Well, I really need to find that longliner and see the name on it. Then I'll get the state troopers in. Could you . . . maybe . . . would you be willing to take me to look for it?"

"Well, I don't know. First I have to look for smoke along the shoreline. I'll have to go along the shore east of Merrifield—Paul may be somewhere past here, washed up somewhere, made a fire. You looked around Point Baker, didn't you? I hope he's safe—just can't believe he's dead."

"I'm sure you'll find him alive."

"Oh, I suppose I could do it after that, look for the longliner. They shoot people though, you know."

"You really don't want to do it," Beringer said, "but I just have to see her name and see if she's towing seismic airguns before we call the troopers in."

"No," Liza said, "I don't want to do it, but since you don't have a boat anymore, I guess I'll have to."

"Thanks," Beringer said. "Thanks so much for looking. And I know you'll find Howard alive—I'm sure of it."

Liza went out and pulled the little raft called *McDuff* onto the stern deck. She didn't want it flopping all over while she searched the shoreline. Beringer climbed back over both rails, and went below to get his gear.

Sam was dancing around wanting to go ashore. She had her own raft in the water, so she rowed to the beach with him. The snow had turned to a fine mist—it was warmer and the wind had dropped. She spotted a helicopter searching the shoreline—they were looking for Paul. Then another helicopter right down the center of Sumner Strait, looking for his body floating. No, she couldn't believe he had drowned. No, no.

When Sam came back, she rowed to the *Salmon Eye* and dragged the inflatable onto the deck, then put it on the cabin top, strapping it down. Her muscles told her what to do, her mind did not.

She started the engine, letting it warm up while she went out on deck to cast off the *Aquila*. Tango came out on deck and said, "We're going home. 'Home is where the heart is.'"

"To Kashevarof?" Liza asked.

"To Kashevarof," he said.

"And then Wrangell?"

"The *Aquila* will return to Wrangell, from whence it came."

Beringer came out on deck with his gear and climbed back over the rail. He'd already told them that Liza was going to help him search for the longliner and they'd have to put an anchor down if they wanted to stay in Merrifield Bay. But Jake was in the wheelhouse now, raising his hand to her before starting his engine. She waved back, went into her own wheelhouse and put the engine in gear. She wouldn't look at the *McDuff*, still tied at the dock, but then she did, watching till it was out of sight. A forlorn boat. And empty. Empty.

A rockbound coast, this north shore. She had the radar set on one mile, and the *Aquila*, she assumed it was the *Aquila*, came and went on it. Right at the edge of the screen, a larger boat passed her, going in the opposite direction. Might it be the longliner? She asked Beringer to go out on deck and try to get a look at it, but he saw no trace of it and came in shaking his head.

Liza scoured the shore, searching for smoke, a fire, anything that would tell her Paul was safe. Beyond a tiny ridge well behind Buster Bay she saw smoke rising. She turned in to the bay. The *Aquila* passed them, the two men waving at them.

Liza pointed at the smoke. "I see smoke over there," she said. "I'm going to look at it, see if Paul's there."

"I'll go with you," Beringer said.

Liza asked Beringer to go out and release the brake on the anchor windlass. He went out to the foredeck and pushed the brake over on the winch that set the anchor—they both listened as the chain rattled down. When it was on the bottom, Liza reversed the engines, letting out more chain, then signaled to Beringer when she wanted the brake set again. She backed down on the anchor to set it.

They put on their wet gear and boots. Liza rediscovered the folded-up newspaper in the pocket of her jacket. "You can read the story about Henry Sizemore getting drowned when we come back," she said. "I couldn't read it. I wrote to his wife, but I didn't want to read the story."

They rowed the inflatable to shore and trudged along Buster Creek. Buster Bay was flat almost to the road, but there was a small ridge that hid the smoke that was rising. From the ridge she looked down on a cabin. Smoke was rising from a metal chimney. A woodstove, she thought. They made their way through the trees to the cabin, and Liza knocked on the door. There were slow footsteps behind it, and somebody opened the door only a crack. One eye looked out, red and rheumy, staring at Liza and Beringer standing on the step in front of the door.

"Have you seen Paul Howard?" Liza asked. "He's a lieutenant with the Wrangell Police Department and he's been missing since yesterday."

"Ain't seen him," the person said, and slammed the door. An old voice, quavery—she couldn't tell if it was a man or woman, but she had her answer anyway. She was in denial. The problem was that she could not imagine why Paul had been rowing that little inflatable. Where was he going? And it had wound up with a bullet hole through it. She shivered.

58

WHEN THEY GOT BACK TO THE *SALMON Eye*, they shed their rain gear and hung them on the bulkhead outside the cabin. The mist that fell had made it all extremely wet. They shed their boots, too, and took them into the cabin to dry.

Beringer sank down at the table to read the newspaper about Henry's drowning. He read it carefully, then scanned it again. "You said Henry's boat was tied up at the dock when you got there. But in the morning it was gone. What day did you go out there?"

"Well, my log is missing, but I have those bills of lading. I can look back through them."

She unlocked the drawer and took out all the bills of lading, searching back through them. She'd had a later load for Point Baker, had to get Avery's transmission to him, and had taken rugs, a sink, troller poles and a gill net to Point Baker. But that wasn't when she delivered the hydrophones. When was that? She went back further, looking for them. Ah, here it was. She'd gone to Coffman Cove, then Kashevarof, then out to Point Baker. November 4. She'd gotten there around nine in the evening. There was a huge longliner coming in right after her.

"November fourth," she told Beringer.

"Wow," he said. "The packer picked up his body the night of November fourth. And you said his boat was tied up at the dock?"

"Let me read that," Liza said. She read it all the way through. "You're right," she said. "His boat was tied at the dock. I went to bed around eleven and his boat was still there. The packer found him about ten forty-five that night. But his boat was gone the next morning. Maybe the packer got the time wrong? But Paul said the crew wrote in their log the position where they found him, and the time."

"Oh, I don't know," Beringer said. "Maybe the day was wrong."

"But the Coast Guard searched for his boat right after November fourth and never found it. And I know I saw his boat tied up at the dock at Point Baker that night and it was gone the next morning. He radioed me that afternoon that he was on to something but he wouldn't tell me over the radio what it was."

"Well, maybe he went somewhere in his inflatable and drowned from that."

"Oh, no. The bartender told me he might have gone somewhere in the inflatable to look for whales, but when I left the bar the inflatable was right on top of the cabin on his boat. Maybe . . . maybe he was murdered."

"Wait. Let's think this through again. His boat was tied at the dock when you came in, and gone the next morning, wasn't it? And you say the inflatable was on it when you came out of the bar? Is that correct?"

"Yes, yes it is."

"So maybe someone else was with him. They could have tied the boat up to the dock and gone out the next morning."

"But the packer picked his body up at ten forty-five that night."

"Yeah, I know."

"There was a huge longliner coming in right after me. They went to the inner bay to turn around and then docked facing the *Salmon Eye*. I never saw the name."

"A huge longliner? Was it black-hulled?"

"Yes, I think it was. In the middle of the night, Sam barked and I heard an outboard start up. Henry's boat was gone in the morning, and the longliner was gone, too. Maybe someone towed his boat out and sank it in the middle of Sumner Strait. And maybe the longliner is towing the seismic airguns. *And* if I'd seen his boat tied up there *after* he'd been murdered, then maybe that's why they're after me."

"Sure, sure, that's right. If you'd seen his boat tied up after his body was found, then you're *It*. Maybe you should radio the chief of police in Wrangell about this."

"Out here in Buster Bay? Tell him we're going to look for that longliner? Those people have criminal minds, Scott. Somebody on that longliner killed Barney Ellis and Jenny Andover, and Tango got out of there just in time. I don't think we should look for it. Let the state troopers do it."

"I just want to see her name, Liza. Just get close enough to see her name and then call the troopers in. Make the identification first."

They argued. Liza told Beringer she didn't want to get shot. Beringer insisted that they wouldn't get shot, that all they had to do was get close enough to the boat to see her name, then turn around and call in the state troopers.

"They might have a sniper rifle aboard," she said. "That'd do us in real quick."

"Maybe not," Beringer said. "The others were shot with handguns."

Finally she gave in and radioed Chief Woods. "This is Liza. We're out here in Buster Bay. Scott Beringer, the whale man, is here with me. I saw smoke coming up behind the ridge at Buster Bay and went to see what it was. I'm in denial, Chief Woods. I just can't *believe* he's dead."

"We'll find him sooner or later and he'll be alive, Liza. I'm sure of it."

"Finally I got around to reading that story in the *Wrangell Sentinel* about Henry. But I saw Henry's boat tied up at the dock at Point Baker on November fourth."

"When did you get there?"

"Around nine," she said. "The packer found his body at ten forty-five that night, and Henry's boat was still tied to the dock when I went to bed around eleven. A huge black longliner came in just after I got there. And Tango said it was a black boat."

"Maybe that's why someone's after you. If you put two and two together, about Henry's boat being tied at the dock after his body was found, they'd have to put you away."

"Henry's boat was gone the next morning, and the longliner was gone, too. I wrote in my log how angry I was at Henry for not taking the hydrophones. I dated it November fifth, but now my log is missing."

"Someone has to kill you. They've got to get you for your knowledge of what happened to Henry. I don't like this. I don't like this at all."

"I heard a big outboard start up in the middle of the night. I thought it might be Henry's boat, but somebody must have towed his boat out and sunk it. The Coast Guard couldn't find it. They searched for forty-eight hours and couldn't find it."

"You have to get home to Wrangell pronto, and then you gotta go away, Liza. Take a vacation or do something! Otherwise we'll have to defend you around the clock. Take up all my deputies to do it."

"I might do that, but who would take Sam?"

"I will, till we get those killers. I'll take him."

"Well, all right, I'll go away for a while if you'll take Sam. This is *Salmon Eye*, clear."

"I didn't want to tell him we were going to look for that longliner," Liza told Beringer. "I don't want to get too close to it—I just hope we won't even see it."

"Well, I want to look for it and get some kind of identification of it—maybe we won't have to get really close to it—you have powerful binoculars so we can see the name."

"Yeah, but they shoot people, Scott. Oh *well*. Go out on deck and release the brake on the windlass. I'm starting the engine."

Liza took the *Salmon Eye* all the way to Pine Point, east of Red Bay, but didn't see any smoke, no sign of life anywhere. She turned around there and made her way back, still scanning the shoreline. When she crossed Buster Bay there was smoke still coming from behind the ridge, but she knew what it was now. No sign of life, no one, no one at all, on the other side of Merrifield Bay, either.

It was mid-afternoon by the time they rounded Point Baker and turned into Port Protection. They searched behind the islands and in Wooden Wheel Cove, and found no longliner.

"There are too many places where a boat could hide," Liza said. "They could be in Labouchere Bay or Shakan Bay. They could have gone into Sea Otter Sound or Shipley Bay, or gone over to Port McArthur, Kell Bay, Bear Harbor on Affleck Canal or Louise Cove, Port Beauclerc, Reid Bay, Alvin Bay on the east side of Kuiu Island. Too many places. I don't want to search all over for it."

"We'll just look in Labouchere Bay and Shakan Bay," Beringer said, "and then go over maybe to Port Beauclerc. We were going over there when we heard your voice on the radio. We can cruise along the east side of Kuiu looking in the smaller bays."

"Oh, all right," she said angrily, "but I hope we don't find it."

She turned the *Salmon Eye* in at Labouchere Bay. She'd been in here many times before, the last time when she'd heard Beringer calling about Tango on the radio. There was no longliner in there. By the time they'd gotten to Shakan Bay it was dark. She went through Shakan Strait and around behind Hamilton and Middle Islands searching for the longliner. It wasn't there, either.

They anchored there and had a quick supper. Then Beringer raised the anchor and Liza steered the *Salmon Eye* back into Sumner Strait. They headed for the tip of Kuiu Island. They could cruise along the east side of it, looking into the bays along it for the longliner.

Suddenly Liza noticed a boat on the radar screen. She pointed to it, and Beringer nodded. They turned around and began to follow it. It was going quite slowly and they were getting too close to it. Liza turned around again and went back the way they'd come for a while. "Crazy, what we're doing," she muttered.

She turned the *Salmon Eye* around again and slowly they gained on the boat that showed on the radar screen. The boat swung way out past Point Baker, and headed along the center of Sumner Strait, keeping well off the north edge of Prince of Wales Island. She was still going very slowly.

Beringer went out on deck with the binoculars, trying to see the boat. "Totally black out there," he said, coming in to the wheelhouse. "Couldn't see a thing."

With great caution, Liza moved forward, trying to keep out of range of a rifle. "It was Mink's gun that shot Ellis," she said. "Paul's still muttering around about Tango being a suspect, but he'd never kill anyone. Not Tango. And now

Paul's disappeared." She took a deep breath, just as he'd heard on the radio when she first told him about Paul.

They kept gaining on the boat and Liza wanted to turn around. "I just want to see the name on her stern," Beringer said. "Then we'll go back to Merrifield or Buster Bay and call in the troopers."

Liza got closer and closer to the boat and Beringer went out on deck again. When he came back into the wheelhouse, he was laughing. "A tug," he said. "It's a tug, dawdling along waiting for the slack in Wrangell Narrows."

59

THEY TURNED INTO MERRIFIELD BAY
AND spent the night there. They slept late—they were both
exhausted. Liza woke up at a quarter to nine in the morning
and Beringer at nine-thirty. They ate breakfast slowly, talking about where they'd go next.

"East side of Kuiu probably," Beringer said. "We can
cruise along there and look in all the bays."

"Too many places," Liza said. "I think we should call the
troopers in to look for her."

"We need to get an I.D. We have to know for certain that
that's the one towing those airguns before we call them in.
There are four longliners in the area, and I've already looked
at one black one, the *Sophie Marie*. But she's halibut fishing—I saw her dragging up her longlines filled with halibut."

"There are just too many bays out here." Liza shook her
head. "Let's set a time limit. We'll look for her for three
days, and if we don't find her, we'll call in the troopers."

"Okay. That's good. We'll set that as the limit. And anyway, I need to get back to Wrangell. Sarah's coming next
week, and I'll have to rent an apartment since my boat was
wrecked."

They were late setting out—it was almost noon before

they headed across Sumner Strait to the east side of Kuiu Island, about three before they got down to the tip of Kuiu. "Should we cruise up Affleck Canal looking for her?" Liza asked.

"Oh, somehow I don't think she'll be in there. It dead-ends at the top, though I guess we could look in Port McArthur and Kell Bay. It might be in either one of those, I guess."

No longliner in either Port McArthur or Kell Bay. "Where'll we go next?" Liza asked.

"East side of Kuiu."

They cruised the east side, the bay off Amelius Island, Louise Cove, Port Beauclerc. Pitch dark by then. Liza turned the *Salmon Eye* past Edwards Island and told Beringer to go out and put the anchor down.

"This is where I rescued the whale," Beringer said when he returned. "I laid my face against the whale and imagined some ancient connection to it. Blood like my own blood, slow-beating heart like my own heart. And I hummed to it— it seems to me that whales like music—the humpbacks sing to each other—and the orcas get very quiet and listen to the wooden flute at the Vancouver Aquarium. So I hummed and sang to the humpback that was beached."

"But you rescued it, didn't you? How did you do that?"

"A principle of Archimedes. I put a fence of alder behind it and just held it off till it floated up. I heard it spouting out in the middle of the bay. It was a lovely sound to hear, a great sigh, a great whale breathing."

"I wonder if it was the humpback that ran into the *Salmon Eye*."

"It could have been, but we'll never know."

They had a late dinner, and Liza read the end of the Jane Smiley book while Beringer looked at the charts of Kuiu Island. When they went to bed, Beringer hugged her and told her, "You've been great to do this. I just don't know how I could have done it without you."

"But I've set a limit, and I doubt we'll find her before that. At least, I hope we won't."

He laughed and shook his head.

In the middle of the night, Beringer sat bolt upright in his bunk. He'd heard a whole series of cracks, louder even than rifle shots. They seemed to come from just south of Port Beauclerc, maybe off Amelius Point, or perhaps a little farther south. He bounded out of bed and shouted at Liza, "Did you hear that?"

"Sure," she said. "I'm not hearing impaired. Those are the airguns?"

"Yeah, I'm sure of it. And the boat's south of here. We'll have to pull the anchor and go down there."

Liza got the rifle that someone had abandoned last spring, a bolt-action Ruger. She'd been a crack shot when Efren used to take her to the rifle range, but she hadn't practiced since he died. Since he was shot to death. She groped through the drawer and found a box of .270s, loaded the rifle, then pocketed the rest. Whoever was out there, she wanted to be prepared. Geologists looking for gold. At night.

Liza started the engine, and Beringer went out on deck to raise the anchor. The rain had stopped, and mist was rising from the water. There was a moon in back of thin clouds. She looked up, saw it floating there, almost full. She went back through the channel south of Edwards Island and turned south, A long way from them was a large vessel towing seismic airguns. They saw them spray up when they were fired.

Beringer wanted to see the name on that boat. But someone on that boat had killed Barney Ellis and Jenny Andover, and Tango had jumped overboard. Lucky he'd washed up on the beach—lucky to be alive. Liza didn't want to go near that boat.

There was enough light on the water to see every feature of the islands, and Liza steered the *Salmon Eye* slowly along the shore of Kuiu Island. The longliner was moving slowly, maybe two knots or less. At their present rate, they'd soon overtake it. She dragged back on the throttle, put the gears in neutral—drift for a time. She certainly didn't want to get too close.

Holding her binoculars on the stern of the boat, she tried to see its name. Something starting with E, and another word starting with S. They'd have to get closer to it to see the whole name. Liza put the *Salmon Eye* back in gear and moved a little closer to the boat. Beringer came in and took the binoculars from her.

"The *Eva Sound*," he said. "That's the one—they're looking for gold. I wonder if they found any. There are maps in a geology journal that show gold deposits in the Pacific Ocean off Sumner Strait. Rivers flow below the ocean bed and carry the gold out there. But they're searching Sumner Strait itself. I wonder if they've found it."

Liza had put the *Salmon Eye* too close to the longliner. They'd finally learned the name of it, and now one of them could call the state troopers, tell them about the killings and the seismic airguns, and they'd come out and find the boat and arrest her crew.

Moonlight on the mist made ghosts rise up, and moonlight on the water showed the longliner clearly, as well as the trees on the island, and the rocky shore.

She turned to port and headed back up Sumner Strait. But someone who had turned that blinding floodlight on Liza and Sam in Kindergarten Bay, and knew the name *Salmon Eye*, was on that longliner. She veered to starboard so they couldn't catch the name on the stern, and saw someone drop a ladder over the side of the *Eva Sound*, descending to, oh *yes*, descending to a big Zodiac. The one Tango was taken away in. Another person went down after the first one.

"Beringer," she shouted, "two people going down the ladder to a Zodiac. I think it's the one Tango was taken away in."

The *Eva Sound* was swinging now, putting the Zodiac in deep shadow. Beringer came in and looked through the window on the door but he couldn't see the Zodiac. She couldn't see it either, but they heard it start up, the huge outboard roaring at them. Liza set the autopilot, waited while it warmed up, then put in a course. She heard them coming back toward the *Salmon Eye*. Suddenly the Zodiac burst from the shadow into the moonlight. It was right there, right in front of the *Salmon Eye*. One of the people carried a rifle.

Liza stood behind the wheelhouse door, her Ruger ready. Sam was barking wildly, circling the wheelhouse. The Zodiac turned sideways. One person crouched and fired the rifle. The bullet smashed through the windshield and pierced the roof of the wheelhouse.

"Beringer, lie on the floor," she shouted, and he threw himself down. "Drop, Sam," and Sam fell to the floor. The person fired again, lowering the sites, and the bullet plowed through the front of the wheelhouse and went over Sam's head. Liza shivered. If Sam had been standing . . . if Beringer had been standing . . . she couldn't think about it.

Could she shoot well enough anymore to hit a tube on the Zodiac? What trajectory would she need to hit it? She'd try it—it was all she could do. She punched out the window on the door with the butt end of the rifle and crouched behind the lower panel. Despite the huge roar of the engine, someone in the Zodiac noted the glass breaking. The next thing

Liza knew, a bullet had lodged in the door frame right above her head.

Siting on the Zodiac, Liza raised the trajectory a bit and fired. Missed. Liza slammed the bolt, raised her sites a bit more, and fired again. This time, one of the tubes exploded, tilting the Zodiac to one side. The engine kept it going forward, despite the list. Both people were staring up at her. Liza dropped to the floor before the person with the rifle fired again. The bullet went straight through the broken window and through the window on the other side. Now most of the windows were smashed.

Liza fired the Ruger through the broken window, missed, fired once more, and someone screamed and dropped the rifle. She fired again and another tube went. There were two more tubes left. She fired again and took another one out. The engine spurted forward, then dragged the Zodiac under. The two people were thrown into the water. They were swimming frantically now, the rifle gone to the bottom.

"I could let them drown," she said to Beringer, who was still lying on the floor. He got to his feet and looked through the smashed window at the swimmers.

"No, no, I can't do that," she said. "I'll have to try to get them out. Scott, get some lines out of the locker at the stern. We'll need to tie their hands and feet before we lower them to the deck."

She turned the floodlight on, took the *Salmon Eye* off autopilot and steered the boat close to the pair of people clutching at each other to try to stay afloat. Beringer came back with the lines and threw them down on the foredeck. Liza lowered the hoist with its sling directly on top of the people swimming.

A man came up first, the man who'd had the fight with Barney Ellis. She lowered him till his feet were a few inches above the deck. Beringer tied his feet, leaving enough line to run up and tie his hands. Liza saw the man had a bullet hole through the shoulder. She'd have to bandage it, but later, later. . . . Then Liza lowered him farther, and Beringer tied his hands, then wrapped the rest of the line around and around him. He was shuddering from the frigid water and the bullet wound.

"Maybe he's hypothermic," Beringer said.

She didn't know, didn't care if he was. The *Salmon Eye* had drifted away from the person still swimming. Liza put it in gear, and set the engine forward just enough to hold it against the flood tide. Then she dragged the sling through the water till it was caught and held by the person in the water. This person was a woman, a woman barely conscious. Liza thought she had a faint resemblance to the woman sitting next to Barney Ellis in the Coho bar. Beringer went through the same procedure, tying hands and feet, wrapping the line around and around.

"Get you warmed up first," Liza said. "Then I'm going to radio the state troopers."

Beringer put his hand under the man's arms, circled his waist, and dragged him into the cabin. Sam was so excited that he raced back and forth along the deck, rushed into the cabin and circled it, tore out onto the deck again while Beringer dragged the woman in.

Liza bandaged up the bullet wound in his shoulder, a pretty good bandage, she thought. They put them in sleeping bags and put duct tape round and round the sleeping bags so they couldn't get out. "Who else is on board?" Liza asked.

Though they were both lying on the floor, they glanced at each other. Then the man said, "Nobody."

"You're the *whole crew*?"

The man nodded.

"There has to be someone left on board just to steer the boat."

The man shrugged.

"Guard," she told Sam. "Guard them."

Liza took the three steps to the wheelhouse in one bound. The *Eva Sound* had turned sideways and was drifting very fast toward the *Salmon Eye*. Almost across her bow now. Somehow she had to lash the *Salmon Eye* to it, or put a stern line on its bow, and pull it into shore where she could anchor it.

Liza turned the *Salmon Eye* sideways, parallel to the *Eva Sound*. She shouted to Beringer, "Get some fenders over the rail." She tried to adjust her speed, finally put the gears in neutral so she'd drift like the *Eva Sound*. The *Eva Sound* was approaching very fast, easily twenty feet longer than the *Salmon Eye*, and much taller, heavier; she was sure it had a much deeper draft.

Now it was against the fenders of the *Salmon Eye*. Teetering on the rail and bracing her hands along the side of the *Eva Sound*, she flipped a line around a cleat on the *Eva Sound*'s rail, fastening it down on the *Salmon Eye*. Beringer ran back, climbed on the rail and flipped a stern line over.

She went back in to check the prisoners again. The man had fallen into exhausted sleep, but the woman was sitting up in the sleeping bag, shivering uncontrollably. Liza put the kettle on the stove and heated water, filled some jars, and squeezed them under the duct tape, trying to position them so they would warm her.

"Guard her," she told Sam. He stood right next to her, staring down at her face. Liza knew he'd watch every move she made.

Both boats were drifting very fast up Sumner Strait, the flood current carrying them with it. Liza glanced out the window and saw the light flash on Beauclerc Island. Maybe she should go back in there, anchor both boats, then radio the state troopers.

Beringer asked her what she was going to do.

"I might go back into Port Beauclerc and anchor the *Eva Sound*," she said. "Maybe you could steer the *Salmon Eye* and I could steer the *Eva Sound*.

"Sure, I can do that. But you'll have to get aboard the *Eva Sound* and start the engine before I cut her loose."

She nodded, stood on the rail of the *Salmon Eye*, grabbed the rope ladder from the *Eva Sound* with both hands, and slowly, with infinite care, mounted it.

She crossed the wide deck and went into the wheelhouse. She would have to start this engine then, and steer the *Eva Sound* into Port Beauclerc. The boats had drifted more toward the center of Sumner Strait. Lashing the *Salmon Eye* to the *Eva Sound* had slowed their progress till they were almost stationary now.

Suddenly she heard a great pounding below deck. Somebody shouting. There *was* somebody aboard. Somebody was pounding on a door back there. But she needed Sam with her before she opened the door. And her rifle.

She went back to the ladder, and inched down it. "Scott, there *is* somebody aboard. Somebody shouting and pounding on the door below decks. But I have to have Sam and my rifle before I open that door."

She checked on her prisoners. The man was still sleeping, the woman opened her eyes and stared blankly at Liza, then closed them. Now and then she shuddered. Liza picked up her rifle, the only gun she had anymore.

"Sam, come," Liza said. He ran to the door ahead of her, waited while she opened it, and they both went out on deck. How to get Sam on the *Eva Sound*? She'd have to carry him up the ladder. No, she didn't think she could do that—he weighed eighty-five pounds. But there was the crane—she could use that to get him onto the deck. She put the sling under Sam's midsection. He struggled, knowing, she thought, what was coming next. Then she started the crane and lifted him onto the deck of the *Eva Sound*, letting him down quickly, dropping the sling onto the deck so he could get free.

Beringer waited while she got the crane going, then went up the ladder ahead of her. "Smoke in the wheelhouse. Where's it coming from?" he shouted. Somewhere belowdecks, someone had set a fire. They must have been leaving the boat for good, Liza thought.

Beringer grabbed a fire extinguisher from the bulkhead of the *Eva Sound* and they both plunged down the steps. There was smoke coming out of the engine room. Liza threw the door open. The fire was far beyond what could be put out with Beringer's fire extinguisher, flames leaping everywhere.

The fire had spread now to the floorboards of the wheelhouse—Liza could see flames shooting up through them. They slammed the door and raced down the hall, Sam ahead of them. When they stopped at the door, Sam went into a frenzy of whining and barking, his tail wagging furiously; he sniffed around the edges of the door, clawing at it. Sam told her, "Whoever is in that room is a friend."

With her rifle ready, Liza unhooked the padlock and swung the hasp back. It was pitch dark in the bunk room. From far back in the room, a man moved toward her. He clenched his fingers around her arms and gripped them tight.

She dropped the rifle to the floor. Her lips formed his name soundlessly.

60

LIZA'S KNEES HAD BUCKLED UNDER HER and Paul held her up, pulling her tight against him.

"Paul," she whispered brokenly, "Paul, Paul, Paul." She was sobbing now on his shoulder, and he rubbed his face across her hair.

"Lizzie," he said, "Lizzie."

They heard Beringer open the engine-room door again, they heard the roar of the fire, the flames crackling at the boards, smoke pouring out and rolling down the hallway. "Gotta get a hose on it," he shouted. "Where's the hose?"

"I thought . . . I found the little raft . . . I thought . . . oh, Paul, I thought you might . . . might have drowned." Her voice shrieked out the last word and she clapped her hands over her mouth.

Paul couldn't let her go, didn't want to take his arms away now that he was holding her so tight. "Lizzie," he said, kissing her upturned face, her mouth. Tears still streamed down her face.

"This boat's *burning up*, Paul—we can't save it! We've got to get out of here—it's already through the floorboards of the wheelhouse."

They heard Beringer try to force the engine-room door

shut. He tore back down the hall shouting, "Get out! Get out!" and pulled them out of the bunk room.

Liza grabbed the rifle and Paul followed her through the narrow hall, Beringer in the lead. Smoke poured into the hall from the engine room.

"We can't go this way," Beringer shouted. "The steps are burning. There's a hatch at the back of the hall. We'll have to go through that."

They turned back, forcing their way through the smoke, their hands over noses and mouths, rushing back down the hall to the hatch. Paul, the tallest one, threw the hatch open and lifted Sam up, shoving him through. Then he made a bucket of his hands under Liza's foot and she dragged herself up by her shoulders. Scott next. Then Liza and Scott dragged Paul up till he lay on the deck, totally out of breath. Everyone was coughing.

"We have to get Sam back," Liza shouted, shrieking above the crackle of the flames. "I used the crane to get him over here."

Dropping down the ladder to the foredeck of the *Salmon Eye*, Liza started the crane. Paul grabbed Sam by the collar and dragged him over to the sling. Sam had his feet planted in front of him, resisting every inch of the way. Eventually, one rigid leg at a time, Paul got the sling under him and shouted, "Lift." Sam hung between the boats, then Lizzie lowered the cable and he was back on the *Salmon Eye*. He streaked away from the sling and hid behind the cabin.

Paul dropped down the ladder, Beringer after him. Just as they got to the deck of the *Salmon Eye*, the diesel tanks began to burn, sending thick black smoke everywhere. Paul could see nothing through it. Liza started the *Salmon Eye*'s engine, and Paul crawled along the deck, finally finding a line that held the *Salmon Eye* to the *Eva Sound*. He dragged it through. At the other end, Beringer pulled a line through, cutting the *Salmon Eye* loose, and Liza backed the *Salmon Eye* away. The *Eva Sound* was engulfed in flames now, listing heavily to port. Sparks were flying all over; Paul stomped the ones that came down on the *Salmon Eye*'s deck.

Liza backed a long way before she turned the *Salmon Eye* up Sumner Strait. Paul stood on the aftdeck and watched the *Eva Sound* go down.

The moon had disappeared. It was dark as a cave out there. Paul stood very close to Liza, rubbing her shoulders as she steered the boat. "Tell me what happened," Paul said. "I heard the outboard on the Zodiac start up, and then later, a lot of shots.

"The Zodiac was right there in front of the *Salmon Eye*," Liza said. "Someone fired a bullet through my windshield and another went through the front of the wheelhouse and right over Sam's head. I told Scott to lie on the floor and then I punched out the window on the door with the butt of the old Ruger and tried to put bullets through the tubes on the Zodiac. I fired and missed, fired several more times and took out three of the tubes. The engine dragged the raft under and the two people were swimming. I considered letting them drown, but that would make me guilty of murder, wouldn't it? So I lowered the sling from the crane.

"I told Beringer to get some lines out so we could tie their hands and feet when we got them aboard. Then I told Sam to guard them, though other things got in the way, like you, Paul. But now he is actually doing it. I looked in the cabin and he's standing right over them. Tell me what happened to you."

"It's a long story, but the gist of it is, something distracted me for a split second and I hit a whale, my big engine conked out, I didn't want to have to go back with the kicker—long trip—getting dark, so I turned in to Merrifield Bay. And before that, I thought I saw a war canoe. I must have been hallucinating, but I heard a drum and then I hit the whale."

"You saw a *war canoe*?"

"Yeah, at least I thought I did. There's a story about Killer Whale gobbling a canoe and taking the men down to the bottom of the sea. But it was a humpback I hit, not a killer whale.

"I called it in to the dispatcher and they patched me over to the Wildlife office. And it was some damned orange thing that I saw out of the corner of my eye that distracted me, motion and an orange thing. When I tied up at the dock in Merrifield, I saw it again. So I got the raft down and started rowing toward it."

"That was a mistake, Paul," Liza said. "Those seas were so high, and the wind was fierce!"

"Yeah, well, I was just going to go to the entrance and turn around. But there was the longliner. I think they'd been a long way away, out in the middle of Sumner Strait when I caught that orange thing, but now they were right at the entrance. They were towing that orange Zodiac behind the skiff."

"So Jenny did go back to the boat. And they killed her and pushed her overboard."

"Yeah, I'm sure that's what happened." Paul nodded, then shook his head. "Bad business," he said.

"Well, anyway, the longliner was barely moving, so I rowed toward the Zodiac. A woman with a rifle came out and shot through a tube on my raft and I was thrown in the water. I swam over to the Zodiac and climbed in and the woman dropped a ladder over the stern. I had to crawl across the Zodiac and then over the skiff. She held her rifle on me till I climbed up the ladder, took my revolver, which was totally soaked in salt water, then shut me in the bunk room; they must have had that lock on the door for Tango.

"I was soaking and freezing cold. I groped around and found a blanket, took all my clothes off, rubbed myself down with it, and hung my clothes on an upper bunk so they'd dry. They only got dry yesterday. I was there for days."

"Steve Woods said you'd gone off in a little boat with a big outboard," Liza said. "I found the raft blown up on the point above Merrifield. It had *McDuff* on it, the same name as the one on your boat with the outboard—I recognized your backpack." Liza turned away from the wheel and put her arms around him, her eyes filling.

"Lizzie, if they didn't need me, they were going to push me overboard," Paul said. "They told me exactly that. Like they did to another man. I'm sure it was Henry Sizemore."

"But they started a fire," Liza said. "They were going to *burn you up*."

61

Liza grabbed the transmitter and called the Wrangell Police Department. "Paul's here," she told the chief, her voice breaking. "He's *alive*."

Paul took over. "Yeah, yeah, Lizzie actually found me. I was on the *Eva Sound*, that longliner I went looking for. It burned up and went down, but we all got off first. The crew are prisoners now. Sure, I'll come in as soon as I get there. See ya, Chief."

Both of the prisoners had to go to the bathroom. Liza put the *Salmon Eye* on autopilot, and Paul cut the duct tape off the sleeping bags. Liza helped the woman, then she and Beringer fed them both, wielding the forks because they didn't want to untie their hands.

"What's your name?" Liza asked the woman.

The woman shook her head, her jaw clenched. She still shivered from time to time, so Liza put her back in the sleeping bag, rolling her close to the stove. The man seemed warmer and was more talkative. Paul had recognized him as Frank Smith, the man who'd come to the police station to say that a crew member was missing. Frank told him the woman's name was Alice Randall. The woman glared and turned toward the stove, her back to him.

"Alice shot Barney on the beach," Frank said. He started

to laugh, his laugh rising toward hysteria. "And killed Jenny, too," he shrieked.

Alice screamed, "Shit, I didn't kill them—you did it yourself!"

Frank, in his sleeping bag, rolled over and shoved Alice against the stove. Alice screamed and fought her way back from it. The next thing they saw was a tangle of sleeping bags raging over the floor, heads beating at each other, their feet tied together but used as weapons. Paul grabbed Frank and held him down, while Beringer pulled Alice away. They were both panting. Frank gave an occasional burst of high laughter and shuddered visibly.

"Cool it," Paul said. "The police'll sort this out. State troopers. Radio for the state troopers to meet us in Wrangell, Lizzie."

She did so, then asked, "What made you think I was someone other than your captors? I didn't want to open that door without Sam. I had my gun, too. Beringer came with me, but I didn't know who was behind that door and I was scared."

"Your feet sounded different on the deck," Paul said. "And after a time, I thought there was only one of you, not two, so I pounded and shouted. I smelled smoke then, and after I smelled smoke there was a long, long silence. I thought you'd gone away, and I had to get out of that bunk room, but there was nothing I could use to get through that door. The next thing I heard was the dog racing along the deck overhead. Then footsteps, barking, the door was flung open, and there I was."

He flung his arms around Lizzie. "Thank god it was you," he said.

The *Salmon Eye* entered Reliance Harbor expecting the state troopers to be there. No one in sight. She radioed again. The dispatcher said they'd had another call that had taken precedence over the *Salmon Eye*.

Paul walked up to the Wrangell Police Department, and both Chief Woods and Paul came back, each with a car. Chief Woods shook Liza's hand and gave her a hug. "Great job," he said. "How'd you find him?"

"We were looking for the longliner, found her, and he was there," she said. "Imprisoned in a bunk room. The boat burned up and went down. They'd set fire to it before they took the Zodiac and came after Scott and me with a rifle. But we've got a couple of our own prisoners—the crew of the *Eva Sound*. The state troopers were supposed to come, but they aren't here, so I guess we'll have to take them to the Wrangell jail for right now."

Paul and Chief Woods pulled the sleeping bags off the prisoners and untied their feet so they could walk. They marched them up the ramp. The chief put Alice in the backseat of his car and drove off. Paul dragged Frank to the waiting car, where he handcuffed him and shoved him into the backseat.

He put an arm around Liza, whispering, "I'll come to Shoemaker as soon as I'm done here. We'll . . . uhh . . . we got some catching up to do."

62

PAUL TOOK FRANK DIRECTLY TO THE hospital. When they got there, Paul dragged him out of the car and handcuffed him to his own wrist.

The doctor said, "What happened?"

"Bullet," Paul said. "Liza Romero winged him."

". . . found the gold found the gold found the gold," Frank moaned. "Ellis was blackmailing blackmailing blackmailing said he'd tell what we were doing. . . ." Frank's voice rose to a shriek at the end.

". . . and Jenny went there and told the skipper that Ellis was missing and said she wrote in her log that Henry's boat was there and we had to get her had to get her she wouldn't keep it to herself she woulda told somebody she wouldn't keep it to herself. . . ." He took a deep breath.

"You have the right to remain silent. Everything you say will be taken down, and may be used against you. You're telling this before a witness," Paul warned him. "Do you understand your rights?"

Frank nodded, but he was shuddering so much the doctor couldn't stitch the wound. The doctor rolled his eyes at Paul and shook his head.

Frank went right on. ". . . like this like this like this Sizemore came aboard and said he knew what we were doing and we shut him in the bunk room and went out to the strait and pushed him over. . . ."

He was shaking so hard now that the doctor stood up and said, "I can't do this. It'll have to wait."

Paul repeated, "You have the right to remain silent."

". . . and we went back and his boat was there and we towed it out and sunk it and it went down to the bottom and Henry's body got found by that packer I heard them I heard them talking in the bar in the bar in the bar. . . ."

He jumped from the stool where he'd been sitting and whirled around, screaming and sobbing; his handcuffed wrists were smashing against his face.

Paul shouted, "You have the right to remain silent. Do you understand?"

Frank looked at him with glassy eyes and mumbled, "Yes, I'll be silent but I have to get out out out. . . ." Then he whispered, "It was me it was me that killed Ellis and Sizemore and Jenny it was me it was me. . . ."

Paul asked, "Could you keep him here? We'll put a guard on him."

"Yes, we can do that. He's pretty crazy. He's had a psychotic break. We'll put him in a room that's locked."

Frank was bending over now, slowly shaking the upper part of his body from side to side, and mumbling words over and over. Paul bent over, trying to hear what they were.

"Blackmail," Frank whispered, "blackmail blackmail. . . ."

"The man's insane," Paul said. "We'll run a guard on him till he gets sent up to Juneau. Or maybe Anchorage. They got a place there for crazies."

He must be crazy, too. A war canoe? Drumming?

When Paul went back to the police station, he went in and talked to the chief. "Where's Alice?"

"She was so sullen and unresponsive, I couldn't get a word out of her. I put her in a cell to cool off."

"I got a confession," Paul said.

"Give him his Miranda rights?" Woods asked.

"Yeah, I did. Three times, in fact. But it all poured out. The doc says he's had a psychotic break. Hospital's keeping him in a locked room and we gotta send someone up there to guard him till they send him to Juneau. Or maybe Anchorage. He killed Henry Sizemore and Ellis and Jenny. The doc was a witness to the whole confession."

63

BERINGER STOOD AT THE FENCE AND watched the Alaska Airlines jet hurtle onto the runway, the engines reversing in an ear-shattering roar. The runway ran right at the edge of Eastern Channel, known as Back Channel by the locals, just over the ridge from the main part of town. The runway ended abruptly just short of a submerged reef known as City of Toledo rock. It was a breathtaking landing area, as were most of southeast Alaska's airport approaches—Juneau in its steep bowl of mountains, the approach over muskeg straight into the glacier, Sitka where all you could see were rocks and surf till the plane actually came to a halt.

The plane stopped short of the City of Toledo rock and taxied back to the terminal. He watched the stairs wheeled out to the door and the door open. Quite a fair crowd for Wrangell. She was seventh in line and he caught his breath as she appeared in the door, waiting for an elderly woman holding the hand of a small boy to get down the steps before she flew down after them. She was so tall. He hadn't seen her for over five months—the worst time to be separated—all these things happening inside her, hormones rampant, my god, how tall she'd gotten. She had disappeared now, behind the terminal, and he raced to the outer door and up the long ramp into the waiting room, standing at the back of the crowd, waiting for their first glimpse of each other.

Tall, lanky, awkward limbs that hadn't yet adjusted to their new length, her face the same, deep-set gray eyes like Andrea's, wide mouth, smiling at him now as she came through the door, perfect teeth that had cost a fortune, the braces gone since he saw her last. She was in his arms and he had to blink fiercely before he could look down at her. Not so far down, anymore.

"Don't say it," she said, trying to compress her grin, hugging him all over again.

"Okay," he said. "Not a word about inches or pounds. Have a good trip?"

"This is such a cool place, Dad. I had a window seat from Seattle and it was clear the whole way. I mean, no kidding, the mountains looked like one of those maps that have ridges—three-D maps?"

"It's a pretty spectacular coast all the way up, isn't it? Ohhh, Sarah, I'm *so* glad you're here."

"I'm glad, too. It isn't too great in San Diego. I mean, like—things aren't too good, actually. That green canvas bag's mine—the one on top of somebody's guitar—I'll get it."

"Here, you take your backpack and I'll grab the bag. The car's across the road in the parking lot."

He'd acquired a wedge against Andrea. Soon he'd do it, but not quite yet.

"I wrecked up the *Keltie* in a storm a couple of weeks ago, but my office found me another boat. I didn't think they'd get me another boat till January, but here it is. Old ChrisCraft, sort of a tub, but we'll live on it for a time before we get another. Pretty good cabin and a lot of space belowdeck. You'll have a little bunk room all to yourself. Ohh, Sarah, I'm just so happy you're here."

Late that night, after Sarah was asleep—she'd loved the little bunk room—she was overjoyed to be in Wrangell with her dad—Beringer called Andrea.

"Scott?" she said. "Did Sarah get there all right?"

"Yes, she did. She's so tall now—an adolescent since I saw her last."

"Well, yes, she's grown a bit. I'm coming home in ten days, not three weeks, so you can send her back sooner."

"I met an old friend of yours. Ted Hilliard. Remember him?"

There was a prolonged silence at the other end of the phone. Beringer drummed his fingers on the table while he waited for a response.

"Scott? I was already a junior partner in the law firm. He left me a note saying he'd just walk away from his past in Vietnam. The whole platoon was blown up, you know . . . well, not you—you had your leg blown away—and Ted was okay but he had his mind erased. I was really sorry he was gone. I thought he might kill himself because he sounded so desperate. I waited a year for him to come back before I wrote that letter to you."

"I'm keeping Sarah. You have no right to custody because you lied to me. You lied to me about Ted's being killed on the freeway, you lied to me about throwing his ashes in the Mississippi River. I'm going to hang up now. We need to say good-bye for good, Andrea."

"Scott? You can't . . ."

He heard her wail as he hung up the phone.

64

TODAY WAS THANKSGIVING. BERINGER
had bought a little turkey and Sarah stuffed it for him. She'd
had to cook for herself because Andrea was never home at
dinnertime. They put two sweet potatoes in the little oven
with the turkey, then went for a walk while they cooked.
They walked past the old Wrangell Institute and Beringer
told Sarah that it was an Indian school till the '70s. "It went
through eighth grade, but the high school was in Sitka. Mt.
Edgecumbe, the high school was called. After the institute
was closed, they found it was full of asbestos. That's a very
toxic material that gets into your lungs. That's why it's
falling down. Beautiful architecture, though."

"It's sad, isn't it? All those tumble-down buildings.
Maybe ghosts live there, like, maybe ghosts of the children
that went there?"

"I suppose there could be ghosts, spirits that wander the
halls and sit at the desks. There are beautiful murals in there,
too. Maybe they're looking at them and thinking about the
past."

"I think they're watching us walk past and wishing they
could walk with us. We're just imagining, though, right?"

"Just imagining. Exactly right."

They walked all the way to the mill. A few tugs still there, though the mill would close soon. They turned around at the mill and raced each other back, Sarah's long legs one step ahead of Beringer's limp all the way.

"Smell that turkey," he said, when they finally reached the boat. "You shower while I pull the foil off and let it brown a little."

Beringer opened a bottle of wine and gave Sarah a little glass. "Don't tell your mother," he said. "I wouldn't want her to know I gave you some."

He knew he had to tell her that she was going to be with him now. And he guessed he'd have to tell her why. "Sarah," he said. "I have something to tell you. You're going to stay with me from now on."

Her face lit up. "I really, really wanted to be with you the whole time, but I couldn't because I had to stay with Mom."

"Well," he said, drawing a deep breath, "this is what happened. I met your mother's first husband. I knew him from Vietnam when we were at war over there. I called her last night and told her I'd met him. She had said he was killed on the freeway and that's why she married me. But he wasn't dead at all. We'll go over to Kashevarof tomorrow and talk to him. That's all I can tell you. I'm so sorry about all this, but at least I have you."

Sarah's eyes were enormous and she was biting her lower lip, trying not to cry. Beringer reached across and took her hands in his.

"So am I a . . . ?"

"I suppose it's possible, if we actually weren't married, but we went through the ceremony and I assumed we were married all these years, so I really don't know. We'll need to look into it. Your mother never divorced Ted because she said he was dead. And maybe she did think he was dead. But here he is. So I just don't know what that makes you."

"I guess we have to wait and see. Will you go back home when you find out what happened to the whales?"

"I've already found out what happened to the whales, and I'm going to stay right here in Wrangell and live on the boat—I'll get a job with the Wildlife Protection Agency—I just hope you'll be happy here, too."

She jumped up, came around the table, and hugged him.

The day after Thanksgiving, Beringer took Sarah over to Kashevarof. The snow-capped peaks behind Petersburg were visible from Zimovia Strait, and a slight breeze wrinkled the surface, but through Chichagof Pass there was no wind at all. It was a bright cloudy day, the sun somewhere far to the south, forests reflected in the water, the water silvergreen. Clarence Strait was very choppy, a fresh southeasterly, funneled by the islands on either side, blowing up.

At the Velvet Moose, he spotted Ted right away, stretched out on the bench, his gray hair in a ponytail. "Sarah," he said, "Ted Hilliard—he's called Tango now—is a bit of an oddball. He talks over the radio all the time using Vietnam jargon, and he's learned most of the world's literature, so he talks in quotations much of the time. He was an English professor and married your mother before he went to Vietnam. He always calls me Baron."

He waved to Mink and then walked with Sarah to the booth where Ted was sitting.

Ted raised his hand to Beringer and said, "'A lovely lady, garmented in light from her own beauty.'"

"This is my daughter, Sarah."

"Sarah, 'Where name and image meet.'" He nodded and held his radio out to Beringer. "I've given up my radio now that my shadowy past has returned."

"You've given it up?"

"I have indeed. I might have to call you on it, though."

"I called Andrea last night," Beringer said. "I told her she'd lied to me about your dying on the freeway, and she lied about throwing your ashes in the Mississippi River. So Sarah will be living with me from now on, and I'm staying right here in Wrangell. I love it here, and I think Sarah does too."

"I'm very fond of this place myself."

"Ted, I need to ask you something. You left her a note telling her you were going to walk away from your Vietnam experiences? She thought you might kill yourself."

"Oh, yes, I did leave her that note. The whole platoon was blown up! My mind did not function at the time. Perhaps it does not function now? I wandered away. 'I walk'd through the wilderness of this world,' until I came to this place. Beyond the end of the road."

Beringer bent over and hugged him.

65

THE CHIEF TOLD PAUL, "HE WAS USING an alias. We sent his fingerprints to the FBI electronically and they called to say they had a record on him. His name is Frederick Schulz, a.k.a. Felton Shuby, a.k.a. Frank Smith. He flew little white crystals across the Mexican border and was busted, spent seven years in jail, got out on parole, skipped, and came up here."

"We'll set Alice Randall free?"

"No, we won't. She was doing something highly illegal with those airguns. We're gonna put her away for a little while. And Frank, or Fred, or whatever his name is, is gonna spend the rest of his life in the Lemon Creek Penitentiary. Or maybe up in Anchorage where they have a place for the criminally insane. And you, Paul Howard, are gonna have a desk job for the rest of your life."

"I don't think I'm hearing you correctly," Paul said.

"You're hearing all right," the chief said. "You're grounded. You went looking for that longliner that wasn't in our jurisdiction, got taken aboard it, a prisoner—hell, yes, you're gonna have a desk job, starting right now."

"We brought 'em back alive."

"Sure you did, but that boat was *not in our jurisdiction*. You should have called the state troopers to look for it."

"Ahhh, sheesh, I had to do it for my own self-respect. Tango was a prisoner on it and somebody from that boat killed Ellis on the beach and Jenny Andover—I had to go looking for it."

The chief stood up. "Maybe I'll see it differently in a few weeks or months. Maybe not for a year. But you have a *desk job* for now."

Lieutenant Paul Howard rose and stalked out of the room.

He drove very slowly out to Shoemaker, heading for the *Salmon Eye*. He was in a foul mood, but maybe Lizzie would get him out of it. He found her at the top of the ramp, taking Sam for a walk before dinner.

"My house," he said.

Lizzie stared at his grim face. "What happened?" she asked.

"Chief says I gotta have a desk job, starting today. I'm grounded for going off after that boat."

"But we brought them back."

"Yeah, but the chief says the boat wasn't in our jurisdiction so I should have called the troopers to look for it. Anyway, I shouldn'a done it. Both of us lived through it though. And we're here and we're going to my house. That bunk's too small for both of us."

"I'll give Sam his dinner and get some clothes."

He followed her to the boat and watched while she gave Sam his dinner. Desk job, hunh.

Lizzie murmured something in his ear, then fell asleep. She was curled against him and he held her in his arms, rubbing his face across her hair. He was wide awake. He didn't want a desk job. He'd retire, do something else. Chief had no right to ground him. He'd quit before he'd do some stupid desk job.

In the middle of the night, the phone rang. Paul groped for it, held the receiver to his ear, said, "What."

The night dispatcher said, *"Chief wants you. A man has barricaded himself with a little boy and a rifle in a public housing apartment. He's got a lot of ammunition and he's firing through the window. Go directly there—Chief's already there."*

"Yeah, I'm going, I'm going. Be there in a couple minutes." Desk job. Hunh.

On the other side of the door, Sam was whining, gave a sharp bark, whined some more. Lizzie was awake now. She looked across him at the clock. He turned to look too. 4:18.

He reached toward Lizzie, put his arms around her, pulling her tight against him, running his hand down her hip. "Lizzie," he said. "You know? You know how it is with cops?"

Lizzie buried her face in her pillow. "Yes," she said, her voice muffled by the pillow, "yes, I certainly do."

EARLENE FOWLER

introduces Benni Harper, curator of San Celina's folk
art museum and amateur sleuth

☐ FOOL'S PUZZLE   0-425-14545-X/$6.50

Ex-cowgirl Benni Harper moved to San Celina, California, to
begin a new career as curator of the town's folk art museum. But
when one of the museum's first quilt exhibit artists is found dead,
Benni must piece together a pattern of family secrets and small-
town lies to catch the killer.

☐ IRISH CHAIN   0-425-15137-9/$6.50

When Brady O'Hara and his former girlfriend are murdered at the
San Celina Senior Citizen's Prom, Benni believes it's more than
mere jealousy--and she risks everything to unveil the conspiracy
O'Hara had been hiding for fifty years.

☐ KANSAS TROUBLES   0-425-15696-6/$6.50

After their wedding, Benni and Gabe visit his hometown near
Wichita. There Benni meets Tyler Brown: aspiring country singer,
gifted quilter, and former Amish wife. But when Tyler is murdered
and the case comes between Gabe and her, Benni learns that her
marriage is much like the Kansas weather: bound to be stormy.

☐ GOOSE IN THE POND   0-425-16239-7/$6.50
☐ DOVE IN THE WINDOW   0-425-16894-8/$6.50